Quantum Genesis

MD Hanley

Copyright

Table of Contents

Dedication

To all the readers who appreciate a great story.
To all the writers on a journey to create and inspire.
To the person who constantly inspires and teaches me,
my mother, Christine A. Adams

Quantum Stone Properties

STONE	POSITIVE ABILITY	NEGATIVE ABILITY
BLUE	Gain Knowledge	Lose Knowledge
RED	Body Healing	Body Death
GREEN	Nature Healing	Nature Death
YELLOW	Strengthen	Weaken
PINK	Speed Up	Speed Down
GREY	Time Forward	Time Back
VIOLET	Truth	Untrue
CRIMSON	Heavier	Lighter
BROWN	Object To	Object From
ORANGE	Teleport To	Teleport From
OLIVE	Compel	Comply
LILAC	Give Protection	Remove Protection
WHITE	Amplify	
BLACK	Nullify	

Cryogenic Stasis Capsules

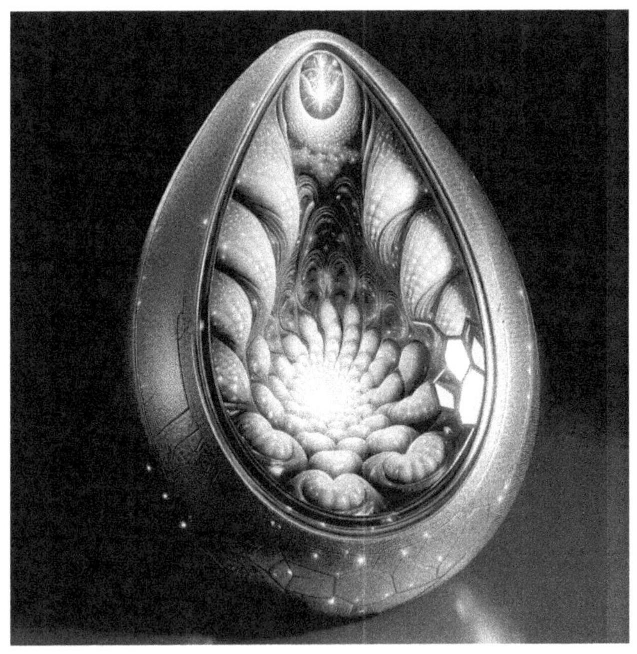

Chapter 1
Wounded Land

ODE TILLMOOK COULD FEEL THE birthmark on the right side of his neck and, just below his ear, start to burn and pulse. This hadn't happened in a long time. Sometimes, when he was angry or frustrated, it would trigger this reaction. Right now, he was getting frustrated and tired. He was in the middle of a very animated discussion with his colleague, Erig Maltok.

Erig managed a team of technicians responsible for monitoring the various regions where Ode's team conducted testing. They were arguing about how to measure the energy being transferred during quantum photosynthesis. They had been going at this for the last hour, and they were clearly at an impasse.

The burning and pulsing sensation of his birthmark was growing increasingly annoying. He was just about to ask Erig if they could continue the discussion another day when the door to Ode's cramped office burst open, cutting him off.

His manager, Bodar Odell, looked at Ode with contempt. He pointed his finger at him and barked, "You! Come with me."

Ode followed him, trying to keep up with his supervisor's quick stride. Ode was tall, but he normally walked at a measured pace. The birthmark on Ode's face became less of a distraction and was turning into anxiety about going into the briefing room. Temporarily, he was relieved of the dull throbbing pain in his neck.

The birthmark on his neck was, ironically, something of an unusual event when he was born. The moment his mother gave birth to Ode was during an intense lightning storm raging outside the home where he was born. In the exact moment that Ode was separated from his mother's body, lightning struck a tree outside the house. Everyone in the room felt the energy of the lightning. The hands of the midwife had glowed slightly, and when she removed her hands to give Ode to his mother, the birthmark was the impression of the midwife's hand where she was holding Ode at the base of his neck and face.

For years, his parents sent him to doctors who tried to remove his unique birthmark. They were worried it would cause him unnecessary teasing, or the birthmark would be a measure of who he was. However, Ode grew up with it and just got used to it. One day when his mother talked about a new doctor who might have a different technique for removing it, he told his mother, "It's part of me now; removing it's like removing a part of me."

From that point on, his parents never brought it up again. They just got used to it like Ode did. It became part of him, and there was never anything harmful or dangerous about it. The mark caused his skin to be discolored there, but it wasn't so visible under most circumstances. Ode learned the hard way that if he stayed in the sun too long, it would be very visible and stand out like a beacon with a bright white part of his skin highlighted around a sea of deep orange colored sunburned skin. A consequence of his sensitivity to the sun was to grow a closely cropped beard that covered his neck.

Ode was generally in good physical condition, however, in the last few years, his middle had grown a little bigger and seemed to settle and stay for good. His lifestyle as a scientist left him more sedentary as he got older. The slight bulge around his middle was the result.

Over the last few decades, the Continental Imperium Ministries and various Regencies sponsored many of the projects for Ode's company. Their mission was for the peaceful advancement of a technologically advanced society. However, the facility's mission has now morphed into a contest to determine which continent has the most superior technology. Overtime, simple competition, and national pride turned into a "win-at-any-cost" mission. The Continental Imperium created new sectors of Regencies to fulfill the goal of rewarding technologically superior nations on Ghia. The Continental Imperium expanded the Law-and-Order Ministries to include additional responsibilities of the Justice Regency and also established a new Regency of Defense to aid in protecting and enforcing compliance of technological superiority.

For example, over the past century, farms developed new technologies to produce food quickly, enabling year-round harvesting. Nothing ever went out of season. A large farm on another continent copied this technique. The farm, which developed this technique, successfully called upon the Regency of Defense to protect their superiority in this technology. The Defense Regency sent police and missiles into the farms where they were copying and using this technique on their crops. They blasted and wiped out half the farms on the Prosun continent. Unfortunately, the people on Prosun weren't a wealthy nation, and many parts of the continent were on the edge of starvation. It took the Ministers of Prosun to actually beg the Continental Imperium for help, since large parts of its population were facing starvation. Shortly after this happened, most people on the continent eventually migrated to large concentrations of populations on Altira or Sunira, hoping to settle down and raise a family in a more stable community.

Ghia boasts six expansive continents sprawling across its vibrant surface. The continent of Avorithea, referred to as the "Land of High Winds," is located at Ghia's north pole and is renowned for its extreme altitude. Here, razor-sharp plateaus pierce the clouds, forever buffeted by howling gales. This is the testing ground for different models of the nearly universal mode of transportation called AeroRovers. These sleek vehicles are designed to tame the planet's turbulent skies and rocky terrain. At Ghia's south pole, lies Zithea, the "Frozen Expanse". Towering glaciers and monolithic ice formations dominate the landscape, a testament to Ghia's diversity of climates. Schools of different large marine animals migrate to this area during certain times of the year, luxuriating in its unforgiving cold.

In stark contrast lies Altira, the "Emerald Embrace." This vast unbroken continent spans the northern hemisphere, equatorial regions, and the southern hemisphere. The continent bursts with life, a sprawling jungle where sunlight filters through a canopy of bioluminescent trees, illuminating a vibrant tapestry of flora and fauna that glows with an otherworldly light. On exactly the opposite side of the planet lies Sunira, the

"Oceanic Cradle," unfolding similarly from the northern hemisphere and stretching its way significantly into the southern hemisphere. In its center, the continent expands dramatically and yields to a vast ocean teeming with life. Sunira's heart is a sprawling coral reef system, a kaleidoscope of color teeming with exotic marine creatures.

Prosun, the "Protected Plains," stands as a geological paradox. Imagine a colossal bowl with a rim of continuous, jagged mountains that encircle the entire continent. These formidable peaks rise from the ocean, acting as a barrier against the elements. But unlike a real bowl, Prosun's center is anything but concave. Instead, it stretches out as large barren prairies of waist-high grass, with its flatness broken only by the occasional hills that rise up. This intriguing topography holds a hidden secret. Steam plumes erupt from cracks and fissures along the base of the coastal mountains, hinting at a network of geothermal vents simmering beneath the surface. These vents offer a tantalizing glimpse of a hidden power source, a potential lifeline waiting to be tapped in this arid land. Finally, Irsun, the "Desert Jewel," completes the tapestry. Here, endless dunes stretch under a relentless sun, punctuated only by the vibrant oasis settlements that dot the landscape, testaments to the resilience of life on this extraordinary planet.

The tectonic plates on Ghia reveal a picture of a patchwork of several smaller tectonic plates that have become fused together over eons. These plates, once restless giants constantly jostling for position, have settled into a state of near-immobility. The once-active boundaries between them have become muted, the telltale signs of stress – tectonic quakes and volcanic activity – largely a thing of the past. However, evidence is pointing to a much more unstable and chaotic plate shifting. For years, Ode has suspected that the activity is directly linked to the product created by his company.

Ode's company, Advanced Aegis Application, is situated in Hulton, a medium-sized city on the Altira continent. The city boasts a sprawling technological park known as Hulton Advanced Aegis Acreage, or H4A for short. Within this vast facility, numerous advanced technology companies, with Ode's being the largest. Their primary product, called Aegis, is an epoxy glue-like substance renowned for its exceptional protective and shielding properties when applied to various solid materials. Builders, road constructors, roofers, shipbuilders, and manufacturers of vehicles and other solid structures commonly use Aegis epoxy in their construction projects. Its strength is such that even a thin layer of this adhesive resin renders a pane of glass virtually indestructible.

Testing primarily takes place on the mostly uninhabited Irsun continent. In the initial versions of this product, the epoxy demonstrated its ability to withstand powerful explosions. As technology advanced, stronger and more explosive devices were developed, leading to the creation of various types of high-yield explosives.

The extensive explosive testing conducted by Ode's company was necessary to ensure that the treated material maintained its super strength and durability. However, the testing process had a significant impact on the environment. The scattering of the testing apparatus and defunct sensors used in the experiments by Ode's company across Irsun resulted in enormous areas of the region becoming a wasteland. The remnants of these tests transformed the once thriving landscape into a desolate and barren expanse.

In the past ten years, the Defense Regency has directed almost exclusive use of Ode's company. The Defense Regencies increased the need for the Aegis epoxy and also increased their technical requirements for increased strength and durability of the Aegis produced. This required even more comprehensive testing. They relocated all their testing of the Aegis material to the Prosun continent in the northeastern Angbok area. This location was also much closer to the H4A campus on the Altira continent.

Ode noticed an increase in tectonic plate movements over the past couple of years. The history of plate movement in this area was extremely rare. However, the movement of the plates, the increased volcanic activity, and new plate fissures opening seem to be a common daily occurrence.

Ode has long suspected that this increased activity was due primarily to the Aegis epoxy and the testing that has been going on. He lobbied vehemently to his boss, Bodar, and Sr. Commander Fulton. It fell on deaf ears. They rationalized that since the area was largely uninhabited, they had no reason to slow down the testing and production of the Aegis epoxy. The only thing Ode could think of was to find out why this area has experienced increased plate activity.

The instability is making it clear that the Aegis product is weakening the planet's surface, making it very brittle. The area surrounding where they have deployed the product is now destabilizing the entire section of the tectonic plate. This complex reaction is causing the tectonic plate to lose all of its ability to keep the entire continent stable. Areas were now becoming so fragile, they were just crumbling and flattening. It was like a sandcastle you made at the beach, and when high tide came in, it just leveled everything it ran over. Even worse, the weakened areas became so unstable they were beyond repair. The bonding properties of the material just stopped.

Ode was about four or five steps behind Bodar as they walked down the long hall to the conference room. Bodar turned to him impatiently and said, "Ode, keep up!"

Ode quickened his pace and jogged forward to catch up. Bodar snapped, "Why are these areas that have been completely stable for the longest time now becoming unstable? Why are they having these upheavals and rising volcanic problems?"

"I think it's the Aegis formula," Ode replied, a little out of breath, and regretted it the moment he finished. "I mean, the Aegis material bonds so strongly to the planet that it makes the surrounding areas without the bonding chemical totally sterile and weak, almost like sand. The planet needs trees and plants and animals to make the planet stronger. I have been working on something that might help. If we could use this inste-."

"No! Absolutely not," Bodar interrupted angrily and stopped mid-stride turned and faced Ode, "You will do no such thing. Don't mention your ridiculous ideas to anyone, especially at this meeting. Do you understand?"

Ode knew when Bodar got like this, there was only one answer to this question. He said, "Yes, I understand, and I won't mention this. What do you want me to say about the problem with the edges of the areas becoming fragile and sand-like?"

"You're the scientist; you tell me?"

Ode quickly thought and said, "We could deploy an application with a weaker bonding property to these critical vulnerable areas. This will have to be deployed and applied manually to the areas showing weaknesses."

"Good. Then, this is all I want to hear from you. Don't say a word about anything new or untested in the field. The crumbling problem you suspect has no concrete evidence of this. Ultimately, you're just going to make the people in charge, the people who pay you and me, annoyed. If they get annoyed, they inform me of how annoyed they are. Guess who will be the next person to know how annoyed they are? Are we absolutely see-through clear on this?"

Bodar turned and stomped off quickly down the hall to the conference room. Ode hurried to keep up for the rest of the way to the conference room. Thankfully, it was in silence.

When they reached the conference room, it was standing room only. Several junior staffers and scientists were standing since they had to give their seats to anyone who ranked higher than them. Scientists were at the bottom of the pecking order, so most of them were standing on the side or in the back of the room.

Ode noticed only one person who was of a higher rank than Bodar, so this told him it was important. Bodar held the second-highest rank in the facility. He was the "go-to" person who had the power to sign off on any projects related to Project Aegis and also any chemicals needed to create it. Ode was in the testing and R&D part of the facility. This gave him a lot of latitude to work on his pick of projects that came up. As long as he could justify its worth. It allowed him to work on a wide range of projects, which he could choose or create the ones he thought would be interesting, as long as it aligned with the mission of the R&D facility.

The commander, who had called the meeting, saw Bodar come in and started the meeting. Her name, Senior Commander Alginna Fulton. She was rail thin with a razor-sharp face and striking coal black untidy hair, but beautiful and flawlessly black. Ode thought she was probably physically much stronger than people thought she was and could probably take down about 90% of the men and women in the room. Her face was a mask of indifference with a granite façade, with no trace or any hint of her thinking. She wouldn't be someone you wanted to play a game of poker with.

She said, "Okay, let's start. Over the last two weeks, we have been registering an increase in seismic activity around the Angbok area on Prosun. The land has become very unstable, and some of the reconnaissance views we have are showing some disturbing information. This information isn't for public consumption, so nothing discussed here is to leave this room. Is that understood?" Her stony gaze looked at all the scientists and staffers around and in the back of the room. Some mumbled a feeble "yes" or "absolutely". She pressed a button, and the wall at the back of the room turned into a large, full wall-screen, which was now showing the pictures from the reconnaissance drones they had sent out. Most of the scientists were standing in this area, and they awkwardly moved to a different place so as not to block others at the table from viewing the picture displayed on the wall-screen.

The pictures were showing a large section of the planet, completely barren and all the same color. It appeared as if someone had created a large, highly detailed map that depicted all the distinct elements found in most large sections of land. A normal map would show large groups of trees and little sections marked by a river or a small lake. The map being shown on the wall was similar, but it looked like someone had taken a large black felt-tip marker and colored in a large section of the map to obliterate any type of difference in the land. Just one large black-colored section with no trees, no rivers, and no lakes.

"The picture you're seeing is what the land looked like one week after the deployment of the missile we sent there. This is what we normally see whenever we have sent missiles out. This is what we are seeing now."

She clicked a button, and the wall showed a new picture. Within the large blacked-out sections, brightly colored red and orange lines of planet magma and extensive areas of fire showed on the same map.

"The air in which the drone was flying caused severe corrosive damage, rendering it useless. Any suggestions of how we can fix this?"

No one dared speak. One scientist offered, "Why don't we just redeploy the compound to the area again? It should bond with the magma and make it solid."

Commander Fulton said, "That is an expensive proposition, but I agree we should redeploy a new missile in the area."

Ode, without thinking, said, "I think the compound could manually get deployed and target only the areas that are showing the weakness of the tectonic plate. We have never applied two deployments of the compound before and aren't sure of the results. We might manually deploy the Aegis material using portable rocket launchers to target the areas manually which are weak and letting the planetary magma seep through. This should fix this issue."

"I agree. Ode, are you volunteering to go to this area of hell?"

Ode regretted saying anything, but it was obvious he had no choice. He said decisively, "Yes, I suppose I am."

"Good. You will leave tomorrow. Put your requisition with the supply master for what you will need. I expect this to be resolved when you're finished manually deploying this compound to these areas. Hope you're not afraid of a little heat on your skin."

She stood up, and everyone left the conference room. Ode could see some of his colleagues visibly sighing with relief they were not going to this area of unspeakable damage and hell.

Chapter 2
Phobons

THE HULTON ADVANCED AEGIS APPLICATION Acreage, or H4A as it was called, always impressed Ode when he commuted to work. H4A stood out among all the other buildings as a magnificent feat of engineering. Two colossal triangular towers, each a dark monolith of smoky, coppery bronze glass, pierced the sky. They were impossibly tall, their apexes scraping the clouds at a dizzying eighty-five stories. It still surprised him what a feat of engineering it took to create these impressive buildings.

As the colossal research and manufacturing facility came into view, it always took his breath away. Two sky scraping glass towers, each a perfect isosceles triangle, pierced the sky, their sharp apexes seemingly scraping the clouds. Their mirrored surfaces reflected the surrounding landscape in an ever-shifting kaleidoscope of color. But it was the connection between these behemoths that truly stole the show. Three sky bridges, transparent arteries of shimmering glass, spanned the distance between the towers. One, a sleek white band, bisected the buildings around the tenth floor. The second, a vibrant emerald, arched elegantly at the midpoint, while the third, a fiery orange, connected them near the very peak.

Sunlight glinted off the glass, creating a mesmerizing interplay of reflections. It was as if a giant hand had carefully placed these immense triangles side-by-side, then woven delicate pathways between them for those brave enough to cross. This wasn't just a building; it was a monument to ambition, a testament to the relentless pursuit of strength, a silent promise that what they built within those walls would hold fast against anything the world could throw at it.

Ode arrived at the H4A facility early in the morning. He requisitioned an AeroRover from the H4A's fleet of company vehicles to get him to the Angbok region of Prosun. His flight would be northwest of the H4A and require a short flight over the ocean. It will take him about three hours to reach the area that was illustrated on the map yesterday in the conference room.

Before he took off, he went to the back of the AeroRover to secure the items he was bringing with him on this mission. The AeroRover typically had two rows of passenger seats in the back. Ode pushed a button, and the seats seamlessly folded into the floor of the AeroRover. This provided Ode with ample space to arrange his equipment. He was bringing mobile rocket launchers. Also, Ode packed a portable rocket launcher he could hold like a rifle and fire missiles from his shoulder. He securely positioned the ten missiles he was going to use and strapped them to a special cradle, which would keep the missiles stationary during the flight to the Angbok area.

There was a small box holding the vials of a special blend of the Aegis epoxy formula. To help guide the missiles was a small 3D headset visor, which would provide Ode with a wealth of information necessary for him to have the greatest precision in targeting.

Not knowing how corrosive or toxic the environment would be, Ode packed a full chemical and fire-retardant safety suit, giving him a little confidence boost of not getting hurt. Of course, this safety suit had a healthy application of the Aegis formula applied to it. Finally, he also packed a spare set of clothes, some limited rations of food and water, and any other essentials he thought appropriate.

He took off in a northwest direction from the H4A facility. Once established on course to the Angbok area on Prosun, he put the AeroRover into autopilot mode. The flight to Angbok would be about three hours. While he was flying over to Prosun, Ode went into the back to set up the gear so he would be ready to go once he landed.

The first thing he needed to do was to swap out the payload of the missiles with a new vial of his special formula. Ode knew these missiles well. Since he was the original designer of this type of missile, he was familiar with all the technical specifications of them. He extracted the payload of each missile and replaced it with a vial containing a special formula of the Aegis epoxy, which he had made the night before. When the missiles hit the area, there would be quite an explosion. He brought a bunch of safety gear with him, so he was reasonably confident he wouldn't blow himself up by doing this.

When he completed changing out the payload of each missile, he put the missile back into the cradle, holding it secure during the trip. After he landed, he would place four missiles into each remote rocket launcher and set them about two hundred feet away from the AeroRover. The other two missiles he would carry with him, along with the portable rocket launcher. Each missile weighed about five pounds. They might be small, but they packed quite a punch. Ode will also use the 3D viewer headset to give him the precise targeting coordinates he is aiming for. The headset would also allow him to connect to the mobile launchers near the AeroRover and remotely fire the missiles they contained.

The headset he brought with him was a typical all-in-one gadget. The visor provided Ode with a real-time display of abundant data, which would be required to fire the missiles effectively. These missiles needed to have pinpoint precision to target the areas he wanted the missiles to hit. If he tried to do this just by sight, it probably wouldn't work. The headset he brought with him gave him the highest degree of accuracy possible.

The device would display a 3D map of the affected ground and could offer him the critical quantum data of the area he hoped to target. Specifically, he was looking for which areas would be best to achieve a *photosynthetic energy coherence event.*

A coherence event is comparable to a group of people clapping in unison. If everyone claps at different times, the sound will be chaotic and uneven. However, if people synchronize their clapping, the sound is loud and clear. A photosynthetic energy coherence event is like a large crowd of people clapping in rhythm. The energy being absorbed by the planet gets perfectly synchronized to allow the most efficient transfer of energy. This efficiency gives the highest reaction to Ode's formula. In the lab, when they tested this, it showed him the areas that would be most susceptible to a breakdown of the Aegis material using photosynthetic energy.

While he was securing the missiles, he thought about the intense discussion he had with his wife, Felisa, last night. The weather last night was pleasant, and it was a familiar habit that he and his wife practiced most nights, weather permitting. These walks usually coincided with the two moons of Ghia rising in the south and the east. The size and beauty of the moons was always a welcome addition to the nighttime sky on their walk.

These walks also gave them a way to get out of the house and talk about their day. It also allowed them to carve a small window of time where they could relate as husband and wife instead of the never-ending responsibilities of being the mother or father.

They followed the path they usually took to a nearby park. Felisa started the conversation with, "How was your day? Did the meeting you had with Bodar this morning go well?"

He hesitated before he answered. One of the standard documents you're supposed to sign when you're hired by the company is a pledge that you won't discuss any of the work being done at the facility with family members. This was one rule he never followed. When they were first married and talked about having a family, they promised each other that they wouldn't put themselves in situations that put them in physical harm. They had five children who depended on both of them, so in order to protect them, he needed to avoid being put into risky positions or assignments.

While Ode was thinking about how to start the conversation, Felisa gave him a concerned look and said, "I guess it didn't go very well. Did it?"

"No, I'm afraid it didn't go well." Ode tried to sound as neutral as possible. He grabbed her hand and continued, "There is an area in the Angbok region on Prosun, which is having some," he hesitated, and said, "let's just say, it's having a problem with the latest applications of the Aegis product. The result is making the area highly unstable. The only way to calm it down is to physically go to the site and use portable rocket launchers to target the problem areas. This is the only way to fix this area of instability. They are sending me into the area tomorrow to accomplish this."

He knew this was going to be hard for her to hear, and her grip on his hand tightened. She knew about his frustration with the Aegis project and how it was damaging the planet. She asked timidly, "How bad is the area? Will you be safe?"

He needed to be honest with her and trust her as he always did. They may not agree, but honesty is a fundamental part of their relationship. With honesty, there also comes trust, and he needed this very much right now. "To be honest, it looks like there is a lot of instability in the area. I saw the images captured by a drone flying over these. It looks pretty bad. It showed a large amount of volcanic activity and lava pooling at the base of one of the mountains. I'll have a full protection suit on, so it should keep me safe from the corrosiveness of the air, which was detected by the drone sent there. Sorry. I know this is difficult to hear, but I really don't think there is a choice. If you don't want me to go on this risky mission, I'll tell them tomorrow, and they will have to find someone else to go to the area."

Felisa was quiet for a few seconds to digest the information that Ode had just told her. He knew she was trying to reconcile this in her mind. Then, she asked, "A couple of questions. Explain to me exactly what it is your company is asking you to do once you arrive in this cursed land. How close are you going to be from the dangerous pools of lava you saw on the map earlier today? Will the protection equipment provide you with enough of a safety barrier so that the corrosiveness of the surrounding air won't harm you? If you applied another application, will this correct the problem?"

These were excellent questions, Ode thought. "Yes, the protection equipment I'll take with me will provide me with ample protection from the corrosive air. My plan is to climb to a prime spot in the area and be able to see which areas look the weakest and will benefit from a new application. I'll use a rocket launcher to target and send missiles into the weakest spots to apply a new application of the standard Aegis product we have been using. To be perfectly honest, I think there is a less than 50% chance of this correcting the problem. However, I might have an alternative solution for this mission."

Felisa turned and faced him. "I suspect your alternative is less safe than this original plan?"

"You know me too well. You know, I have been working on a different formula for the Aegis project to undo the bonding of the chemicals. Once something gets bonded, we can't break it or reuse anything we have applied the product to. This is a tremendous waste of material. I have told you about a lot of the various breakthroughs we have made over the last year. This new chemical application I have developed will start a chain reaction at the quantum photosynthetic level. My hope is that the chain reaction will spread the properties out to other areas around it. This new chemical application could actually fix these wounded areas of our planet."

Ode paused for a second to let this register with Felisa and then said, "This would be a great opportunity to give it the first field test. If we applied this to an area with the Aegis product applied to it, it could revert the area back to its original form before the Aegis product was applied. If this works, and I'm reasonably certain it will, we can correct a lot of areas of the planet which we have destroyed and made into wastelands. All I really need to do is target the area. I don't have to be close to the damaged area, but I must see it so I can target the areas for the missiles. I know it isn't perfectly safe, but I really think this will be a big break in our quantum chemistry science."

They were coming up to a part of their usual walk, which was the midway point, and there was a bench they would usually sit on to talk. Felisa was quiet, lost in her own thoughts. Ode knew well enough to let her think and digest the facts of what he had just told her. When they reached the bench and sat down, he could see his wife was still trying to weigh out in her mind her concerns and fears for Ode and what the correct course of action is for him to take. She has always been his biggest supporter and wanted him to be successful and to have a purpose in his work. Science was his purpose, but he would walk away from it if it threatened his family. She knew this, but it would change him. He has put a lot of work into this new product, and she felt as he did about it. It was finally using science to do something smart and useful rather than stupid and destructive.

Her voice caught in her throat, and the hurt was plain to see. He could see in her eyes the firm determination he had grown to know and respect for so long. She said, "Ode, I'm uneasy about your safety while going on this mission. We have always been honest with each other about these types of things. I'm afraid you might get hurt, but I know you will take all the precautions you need to be safe. However, as much as I'm afraid of you going on this trip, I'm more afraid of you not going on this mission. If you don't go, you will never know if you could correct the damage we are doing to the planet. This is a mission that you need to do, not only for yourself, but also for the sake of the planet."

"Felisa, are you sure of this? If you're not okay with my going on this mission, I will have them send someone else. I think this could be an important step for our planet. I can train someone to go up at a later time to test this out."

"No, Ode. Thank you for saying that, but I know you need to do this yourself, and no one else. I don't want to tell the kids before you go, since it will worry them needlessly."

"Yes, I understand," and Ode grabbed Felisa in a big embrace, whispered in her ear, "You are my rock. I don't know what I would do without you."

Felisa whispered back, "I love you too."

As he replayed the conversation with Felisa, Ode was even more determined now to find out if he could indeed fix this problem.

Ode wanted to have other future scientists help him with researching this. He wondered about some of the additional practical usages of photosynthetic energy could be. He had tried several times to get this into the main pipeline of projects they were working on. However, the facility that Ode worked at was strictly focused on the Defense Regency projects. There used to be different centers on the planet that operated truly just for the advancement of science. Most, if not all, of them have been closed or converted to being used for the development of Imperium defensive or offensive applications.

None of this ever made any sense to Ode, but it was something that kept him in the lab and was just easier *to go with the flow* of what the different regents or ministers wanted. At one point, when he was younger, he would dive into any new area of science just for the sake of science. As he got older, his priorities changed, and family became his driving force.

Ode was getting closer to the affected area. He was optimistic about the positive impact his project would have. His concoction would hopefully be effective when the explosive force caused the particles in the mixture to react in a quantum cascade effect. The chemicals inside would cause a change in the photosynthetic properties of everything it touched. At a quantum level, it would take whatever photosynthetic structures currently exist in any of the atoms of the planet and restart them quantumly. It wouldn't just restart the photosynthetic properties of the atoms; it would multiply them by a factor of 1000 times. It was like spreading a quantum virus into the atoms of the planet.

This brought back memories for Ode, when his eldest son, Dulvod, was only six years old and once asked him, "Dad, how do plants eat?" He chuckled a bit at the question, taking a moment to think before answering and simplifying the complex process for his son to grasp. Ode replied, "Well, you see, plants have a unique way of eating. It's completely different from how you and I eat our food. For plants, their food is actually the light that comes from our sun, Tol. They thrive on the nourishment that Tol provides."

Before he could have continued, his son asked, "Is that all they eat is light? Is this why it gets dark at night, because they ate all the light up and Tol has to make some more while we sleep?"

Ode laughed and said, "Well, not exactly. Tol never runs out of light. Our planet turns around so the other side of the planet can get some of Tol's light. But Tol always has enough of its warm orange sunlight for all of us, including all the plants. Plants are made in a very unique way. They have an incredibly efficient way that they eat light. There are special organs in a plant called antennae. They are extremely small. So small you can't see them. Now, when the light from Tol comes to us, we feel the warmth and enjoy the light that it gives to us. Now, the light we receive contains tiny particles we call photons. Do you remember the toast we ate yesterday, and you grabbed it in your hand, and it broke apart and made a mess of crumbs all over the table? Well, light is like toast. If you keep breaking up the toast into smaller and smaller pieces, you will eventually have a very large number of crumbs to clean up, right?"

"So, all those crumbs are called phobons?"

Impressed by his son's efforts to understand, Ode responded, "Yes, but they're actually called 'photons,' and each photon carries a significant amount of energy. When these photons come into contact with plants, they interact with specialized tiny cells that act as antennae. The photons become incredibly excited and transfer this excitement to the plants as energy. Various proteins and chemicals then absorb these energized particles. The plants utilize these chemicals to fuel their growth. This process is called photosynthesis in scientific terms. You can impress your mother later during dinner by explaining how plants eat. You can tell her you've already absorbed all the photosynthesis you can for the day."

They both laughed at that.

Even though he had to break it down in the simplest way, it was actually close to the truth. His plan for the day was to take his missiles to the affected areas of the northeast area of Angbok. The new payload of these missiles would explode in the weakest areas of the disturbance, and then set off a chain reaction of photosynthesis. His chemicals will react to the tiniest amount of light from Tol or reconstruct any photosynthetic structures that exist in the atoms.

The power of photosynthesis was truly an amazing science and, sadly, not reused in a majority of possible applications. Ode could see many practical applications for energy creation and storage. At the very least, what they could accomplish was to double or triple the yield of the food grown on Ghia. The only reason Ode was using it was to be more efficient in the lab, but he had been dying to try this out on repairing the actual damage the Aegis project was doing to the planet.

In order for the "fix" to be considered successful, the chlorophyll molecules must capture the photons of light and elevate them to an excited state. This excited state promotes the electrons to a higher energy level called excitons. Quantum coherence helps with energy transfer, which allows the chlorophyll molecules to interact with each other in a more coordinated way. This can lead to faster and more efficient energy transfer, which can ultimately lead to more organic cells being produced.

His second missile needed to be timed to explode just as this electron transferred its energy. All the chemical and amino acids, proteins, and any other chemical used in the process will fire off every atom in the area into this excited state of sharing electron energy to the matter all around it. This should reduce all the Aegis compound resin and the planet's bits into its basic elements, like carbon, iron, silicon, and oxygen. This reaction will force them to rebuild themselves based on the fundamental atoms that make them up. For example, even though there might be black dirt on the planet, the chances are it wasn't always dirt and only became dirt through the decomposition of something. Maybe it used to be part of a tree or a bush or a water droplet or whatever.

In a sense, it's like restoring the toast by gathering all the breadcrumbs that his son had scattered when he broke the bread in two. Ode is actually going further than the toast example, he told his son. He's rebuilding the toast from the original wheat the bread started from. At least, this is his hope for what will happen.

Ode thought back to why he had helped to create this new resin for the Aegis Project. When he joined the facility, they were looking for someone who was a generalist in several different scientific areas to work on a project called Aegis. The purpose in the beginning was to produce material they could put on the surfaces of buildings and structures to make them impervious to any type of armed attack.

When he first joined this facility, he was excited to dive into the science and chemistry of the project. The team of other scientists he worked with were very skilled and extremely talented. Each scientist had their own expertise in an area of the project. Ode worked with each of the scientists in the beginning, when he was trying to learn more about the Aegis Project. It didn't take long before Ode became the most knowledgeable person who could jump in and help in any of the areas that needed help. It also made him the person whom the commanders or the high-level visitors wanted to talk to since he had the most knowledge of all the different parts of the project.

Ode was also a very competent scientist with a keen mind and an understanding of how all the pieces of the project worked. He became involved in many of the design meetings and could quickly assimilate all the details of each area and provide valuable technical direction for the project.

They achieved their project goals long ago. Over the past few years, they have been refining the chemical to enhance its binding properties, making it one of the strongest materials for buildings and structures. Nothing has been able to breakthrough anything with this material applied to it.

Chapter 3
Bullseye

Angbok Region

ODE NOTICED HIS ARRIVAL IN THE troubled area as the terrain beneath his vehicle underwent a sudden and striking transformation. Previously, he had soared above flat prairies with lush grass and the occasional glistening lakes, but now, the scenery shifted dramatically. A desolate expanse stretched before him, devoid of any signs of life. The once green landscape had turned into a vast, featureless wasteland, its surface an unforgiving black void.

Ode observed an unusual phenomenon in the desolate landscape. Small mountains appeared suddenly, as if they had come out of nowhere. These miniature mountains, unlike anything seen before, reached heights of several thousand feet above the ground. Strangely, they seemed devoid of any distinctive surface characteristics. The foothills leading up to each mountain displayed smooth inclines, ranging from twenty to thirty degrees. Although it would be a steep ascent, they appeared to be climbable.

He could see four or five mountains clustered in one area. Looking at his navigation holographs, this is where the source of the instability was located. There was a large pool of molten lava at the base of one mountain. Two rivers of lava were flowing off from this large pool of lava. Ode knew instantly this was where he wanted to target the missiles at.

Ode flew around the area to get a sense of where to land and start his work. He didn't fly over the pool of lava and the rivers, knowing the air above them would be too unstable and corrosive for the AeroRover to fly. He determined the best place to launch the missiles would be on top of the tallest mound in this area. This would give him a great vantage point to have enough distance away from it, but also be able to target the areas he needed the missiles to go to effectively.

Ode was a little disappointed that he wouldn't be able to just land on top of the mountain and start from there, but the area at the top of mountains didn't look large enough or stable enough for him to land safely. He would have to hike up this mountain to get to the best place to target the areas. It was mid-morning, and it would take him a couple of hours to climb to the right spot.

Landing his AeroRover near the foothills of the mountain, Ode set up his two remote mobile launchers. Despite their weight and bulkiness, he successfully positioned them 200 feet apart and loaded four missiles into each. Additionally, he carried two missiles with him, intending to launch them from the portable missile launcher. His goal was for the missiles to pinpoint the mountain's weakest points, allowing his new formula to work effectively. Taking a moment to test the communication between the launchers and his control pad, Ode confirmed everything was functioning properly. Now, all that remained was for him to make his way to the mountain's summit.

Before he started his hike, he made sure that all his protective equipment was air tight and securely fastened. He grabbed a couple of drinks and some food to bring with him. Then Ode strapped the rocket launcher to his back and made sure everything was securely in place.

When he flew over the area, he determined his ascent to the top would need to be executed in a couple of stages. The first stage would require him to walk up a twenty or thirty degree incline. About two-thirds of the way up, there was a steep rock wall that would be impossible to walk or climb up without some help. Jutting out from this sheer wall were three stone spikes, which looked strong enough to hold his weight. He brought a grappling gun, which he would use to snare the first spike, which was about halfway up this wall. Using a motorized winch would bring him up to this first spike.

Next, he would use the grappling gun to snare the second spike jutting out at the top of the wall. The last section of this mountain was the climb to the summit. This last part only looked to be possible from a part of the summit which was on the backside of the mountain. If his plan of execution was correct, he could probably reach the top in about three hours.

Ode began his ascent up the first part of his plan, finding himself surrounded by a desolate and lifeless landscape. The eerie emptiness sent shivers down his spine. As he looked around, he noticed that some of the neighboring mountains had slopes covered in molten lava and large pools of exposed lava from the planet. The surrounding areas, which had exposed molten lava, generated an intense amount of heat. Ode's suit offered him protection against the scorching temperatures and any corrosive substances in the air. However, as he climbed higher, the heat and corrosiveness seemed to intensify, challenging his progress.

The area felt like it was on the verge of boiling over. His birthmark was pulsing like it has before under stressful situations. He could feel some slight tremors underneath him, but nothing too destabilizing to cause him to lose his footing. The closer he got to the rock wall; he could feel the ground vibrating constantly now. The vibration felt like it came from the rock wall. Ode wasn't sure what this meant for him, but he knew there was no stopping now. He quickened his pace as much as he could, but it was exhausting on an uphill grade and his internal body temperature skyrocketed. The birthmark on his face and neck got hot and stung.

Ode finally reached the rock wall and had to stop to rest for a minute and drink some fluids. When he took off his mask, a strong chemical smell of chlorine, ammonia, and sulfur assaulted him. Ode quickly drank as much as possible and then quickly put his mask back on. He had suspected it would be a horrible mixture of extreme heat and noxious smells. This was literally the ground being boiled down to its basic elements.

Finally, he approached the base of the rock wall and aimed his grappling gun at the spike almost halfway up the wall. The big clamp securely fastened onto the spike, gripping it tightly. Ode tested the hold of the clamp. It seemed strong enough to hold his weight. He attached the motorized winch to the line and also hooked this to the front harness of the protective suit.

Ode pressed a button, and the cable reeled him up the sheer rock wall. He didn't need to do anything except use his feet to guide his direction up the wall. He didn't realize how steep the wall was until he was getting pulled up to this first spike. Ode was thankful for the clamp reaching its target and holding fast. In about ten minutes, he was reaching out for the middle spike to allow him to pause for a couple of moments. Ode grabbed another grappling hook and length of rope. He loaded the gun and aimed it for the spike which was on top of this sheer wall.

His initial attempt to capture the top spike was unsuccessful. Although it appeared to secure a grip, he sensed it vibrating and slipping off before the clamp could fully tighten and affix itself to the spike. Retrieving the clamp and resetting the gun took about five minutes. Determined, he aimed again, this time successfully enveloping the top spike with the clamp, securing it tightly. Despite his precarious position, he tested the hold as much as possible and felt confident that it would remain secure.

The vibrations were getting more and more intense. It felt like something was about to explode. Ode wasn't exactly sure of what or where it would explode, but he knew it wouldn't be good. There was no choice. It was now or never. He pressed the button to raise himself up to the top spike.

The world pulsated with an intense vibration, a symphony of sound that rattled his eardrums. It echoed like the forceful shaking of a bag of stones repeatedly hitting the ground. The air itself seemed to tremble, relentlessly pushing against him from all sides. Each vibration felt like a physical slap, tolerable for now, but gradually wearing him down. Time was of the essence, urging him to hasten his pace.

Ode had finally reached the top spike and stood on a small plateau, only about two feet wide. Fortunately, there was a little ledge that he had pulled himself up to. It was just wide enough for him to walk over to a wider ledge that encircled the back of the mountain. This alternative route would allow him to gradually and safely make his way to the summit. The rock wall he had just climbed continued upwards, albeit at a slightly less steep angle, leading to the summit. However, the slope was still too steep for him to traverse from this side of the mountain.

Ode briskly made his way up the summit, his pace quickened to a half jog. The scorching heat and sheer exhaustion forced him to halt momentarily. It felt as if he was trudging through a stifling, suffocating jungle, the air heavy and humid. During his earlier flight over the area, he had observed that the only feasible route to the summit was on the other side of the mountain top, offering a less steep path.

The oppressive warmth of the air surrounded him, filled with corrosive chemicals, which ate away at his protective suit. The seams of the suit showed little singe marks, evidence of the sulfur, ammonia, and chlorine slowly breaking it down. The distinct colors of the singe marks revealed trace metals in his suit, like copper, nickel, and manganese. The copper reacted with the ammonia, displaying a vibrant blue hue. The chlorine attacked the nickel, resulting in a ruddy greenish color. Lastly, the sulfur assaulted the manganese, causing a bright pinkish purple shade to appear.

After another twenty minutes, Ode finally reached the summit of the mountain. The vibrations and trembling grew stronger with each passing moment. He activated the 3D headset within his protective suit's helmet. As he observed the surroundings, Ode noticed several areas of molten lava, emitting bright orange and fiery red hues, scattered across the terrain. A river of molten lava flowed from a nearby mountain, widening as it made its way down. Taking a moment to survey the area once more, Ode devised a plan for the target points of the missiles.

Ode quickly connected to the interface of the remote mobile launchers back on the ground near the AeroRover. They connected immediately, and he programmed a set of coordinates to target the mountains with the greatest chance of success. The timing of the explosions was critical. Each area would receive two missiles. Once the first missile exploded, the second missile would explode nanoseconds after it. These timed explosions were critical to the success of Ode's formula.

He planned to distribute the missiles strategically. Two of them would target the base of a mountain, located about a mile away. Another two missiles, he would aim at the middle of the molten river path, and he would aim two more to target the end of the river path. Ode would launch an additional two missiles into a large crack, which had formed approximately four miles from their current location. The idea was to detonate one missile in each area, followed by another missile just nanoseconds later. He expected this approach would enhance the effectiveness of the newly deployed substance through a multiplier effect. The goal was to trigger a chain reaction that would amplify the quantum effects, resulting in increased energy transfer of the excitons within the microscopic bacteria. Ultimately, this process would lead to quantum electronic coherence in the surrounding matter.

Ode unstrapped the shoulder missile launcher and got ready to start the chain reaction. He got down on one knee and raised the missile launcher up to aim it, about a mile away from him, at the top of the mountain. Ode lined up his target, and just as he was about to press the fire button, the vibrations from the ground caused him to hit the fire button prematurely. The missile fired, and it impacted just below his intended spot. He quickly reloaded a new missile into the launcher, and this time, when Ode aimed the missile, he took a deep breath and held it while he felt the rhythm of the vibrations and timed his pressing of the fire button correctly this time.

The missile reached the mountain and exploded correctly where he aimed it. Ode activated the other missiles and watched as they all took off and soared through the corrosive air and hit each target in a loud, staccato boom-boom of explosions. Ode used the 3D visor to zoom into the areas where the missiles exploded. Nothing seemed to happen at first. Ode expected this, and he kept looking at it. Sure enough, after a few seconds, he saw the pool of lava sputtering and splatter in all directions like it was a pot of spaghetti boiling over. The pool was violently spewing molten magma and bits of the planet high into the air. He hoped this would be the extent of it and not go into full volcanic explosive activity. If it did, it might throw molten bits of the planet all the way back to him. If that happened, he could be in a dangerous situation.

Ode carefully surveyed the areas along the river where the missiles had detonated. He observed that the once-rapid lava flow had slowed down, gradually seeping out of the cracks, and overwhelming the banks on either side. The molten lava was now spreading across the surrounding land near these fissures. As the lava continued to spread, so did Ode's formula. He couldn't help but feel a glimmer of hope, wondering if his plan had actually succeeded.

Ode zoomed in on the area containing a pool of molten lava. The sputtering had diminished, and now the pool was expanding, overflowing the retaining walls, and cascading down the sleek, desolate mountain surface. This is good, and he was expecting this.

Bullseye! Great, it's working!

Ode would have jumped up and down for joy, but he didn't forget how toxic the air was right now and it would still be very toxic for a period of time. How long of a time he didn't know. The vibrations still continued as strong as ever though. Time to get out of here.

Ode was so consumed with the targeting of the missiles, he didn't realize the ground he was standing on was slowly moving. He found himself ankle-deep in a muddy concoction of soil and water vapor seeping out from the ground. He couldn't afford to waste any time. With a struggle, he lifted his foot and attempted to gather his equipment. After picking up the rocket launcher, he endeavored to move forward, only to realize that both of his feet had sunk further into the muddy blend.

Ode found himself immobilized, unable to move no matter what he tried. Even if he freed one foot and place it in another spot, it would sink down just like before. The vibrations in the ground were aggravating the situation, causing him to sink deeper and deeper. The thought of being swallowed up in a quicksand pool was a horrifying possibility he preferred not to think about. Desperate for a solution, he used his body to anchor the shoulder rocket launcher into the ground. By balancing his weight on it, he managed to alleviate the sinking sensation slightly. However, this was only a temporary fix. Now he had to figure out what to do next.

To his horror, he noticed that the ground was moving with the vibrations. It was sliding off the top of the mountain. This entire top of the mountain was about to experience a massive mudslide. Ode was completely stuck. An even scarier vision was seeing where the mud was sliding toward. Now, he was sliding to the sheer vertical drop off and he had no way he could prevent it. He was only about a foot away from it now. There was nothing he could do as he felt himself being pulled off the top of the mountain and sliding down the steep section without the spikes.

Could he somehow grab onto one of the two spikes at the top of the sheer wall he climbed earlier? Or would he get impaled by one of the spikes? Or, even worse, would he just fall straight down 2700 feet? A horribly gruesome thought. As he fell and slid lower down the inclined surface, he saw the spike at the top, but he was too far away to reach it. Suddenly, Ode tumbled over the edge and plunged down a thousand feet, landing directly on the very first spike he had climbed earlier in the day. The impact was so severe that it rendered him unconscious. The spike halted his fall and pierced his ribcage on the right side.

Ode had landed so hard on this spike it stopped his fall, but this was short-lived. The spike broke off from where it had caught Ode, and with nothing else in the way to stop his fall, he plummeted another four hundred feet to the base of the steep wall where he used the grappling hooks. Ode lay on the ground perfectly still and only moving to the vibrations from the ground. Ode was desperately clinging to life by the slenderest of threads.

Chapter 4
Questions

As the vibrations intensified, cracks formed in the ground, splitting it apart like a shattered mirror. The effects of the vibrations caused the land to shake back and forth, produced a high frequency buzzing sound heard throughout the entire devastated area. The buzzing sound grew deafening, piercing through the air. The vibrations were breaking up and pulverizing the hard, glue-like surfaces of the featureless mountains.

A magma pool halfway up the mountain overflowed. It oozed out and flowed down the mountain like it was perspiring magma dripping wet down its featureless mountain face. The lava flowed sludge-like across the charred surface.

Amidst the chaos, the mountains transformed into a chaotic dance of destruction. The ground itself seemed to writhe and convulse, as if in agonizing pain. No, it wasn't pain and death. It was a rebirth. The land was transforming into something new. The once towering mountains transformed into gentle hills that stretched across the land.

Ode lay on his side, twisted at an awkward angle, his body barely clinging to life. Silt and mud cascaded down the mountainside, coming to rest near him. A thick layer of mud covered most of his body. The protective suit's helmet broke in the fall and now it lay in two pieces, next to his head. The suit had a large tear from the spike he landed on. In a crumpled position, his legs and face were both bleeding, the blood mingling with the mud. Ode's wounds oozed, their contents blending with the muddy flow down the mountain. Thankfully, he remained unconscious, spared from the excruciating pain. Nevertheless, his body was losing the battle to survive, as his injuries were too severe.

The mountains with molten veins convulsed in its final throes. Explosions, once the fiery chain reactions of forced quantum energy coherence, breathed life into this wounded and desolate land. The Aegis resin made one last gasp and cough of an explosion while it relinquished its deadly bonding grip of the wounded land. At the base of the traitorous mountain, Ode lay in a heap. This insignificant lifeform has forever changed this part of the planet. As the sun, a weary traveler, dipped below the horizon, the planet's tremors quieted to a shuddering sigh. The fiery ballet waned, each final detonation a lone rebel yell echoing through the ash-choked air.

Ghia watched dispassionately as Ode fell off the mountain. It was just another life form dying. Ghia is aware of all things happening in and on the planet. Ghia can sense and feel everything all over the planet. Sometimes, it would focus on one area, while its senses of the rest of the planet still felt and recorded everything happening, but more in an "auto-pilot" mode.

Now, the impact that this life form has had on Ghia is truly perplexing. When it launched those missiles into the planet, it somehow altered Ghia as a whole. Ghia's essence underwent a profound change. Well, to be more precise, Ghia attempted to analyze all the data it was currently experiencing. It became apparent that this life form had indeed changed something within this region. On the opposite side of the planet, there existed another continent the human species call

Irsun, which had also experienced a strange numbness, rendering it unable to perceive any occurrences in that area. As time went on, this region gradually felt detached and devoid of its usual sensations. The composition of this substance, they call Aegis, dramatically changes Ghia's connection to the affected areas, numbing it and preventing any perception related to them.

This part of Ghia, they call Prosun, was weaker than the other continents. The glue-like substance hadn't been able to take as strong a hold as it had on Irsun. The edges of where the substance was applied would change from being hard and solid to being soft and fragile. Ghia could feel the vibrations rocking the area. The vibrations were causing the adhesive substance to rapidly deteriorate.

My friend Tol, the beautiful star off in the distance, shining its wonderful orange light on Ghia, was always a joy to receive. This wonderful light fed energy to all the plants across the surface of Ghia, and the photosynthetic reaction was always pleasant. This was different. The light was causing a different reaction focused in this area where the humanoid was lying on the ground, dying. The light Tol sent to me reacted powerfully with the glue adhering to the planet. Tol's light, shining in the places where the glue substance had been applied, silently triggered the bonding properties to explode and eradicate all traces of the glue material.

At the atomic level, everywhere Tol's light reached would excite the light photons to a state of quantum coherence. Quantum coherence resembles multiple pathways for light energy transfer within an atom. These pathways converge at the reaction center of plant atoms, maximizing the efficiency of energy conversion. However, this coherence is incredibly short-lived, lasting only a picosecond or, at most, a nanosecond. During this fleeting moment, the quantum coherence transfers an impressive 99% of its energy to Ghia. Each energy transfer manifests as a small explosion at the atomic level. The reaction center antennae of microscopic and atomic bacteria are the recipients of these energetic bursts. New proteins and amino acids absorbed the chemical energy, leading to their rapid multiplication exponentially.

Ghia could feel each little explosion happening. The explosions were so nourishing to Ghia. Tol, my friend, was giving me energy with each photon it tossed to my surface. This energy felt so wonderful. Every photon was coming to help Ghia. Every vibration which was felt on Ghia's surface were actually tens of millions of little atomic explosions happening in each vibration. In this state of quantum coherence, all these particles were rapidly transferring energy to new structures and creating new chemicals.

This cycle of photonic explosions was causing a massive and rapid growth of microscopic algae and bacteria. The microscopic algae and bacteria were creating glucose, which had oxygen and water as byproducts.

The oxygen and water byproducts were the cause of the molten lava spitting and creating lava droplets coming off the front edge of the lava flows. The water was cooling things down considerably. Everything was brown and barren as it was before, but soon little bits of green and orange broke through the surface and grew. The soil of Ghia held the roots, while they were furiously growing deeper in the ground. The roots grew above the soil and then, almost magically, plants began forming.

How is this possible? Did this humanoid called Ode cause this to happen? He was severely damaged and would probably not last much longer. Ghia was feeling wonderful from all this energy and

pondered what it should do. Should it just let Ode die and reabsorb its raw resources? Was Ode responsible for this change? This question really intrigued Ghia. Why?

It only took less than a millisecond for Ghia to decide what to do. It was curious what had happened. It might regret this later, but it had decided to heal Ode. It rarely healed living things anymore, hopefully it could remember. It laughed a little when it thought of how silly that sounded. Of course it could heal Ode, it could heal anything alive on the planet. Ok, then let's heal Ode.

Ghia turned Ode's body, so he was lying flat on his back. Ghia used gravity and forced his protective suit to be removed from his body. The planet levitated Ode above the ground and floated over to a place at the foot of the mountain. This area contained a small pool of water, which Ghia gently lowered Ode's body into. The small pool was just deep enough so Ode would have his entire body submerged. The silt and dirt on the bottom of this little pool swirled around Ode's body and formed a thick layer of mud all over him. Ghia floated Ode out of the water and laid him flat on a surface of soft mud and leaves, which had formed recently in this area. The mud covering his body also created a thick, velvety layer of moss that adhered to his body.

The mud and the moss gradually healed the damage to Ode's leg and muscles that were hurt by the spike. His cuts and bruises were gently healing. His head had suffered a concussion and his brain would need to heal at a slower pace. The mossy material held and stored the energy of Tol so it could still heal Ode while the light of Tol faded over the horizon.

While Ode was healing, Ghia was still pondering what this lifeform had done? More importantly, Ghia wanted to know why it had done this? This was all new to Ghia, so it really wanted to understand these questions.

In all the time of Ghia's existence, it never intentionally interacted with any lifeforms on the planet. It could have done this, but it just never felt the need to. This would be a novel experience for Ghia.

One day later

Ode remained unconscious for the rest of the day, following his fall from the mountain, and well into the next day. Gradually, he began to faintly perceive his body and the world around him, as if he were in a dream-like state. He was aware that his body had endured some sort of terrible trauma, but the exact details eluded his memory. Perhaps it was for the best. Did he truly want to know the specifics at this moment? Surprisingly, he felt no pain. However, he hesitated to make any movements. For now, he found comfort in his current state of blissful ignorance regarding what had transpired. For the moment, maybe it was best to just be still. He didn't open his eyes, but just lay there, not moving.

Ode heard something. Was it something near him or something he was imagining he was hearing? He was a little confused as to the source of the sound. Wait, it wasn't really sound; it was something he was hearing in his mind. It felt really odd because he knew the sound in his brain wasn't his. Someone who was calling his name in his mind. Was this some kind of telepathy or some kind of mind-to-mind communication? This feels strange, Ode thought. However, he was curious though.

Ode Tillmook! Ode Tillmook, can you hear me? Can you understand me?

Yes, I can understand you. Who are you?

Who I am is a big question. I am not sure you will believe me or understand. I'm not sure I understand it myself, but it is what it is.

Try me.

Your people call me Ghia. I am the consciousness of the planet. Since the ancient times when I was just formed, my consciousness developed to exist within the universe and revolve around our life-giver you call Tol. Since that time, millions of your years have passed and my course around Tol has always been the same. Tol gives life to everything that lives on me. It is a very complicated system of life and death. I have watched everything live on my surface and underneath it, and I have watched everything die. I have always been watching and never interacting or interfering. Your species has caused many living things to die on my surface and your species has hurt a large part of me. I haven't interfered. That isn't my reason for existing.

Ghia? Really? Ghia is our planet and doesn't have a consciousness. This must be my mind playing a trick on me.

Ode, can you move your finger?

Ode tried to move his finger, but it seemed to be disconnected from his body. He tried to move his finger just a little, and he knew it had not moved. He could sense his finger, but it wouldn't move.

No. What is this? A joke?

No, this isn't a joke. Try now.

Ode tried to move his finger again and this time he could feel it move slightly. It felt like his finger was in a soft powder. It was smooth and calming.

Ok. I can move my finger now. Nice trick.

Ode, your body was severely damaged and I'm healing it now. I am conversing with you in your mind. Your body is being kept still to continue your healing. Your finger was undamaged and two toes were undamaged. I figured the finger would be easier to move than the toes, but if you want to test them, I can unfreeze their movement.

No, that is fine. I trust you. You said we hurt you. Are you talking about the other continent on the other side of the planet?

Yes.

You said you haven't interfered in the past and that this wasn't your reason to exist. Why are you talking to me now?

Ode, you have taken steps to rectify the damage caused by your species. Your chemicals have left this area and another nearly devoid of life, save for microscopic algae and bacteria deep underground. Whatever actions you have taken are now helping to reverse the harm that had made this land almost lifeless. I do not intend to meddle with your species to stop this process. My role is to provide an environment for life to exist. Your company sent you here to apply more of the adhesive-like substance you refer to as Aegis. You chose not to. Why?

Ode hesitated. This sounded suspicious. It sounded like something one of the commanding officers would ask. Maybe he was being interrogated by some sophisticated mind serum to give condemning information about him switching the payload of the missiles. He didn't respond to the question.

In his mind, he wasn't sure at first, but after a second or two, he was sure he was hearing laughter.

No, Ode, I'm not trying to trap you with this question. I simply want to understand why you decided to repair the land instead of destroying it. It's worth noting that prior missiles horribly fractured the tectonic plate you're on. Amazingly, the tectonic plate in this area is whole again, bringing stability to this area. Your initial idea of adding more of the Aegis chemical wouldn't have been effective. What you did today has prevented continued volcanic eruptions originating in the planet's core.

I'm a scientist. I investigate. It is important to understand all the forces around us so we can use them better. I want to create things, not destroy things. It was an obvious choice for me to change out the payload of the missiles being sent out into the area. I thought, if I could try to restart the photosynthetic energy of Tol, it might help repair the damage. Tol gives us this energy freely, and nature has been efficiently using this to provide us with life for eons. I thought, why not use that? I wasn't 100% sure it would work, but you said it worked.

Yes, it worked very well. The glue-substance you call Aegis is gone. Life is restarting at an accelerated rate and soon this area will be lush with plants and life. Soon after that, the animals will come back and inhabit this land again. Furthermore, the pain has subsided, for which I am thankful.

Can you let me see it? I can't open my eyes and I would like to see it if possible.

Ode, you need to heal for another day. I cannot release you at the moment, but I'll give you an image of what it looks like outside of where you're being kept. I hope this will suffice.

Sure.

A vivid image of the surrounding area materialized in his mind. The majestic mountains had vanished, replaced by a vast expanse of flat ground adorned with varying lengths of lush, green grass. It seemed likely that the grass would eventually give way to bushes and trees in the future. The once raging rivers of molten lava had now transformed into gently indented furrows, through which water meandered at a leisurely pace. The entire area transformed into an immense field, with vibrant green and orange grass stretching as far as the eye could see. Some sections appeared bare, with small pools of water beginning to form. He envisioned these pools growing larger over time, eventually connecting in a complex and intricate dance with the rivers. It was a delightful sight to behold, witnessing the remarkable changes that had taken place in the land.

Thank you.

Tomorrow, when you wake up, your body will be healed.

Chapter 5
Doomsday Clock

Two days after Ode's fall...

GHIA COMPLETED THE HEALING PROCESS of Ode's injuries that he sustained from falling off the mountaintop. The injuries were severe, including multiple broken bones, four fractured ribs that punctured various organs, and a severe concussion. As Ghia worked tirelessly to repair Ode's broken body, **IT** couldn't help but wonder why this lifeform had gone to such great lengths to heal an area of the planet that it had damaged. On Ghia, all life was constantly engaged in a reciprocal relationship with the planet, giving and taking life.

Throughout the countless ages that Ghia has orbited around Tol, a multitude of lifeforms have thrived and adapted. Yet, amidst it all, one constant prevailed: natural selection always emerged victorious. Under this rule, species would evolve and adapt to changes in their environment or **IT** went extinct. The human species evolved to be the dominant lifeform. Throughout **ITS** existence, humanity's actions have inflicted far more harm than good upon Ghia, leaving a trail of destruction in their wake. In the grand scale of Ghia's existence, it was merely a fleeting moment. Ghia has endured for millions upon millions of years, and very little could permanently harm Ghia. Yet, Ghia contemplated humanity's environmental destruction, questioning how their damage to the planet could threaten their own existence.

While healing Ode, Ghia could have removed the birthmark on Ode's face and neck. However, the birthmark held an unknown significance that Ode was still unaware of. Therefore, Ghia left it unchanged for the time being. There would come a point when Ghia would explain the meaning behind the birthmark, but right now, there was something of much greater importance that Ghia needed to share with Ode.

Ode awoke, his eyes fluttering open. He was lying in a grassy expanse, nestled upon large leaves that resembled a cozy blanket. Towering bushes surrounded him, their branches adorned with blooming flowers in all their resplendent glory. The warm air embraced him, gently rustling through the bushes, carrying with it the delightful fragrance of freshly cut grass and vibrant flowers. The intoxicating scents filled his senses, inexplicably invigorating him. Strangely, despite being completely unclothed, Ode felt neither cold nor uncomfortable.

Next to him was a small pack. This pack contained some emergency supplies in case he got stranded somewhere. It also contained a new set of clothes and shoes. He wondered how the clothes got here. He knew he left this pack back on the AeroRover. How did it get here? Ode remembered that his mission was to fix the area with the dangerous volcanic activity.

Ode remembered how upset and worried Felisa was before he left. She understood the importance of it, but he couldn't help but feel guilty about making her worry. Despite making her more upset, he assured her that his new formula would work and everything would be okay. This was his first thought as he woke up in the grassy area.

Ode and his team have been developing different versions of the formula for the Aegis compound. Their goal was to make the strength and durability bond permanent. However, they faced a new problem - how to reverse this permanent bonding.

To test the Aegis compound, they needed to apply it to a wall and run tests with a thousand different variations of testing criteria. The criteria might be temperature, acids, radiation, explosive forces, and many others. This meant they needed a thousand walls, each treated with a different aspect of the testing criteria. This experiment would be inefficient and a waste of resources.

The task now was to eliminate the bonding and begin as if there was no bonding material at all. Despite Ode's efforts, his attempts to undo the bonding qualities of the Aegis epoxy failed. It seemed like nothing he tried could break through the surface until one day he noticed a flower sprouting from the cracks of a road treated with an Aegis treatment. He laughed at first, seeing the little weed-like plant desperately trying to break through the cracked surface. Then it hit him like a sledgehammer—photosynthesis.

He went back to his lab and created several experiments where he could focus on photons coming from certain lights to capture the energy that was transferred from the photon to different surfaces. He used artificial lights and natural lights from Tol. The photons coming from Tol were highly efficient. Energy from a photon transferred to microscopic algae and bacteria, the photon would release almost 98% of its energy to these organisms. They could replicate and grow. His theory was to discover a method for multiplying this effect.

Ode conducted various experiments to multiply photons using different solutions. These solutions could split one photon into two or more. However, the split photons remained active for only a nanosecond, an incredibly short duration. Remarkably, Ode achieved multiple splits within this nanosecond, around five or six times. After splitting the photons, Ode used them on microscopic algae and bacteria. The results were astonishing, as the algae and bacteria in the experiment exhibited exponential growth.

Ode was well aware of the danger posed by this discovery. The potential to harness energy from photons intrigued his superiors, but he knew their interest was driven by a desire to exploit this power as a destructive force. To protect his research, he kept it and his notes hidden from public view on the main servers. Eventually, he would have to disclose his findings to his superiors, but he was determined not to allow this to become yet another weapon under Defense Regency control.

Ode had a vague recollection of his plan: to replace the payload of the missiles with his new formula. This formula unleashed the quantum powers of photosynthesis on the land. Judging by his surroundings from where he lay, he suspected his plan had been successful. However, he was unsure of his current location. The last memory he had was being at the summit of the mountain, sliding down because of the muddy terrain. After that, everything was a blank slate.

Did his plan actually work? Ode wasn't certain at this moment. He stood up, attempting to gain a clearer understanding of his surroundings. The bushes towered above him, extending well beyond his head. He cautiously pushed them aside, hoping to discern his location. However, all he could see was an endless expanse of bushes, stretching out into the unknown. He couldn't help but think, returning home is going to be much more challenging than he had initially expected.

Once again, Ode surveyed the surrounding bushes, contemplating their thickness. He wondered if there was any variation, or if they formed a consistent wall all around him. Concluding that it was likely the same all around, he settled back onto the bed of leaves, deep in thought about his next course of action.

When Ode looked back at the area where he had awakened, he noticed some fruit next to the pack that had held his clothes. Among the fruit were three round pieces called *jalkor*, one of Ode's favorite treats. As he admired the fruit, a thought crossed his mind - how nice it would be to have a little snack right now.

Just as he began eating the fruit, he heard a voice in his mind. It sounded familiar, the same voice he believed he had heard while he was healing. Initially, Ode dismissed it as a mere dream, considering it unimportant.

However, deep down, he knew it was more than just a dream.

Ode? This is Ghia. Do you remember the conversation we had yesterday?

Yes, I remember it. You healed my wounds. You also wanted to know why I changed the payload of the rockets. Is all this growth of bushes and land a result of those changes I made?

That is correct. You have done tremendous things for this part of the planet. I am indebted to you for this.

I'm glad to do it. How long have I been unconscious?

You have been healing for two days since you sent your missiles into the ground. The entire area has undergone a dramatic change. I kept your aircraft safe while this was happening, so it is undamaged. All electronics had to be turned off since your employer is searching for you. They stopped receiving alarms about the instability of this area and want to investigate. If they find this land completely changed, they might blame you for undoing what has

happened here over the many years of testing here.

That is Ok. I'll tell them this part of the land has a different composite makeup that differs from Irsun. The formula which worked on Irsun just won't work here. It will just make the land unstable. Further use of the chemical in this area of the planet will risk having the planet open up and cause the same consequence. They might believe it. If I can, when I get back, I'll see if there is a way to spike the vats of this chemical we have stored there at the plant with my new formula. This facility is the only one on the planet which has this chemical stored there.

That would be very helpful, thank you. Ode, this isn't the only reason I healed you. There is a great disaster coming toward this planet. There is a significantly large asteroid destined to collide with the planet. This asteroid will cause planet-wide destruction upon impact. All life living on the surface will die.

This asteroid has gone undetected by your scientists because a blue

supergiant star's brilliance and enormous mass has hidden the large asteroid. Your scientists and astronomers call this star Cerulastra. The asteroid has broken free from the gravity of the supergiant star and is now being pulled into this planet's orbit by Tol.

If you want to find this asteroid, point your quantum telescopes to the Lyra constellation, and you should be able to find this coming toward Ghia.

Wait. So, you're saying all life will die when this asteroid hits you? When is this asteroid going to hit Ghia?

Ten months from now.

That's not really much advanced notice. Why did you wait until now to tell us, or rather tell me?

I have the ability to protect a wide variety of animal and plant species. They will follow their natural instincts or innate drive for preservation. In contrast, humans do not always prioritize instinct or the preservation of the entire ecosystem. Your species tends to focus

on self-preservation rather than the preservation of the whole.

Ode was stunned. He was trying to unravel what Ghia had just told him. The part about preserving the "one" versus preserving the "others" isn't very far from the truth. If the planet's population knew about this, it would totally unravel society. As a scientist, an asteroid coming to pay a visit to your planet isn't a simple thing to correct. He started thinking about maybe there was a way to blow up the asteroid so it would break up in the atmosphere or divert the course of the asteroid so that it could burn up in Tol. There must be something they can do to change the outcome than total annihilation. Ode wondered why Ghia would bother healing him if he was going to die in ten months because of the asteroid. There must be more to this story than Ghia was telling him.

Ghia, if I'm just going to die in ten months from this asteroid, why did you heal me?

Ode, my son, I didn't heal you to watch your species go extinct. I've been around for billions of years, nurturing life's cycle. Tol blesses me with its marvelous energy, and it flows through me to sustain all life forms. Our symbiosis was simple and straightforward. Your selfless gift to me requires a necessary change.

Can we avoid the asteroid?

Surviving it is possible, but it'll take effort and trust. I need your help to tell people about this disaster coming. There are several areas on this planet where the crust is thickest and will provide ample protection for you and your species. These areas are all underground and everyone will need to stay in these special areas for a long time. I can induce hibernation to help you survive the destruction and reconstruction.

Can we stop or divert the asteroid?

No, I've checked every scenario. The moons, Druna and Noth, might be safe, but if the asteroid hits them, they'll crash into the planet. If that happens, no life will survive. You will need to tell everyone preparations are being made to create areas underground for them to survive this catastrophe.

I'll try, but they won't believe me. The Defense Regency will probably try to blow it up.

I'll prepare space for everyone to go underground. I have already begun

preparation for the animals and plants to survive until the planet becomes habitable for them. I will create and prepare an additional six places underground where your people can survive in a state of suspended animation until the planet becomes habitable again. Your AeroRover has the details of all the coordinates and all the relevant data for the asteroid

I'll do my best. I should go home; my wife must be worried.

After everything is complete, I will contact you. Good luck, Ode.

Ode picked up his pack and was pondering how he would get to his vehicle through the heavy brush. Then the bushes and heavy growth slowly parted and gave him a path outside of the jungle-like area and he could see his AeroRover sitting in a clearing of grass.

He walked over to it and could see it was exactly as Ghia had said; it was untouched by the hostile ground over the last couple of days. On the bottom landing pads he could see a couple of scorch marks, which he presumed were from the volcanic activities he saw from atop the mountain. He went inside and saw there was a new message on the console of the AeroRover information screen. This message contained all the information Ghia could provide to him about the location of where to look for this asteroid.

The AeroRover took off. Ode could now see a much better picture of what the land looked like below. Ode looked down and saw nothing but green and orange. Extensive areas contained clumps of more advanced growth vegetation, like the one he walked out of. Some areas in the foothills of the mountains were teeming with larger trees and bushes. There were also areas of flat plains with wild, growing grass. It was incredibly exciting to see the transformation the land had undergone in just two days. This would be hard to explain back in his company. They wanted things that were strong and invulnerable. Trees and bushes were not invulnerable. He was going to have to think extra hard about what explanation he would need to come up with, which would be convincing enough for his superiors and his peers.

Chapter 6
Back Home

Late morning…

ONCE THE AEROROVER WAS on autopilot back home, Ode called Felisa. He knew she would be worried sick about him being gone so long with no contact. Their discussion on the night before coming out to the Angbok area was still fresh in his mind. The weight of his Aegis gamble was just now settling with him. *He fell off a mountain! The planet healed him! He should be dead!* Ode took a sharp breath, inhaling deeply. This last statement running through his mind hit him like a dive into icy cold water. Family is the most precious force in his life. But Ghia healed him? No! It was stupid and foolish to risk all he loved to satisfy his curiosity about a scientific problem.

Ode's mind was spinning out of control, and he needed to get his bearings. Using his own holographic communicator, his *eidolon,* to call Felisa.

His wife answered his holo call almost at once. "Ode! I've been worried sick about you. Are you Ok?" Her face was full of concern and worry. She let out a tremendous sigh. A sign known only to Ode, and at that moment he saw her release a torrent of worry and concern. Felisa said, "I was terribly worried about you when you didn't come back home. I tried to contact you several times, and I just prayed you were safe."

"Yes, I'm safe. You married a fool, though. I'm so sorry to have put you through this. It was selfish of me to go on this trip just to satisfy my curiosity about a scientific problem. I can't tell you how glad I am to see you."

"Yes, I know I married a fool. Fools are more challenging and fun. We get them to treat their wives as they ought to treat them. If you were just ordinary and safe, it wouldn't be any fun." The wry smirk from Felisa lifted him higher than the mountain he just fell from.

"I wasn't able to contact you until now. The reason I came out here turned out better than expected. I have so much to tell you. If you can wait until I get home later tonight, I can tell you face to face. I need to finish a few office details. I'll come straight home as soon as I'm finished. Ok?"

Felisa caught on to the phrase *"face to face."* It served as a secret code between them, indicating that what they were about to discuss was truly life-changing and not suitable for conversation on the eidolons. She said, "Sure, that will be great. Dulvod is going to be at Cheru's house tonight. Lumi was wondering where you were. He will be excited to see you later tonight, though. His school picked his final science project about the travel lanes between Ghia and the moons. He is eager to show you what he did. I told them you were doing some overnight testing in an area having some problems. It's doubtful they believed me. Dulvod suspects anything sponsored by the Defense Regency."

Felisa knew the Defense Regency usually sponsored most of the projects out of H4A. Changing topics, Ode asked, "Hey! Do you want to take everyone to the Crestin mountains this weekend? After this trip out to Angbok, they owe me a couple of days off. It'll be good for us as a family to get away."

"Sounds great. The kids would really like that. Helliod will probably ask if Kotlid can join us. Honestly, I would rather it just be the family this weekend."

Ode was relieved his wife said this. He knew they both had a strong liking for Helliod's fiancé, but he preferred discussing the upcoming months with his family before sharing the details with others outside the family. At least, that was his hope. He said, "I agree. No offense to Kotlid, but let's keep it to our family going this time. It has been a while since we have all done something together. I can call her a little later."

His wife sighed, but then smiled. "Ode, you would cave in at the first sign of resistance from your daughter. She knows you will never say 'no' to her. Helliod just has to look at you with her sweet smile and you can't say no. I'll talk to her. She won't say no to me."

Ode smiled back at his wife. "What can I say? I'm just a big softie when it comes to the kids, but you're right. You're right, I would give in too easily."

Ode contemplated not waiting to tell Felisa about the enormity of what happened to him, but he didn't want to put her through anymore anxiety unless he was with her. Ode disconnected the call and was slightly relieved he would have some more time to plan exactly how he was going to tell his family about the impending doom.

He was still trying to shake off his slight disbelief about what happened to him. Was it some bizarre hallucination he experienced, or did this really happen? As a scientist, he had to approach this with data and facts. One way he could test this was with the samples of the ground he had gathered before he left the area.

His company had spent a considerable amount of money and effort on monitors and sensors to gain a diversity of information to assimilate and analyze. Ode suspected the transformation of the area was so drastic, it would be surprising if any of the sensors or monitoring equipment actually survived.

When he had first arrived at this area, the ground was vibrating and shaking him violently as he was climbing the mountain. The tectonic plates were under extreme pressure and bound to erupt at any moment. He seriously doubted any sensors captured what he caused to happen with his new concoction. Ode felt pretty sure that his superiors at H4A would find it a lot easier to blame him for the loss of all their sensors and monitoring equipment. He felt a little guilty of the deception, but he knew this was trivial to what Ghia told him of the coming months. Regardless of how H4A reacts, the first thing he needed to figure out is what, if any, equipment was still functioning.

Ode believed Bodar would order a fresh set of sensors and equipment back to Angbok quickly. Bodar would undoubtedly face pressure from Senior Commander Fulton to make this happen. However, Ode's task was to persuade Bodar to hold off on sending new equipment to the area. Such an action would be an unnecessary waste of funds, which contradicted the principles of their company. Additionally, it would grant Bodar the much-needed justification to delay the deployment of any new equipment for now. Of course, this reprieve would only be temporary, as Senior Commander Fulton would eventually enforce the installation of new sensors in the area. The Senior Commander held immense power in the Continental Imperium as the head of the Defense Regency.

Using his personal *eidolon*, he made another holo call to his friend Erig. He could tell him exactly what information was coming out of the sensors right now. Ode would also need to convince Erig how unstable the land was. If he could convince Erig, it would go a long way to strengthen his pitch to Bodar.

When Erig answered, Ode said, "Hi Erig. How are you?"

"Ode! What happened to you out in the Angbok area? People have been going a little mental here about all these sensors' alarms going crazy. They told me you got sent out to the area where we were having all the problems. Whatever you did out there, it stopped all the alarms going off. However, now all my sensors in that area are showing up as offline. Your boss asked me to create a report of what signals we were receiving before you went and what signals we are receiving now. Wanna help me understand why 95% of my sensors are showing up as offline?"

Ode paused and explained, "Erig, I targeted some of the area which showed up as brittle tectonic plates and they were on the verge of erupting into a tremendous explosion. I intended to quiet things down, but it had the opposite effect. The total area is a complete mess. The areas that have the Aegis applied to it are breaking down, and the crust is deteriorating and allowing hot lava to flow out onto the surface. The parts of the land, which are relatively flat, have a thick layer of fresh lava covering it. It will take a while for this area to cool down."

"So, what exactly are you saying? Do we need to wait for it to cool off before sending new equipment out there, or are you saying that we need to do a whole new site analysis?"

Ode replied, "Yes. It would be a waste to send anything out there until everything has cooled off. Will this cause you any major problems?"

"No, we can wait for a new site analysis in a couple of months. The commanders won't be happy about this," Erig said.

"It would make them angrier to send new equipment out there that lasts for only a couple of days."

"Well, this is your call, but this explains why my sensors aren't reporting any data. Can you tell me a little more about what it looks like out there? Are you still in that area right now?"

"No, I'm heading back to H4A. I can explain it in more detail when I get back, but can I ask you to do me a favor and hold off on submitting that report until I can give my report to Commander Odell?"

Ode sensed a slight hesitation in Erig before he answered. He said, "Sure, I'll tell them I'm still trying to figure out why I'm not receiving any information from the sensors. It will also be better to have your bosses get your information first before they blame my group for not getting any data for them. I'll deliver it to them tomorrow."

"Thanks, Erig. I promise I'll fill you in on everything later today when I get back to the facility. I really appreciate this."

"Ode, when can I send out a new batch of sensor arrays and monitoring equipment? I have been working on some new versions of monitoring equipment. They are three times as powerful and can collect a lot more information than what we are currently receiving. I'm itching to send these out to give them a trial run."

Ode hesitated, and said, "It could be months until the lava cools and the climate improves. Anything you send right now will become defunct in a short amount of time. Your new equipment sounds really interesting, though." The urgent severity of the planet's fate overshadowed his dislike for untruthfulness and manipulation in omitting this information to Erig.

"Ok, I'll wait for a while before I send anything out to this area. We can put in a request for a new site survey in what, about two months?"

"Yes, two months sounds like a good time to get the survey. Assessing all the survey data will take approximately a month. Hopefully, the area has calmed down, and the lava has cooled off sufficiently," Ode said.

He was consciously making sure his face didn't register the relief he was feeling. He wanted to tell him an asteroid is coming to the planet, and it would be a tremendous waste of effort putting new equipment out there. Self-consciously, Ode made sure he kept his face in check.

"Alright, we can send out more equipment there when it's appropriate. It will also give my team a little testing time as well. I'll continue with the development of these new sensors we are working on. You should stop by sometime and I can go over the technical specifications we are putting into these new sensors."

"I'll come by your office soon and we can go over all the bells and whistles that I'm sure you're loading these new sensors with. Thanks again for your help. Bye."

Ode didn't feel right about manipulating Erig when he disconnected the call. He was uncomfortable telling him outright lies. He gave him a lot of half-truths and a heightened emphasis on just how unstable the land was.

Half-truths were still lying, though, and it made him uncomfortable telling his friend this. Eventually, he would disclose the complete truth to Erig and rely on his support to persuade similar individuals of the upcoming asteroid's catastrophic impact on the planet ten months from now.

He was relieved the sensors were not reporting the fresh growth and transformation of the land. Most likely, all the sensors would have to be replaced, which was unfortunate, but if what Ghia had told him was true, then, it was irrelevant.

His next call would be a more difficult one to make. Ode called his commanding officer Bodar Odell. The receptionist put him right through to Bodar's *eidolon*.

"Ode, what the heck happened out there? Why didn't you come back yesterday?" Bodar snapped at him in his choppy bark, which most of the commanding officers developed as they ordered their subordinates to act.

In response, Ode promptly replied, "Upon my arrival in the vicinity, the situation was highly unstable. The planet's crust showed extensive cracks, from which molten lava was seeping and collecting in large pools. Two areas suffered significant damage, with open fissures in the crust. Lava was steadily streaming out from various weak points in that region. Consequently, I directed all the missiles towards those specific areas. This approach appeared to subdue the volcanic activity. The ground was trembling and vibrating upon my initial arrival, creating a sense of imminent eruption. To position myself for missile deployment, I climbed a mountain which I could get the most accurate targeting place to send the missiles."

"So, it took you two days to climb up and down one mountain?" Bodar snapped, slightly annoyed.

"No, but when I fired the missiles into the weakened surface of the planet, it caused an explosion which vibrated the ground so violently it knocked me off from the top of the mountain. I fell several thousand feet all the way to the bottom. Thankfully, the side of the mountain I fell from was extremely smooth, like glass. It is a miracle that I survived after falling almost 2500 feet to the ground. I attempted to climb back up, but gaining traction proved impossible."

"Wait. You said it took a while to climb up it, but then you got down to the bottom in no time. So how come it took you another day to start back?"

Ode tried as hard as possible to not let his anger toward Bodar show on his face and said, "All the equipment I used to get up to the top was still up there. I had to traverse around the mountain to the front side where I had originally climbed up. I went back to the AeroRover to retrieve the extra grappler hooks I had packed, and then I had to climb up the mountain again so I could retrieve the first grappler, sitting up at the summit. Climbing up and down the mountain twice took me almost two days to complete."

He could see Bodar chuckling a little. Even though part of this story was untrue, Ode felt annoyed as Bodar found it funny that he fell off a 2500-foot mountain. He would be dead right now if Ghia hadn't healed him. "Well, whatever you did, it appears to have settled down the area and the alarms are quiet. Where are you now?" Bodar asked.

"I'm on my way back now. Should be at the facility in about two hours," he replied, not daring to give out any more information than was necessary.

"Ok, get back here and check in when you arrive. When can you get me a report on this?"

"I can get this to you by the end of day tomorrow if that is Ok?"

Bodar, of course, wanted it right now, but he gave Ode a little slack and said, "How about tomorrow morning?"

"Yes, I'll have it ready for you tomorrow morning."

Ode disconnected from the call, and he was pleased that it had gone as well as he could have expected. Ode could do the report right now while he flew back to the facility.

Ode got out his electronic notepad and created the report he would turn in to his boss. It was going to be a wonderful tale, full of embellishment and half-truths, like the mountain sliding and slipperiness of the epoxy resin adhering to everything there. He was finishing this report when the navigation on the AeroRover beeped a signal that they were nearing the H4A building.

Later that night

When Ode finally arrived home that evening, his youngest son Lumisod, (or Lumi to friends and family), nearly tackled him. With freckles and bright red hair, Lumi is a tall, lanky boy. He has a friendly smile and a mischievous glint in his deep blue eyes. He takes after his mother as a compassionate boy, who usually puts others before himself.

His wife gave him a big hug and the relief of seeing him being safe at home was visible on her face. Felisa has long, blond hair cascaded down her back in an intricate braid, like a river of gold. Her face is soft and open, with a warm smile that could light up a room. Her eyes are a deep emerald green, and they sparkled with intelligence and compassion. She was a beautiful woman, but her inner strength and kindness only surpassed her beauty. She was a loving mother, a devoted wife, and a loyal friend.

His sons and daughters were thrilled when Ode came back home. Ode and Felisa had five children - a pair of twins and a set of triplets. While twins and triplets were not common on Ghia, they weren't unheard of either. The eldest twins, Dulvod and Helliod, were highly intelligent and had strong opinions. They were usually easygoing, but could become quite stubborn on issues they cared about deeply, much to Ode's concern. The younger triplets, Melliod, Kelvod (or Kelvi to friends and family), and Lumisod (or Lumi), were just as smart and stubborn as their older siblings. Lumi stood out as the most intelligent among all the children. He was quiet by nature and tended to withdraw in uncomfortable situations.

Lumi's reserved nature often concealed the depths of his intellect, surprising those around him with profound insights when he chose to speak. While his siblings' strong personalities shone brightly, Lumi's quiet strength emanated a different kind of brilliance. Ode and Felisa watched with pride as their youngest child navigated the world in his own unique way, shaping his path with wisdom beyond his years. In the bustling household filled with lively debates and passionate discussions, Lumi's silent presence carried a profound weight, grounding the family with his quiet wisdom. As the days passed, it became clear that Lumi's voice, though soft-spoken, held a power that resonated deeply with all who had the privilege to listen.

They all asked why Ode was gone for the last couple of days. He told them the project he was working on had run into some complications and required him to stay later than he wanted. Felisa sensed there was more to the story than what Ode was telling everyone. She quickly changed the subject, telling them she had made a delicious pie made from Zythor fruit for dessert. Zythor is a vibrant purple, pear-shaped fruit. The inside of the fruit is both a tart and a sweet blend of flavors.

After dinner and some pie, Ode asked Felisa if she would go for a walk with him. He knew she wanted some time alone with him to find out the actual story of what had happened in the last couple of days.

Once they were a suitable distance away from the house and out of earshot, Ode began, "Felisa, going out to that devastated area was a completely surreal experience. It was unlike anything I have ever seen. I can remember everything that happened to me, almost perfectly, up to a point. My mission was to inject some more of the Aegis product into the weak areas of the planet's crust. As I told you the night before I left, my plan was to substitute the payload of the missiles with a new compound that I have been developing. I had to climb up a tall mountain to deploy the missiles correctly. The entire area was vibrating so forcefully, you just can't imagine how powerful it was. A sandy-like surface covered the top of the mountain. After I fired all the missiles into the planet, they caused the planet to produce some massive explosions. The whole top of the mountain just slid off. The surface had me trapped, and I found it impossible to move. As everything slid over the edge, it carried me with it. There was nothing I could do to prevent it and I fell to the bottom of the mountain."

His wife took a deep breath and stopped in the path they were on. Ode put his arm around her shoulders to help give her support. He didn't sugarcoat anything and promptly informed Felisa about the events, swiftly moving on to the part about Ghia. Ode knew she was gathering strength to hear the rest of the story, which he knew she felt compelled to listen to. Silently, she nodded and continued walking with him.

"It was terrifying knowing I had no way of stopping myself from falling over the edge. I fell to the bottom of the mountain. Near the bottom there is a sheer wall of stone which has a couple of protrusions jutting out of it. I landed on one of these spikes and it speared me right through my side. The force of me falling on it broke it off, and I then fell another couple hundred feet. When I finally landed at the bottom, I knew this fall was going to be the end for me. I remember the pain of it and then everything gets a little fuzzy."

Ode carefully looked into his wife's eyes to see how she was handling this information. He knew he had to tell her every part and not try to protect her from just how badly hurt he was. He could tell she was handling this Ok. They came across a small bench in the path, and he guided them over to sit for a bit.

Ode continued replaying the next part of his story and said, "I know it's going to sound a little strange, but something was talking to me after I fell. It was a strange sensation of being very aware that I was unconscious and probably mortally hurt, yet I could carry on conversations with another consciousness. Kind of like directed dreaming, sort of. This other consciousness was asking me why I changed the formula of the Aegis project to unlock the power of photosynthesis. To be honest, my first thought was, it was a trick, and my company was interrogating me to find out why I had gone against an order. I felt suspicious, like if I confessed anything, then they would definitely punish me. It laughed when I thought it was a trick or some kind of truth serum to make me confess what I had done."

"What did you tell this other consciousness when it asked you about switching the chemical compounds in the missiles?"

"I just told it the truth. My motive for this was to heal the land. I wanted to make it go back to its natural state. Apparently, it believed me. The consciousness told me it was actually the consciousness of the planet. This was Ghia talking directly to me. Even saying that sounds like a crazy person, but I have no way of proving or disproving it. Anyway, Ghia told me it was grateful for helping to restore this part of the planet back to its natural state."

"I'm just glad you're alright. I think I can understand the notion of our planet having a consciousness or a kind of being." Felisa smiled and said, "I have always believed that nature was the heart and the mind of our planet. Nature is all about living and, unfortunately, it is also about dying. The one question I have, though, is why, after all the eons that this planet has taken shape and formed, why is it reaching out and connecting with us now?"

Ode said, "Curiosity? Surprise? I'm not really sure exactly."

He said sarcastically, "As a species, we have always taken away from the planet. We cut down trees, hunt animals, spoil its air, make the water not drinkable, and on and on. As a species, we seldom give anything back to the planet. Our sun constantly sends energy to the planet to help it grow and provide a space for all the living things on this planet. I gave it something which our sun gives it every day. Only the substance I gave Ghia was a concentrated burst of energy, like a sun going super nova in the amount of energy transferred. I basically gave it a year of energy in about a nanosecond."

"So that is why everything grew so quickly?"

Ode smiled. He was once again surprised at how quickly his wife could assess a situation and sense what the big picture was. "Yes, exactly," he said and continued, "Photosynthesis is normally a slow process of each plant receiving this energy and using it to create chemical reactions. These chemical reactions create new plant mass and different byproducts like water and oxygen to feed the plants and help them grow. The trick with my formula was that it transferred the energy from Tol in a super concentrated and exponentially faster way. However, it was Ghia who healed me from a definitely fatal fall for a reason."

Felisa looked at Ode, and she visibly seemed to relax more. He could sense she was pausing herself to gather all of her strength together in anticipation of what he was about to tell her next. Ode could read his wife very well. He also realized if he could read his wife this well, then she also could read him just as well.

Ode took Felisa's hand, and he looked into her deep green eyes. He felt a pang of sadness. He knew what he had to tell her, and he dreaded the look on her face when she heard it.

"Felisa," he whispered. He took a deep breath. "Ghia informed me that an asteroid is approaching our planet. It will collide with the surface, and there is no way to prevent it. The asteroid is of considerable size and will cause catastrophic devastation."

Felisa's face went pale. "But what can we do?" she asked.

"Ghia has a plan," Ode said. "But it will be very difficult. We need to gather everyone into six different underground caverns scattered around the planet where the crust is thickest. These caverns will have a capsule for every person. When we are in these capsules, we will sleep. It will be like a hibernation state. All bodily functions will slow to their lowest level."

Felisa let out a sigh, and Ode could see the questions forming in her mind. She asked, "When will this asteroid hit Ghia? How long will we be underground in these capsules?"

Felisa gazed at him for a moment before adding, "No one will believe this. We need to have proof of this."

Ode agreed, "Yes, you're right. We will need proof of this. It must be done quietly though, otherwise this information could cause massive panic. There is a lot of planning and things that we must get done before we go underground. I know contacting a few of my friends from university who might help us verify the asteroid's existence and its trajectory. Ghia told me the asteroid will hit the planet in ten months."

Ode continued, "Ghia didn't specify the exact duration for us to remain underground. It might be decades or even centuries. As the asteroid approaches the planet, we will have a clearer understanding of its size. Currently, it is too distant to determine the impact on Ghia. Once the asteroid penetrates the atmosphere, it will fragment into several sizable meteorites. The size of these meteorite pieces and their impact locations on the planet are aspects that still need to be determined."

Felisa looked at him for a long moment. Then she nodded. "I'll help," she said.

Ode smiled. "Thank you," he said. "I knew I could count on you."

He took Felisa's hand, and they held each other tightly. They were facing the end of the world, but they would face it together.

Chapter 7
Weekend Trip

Cabin at Crestin Mountain

THAT WEEKEND, ODE AND HIS FAMILY embarked on a serene retreat in their cherished cabin nestled amidst the Crestin mountains. The cabin, perched on the tranquil lake's edge, offered a breathtaking view of the bald-faced Crestin mountains, majestically towering over the glistening waters of Crestin Lake. This idyllic setting held a profound significance for Ode and his family. This weekend would be a time for them to enjoy some undisturbed time together, free from the usual day-to-day distractions.

The land around the Crestin mountains was a tapestry of vibrant, orange hues woven by Tol's light. The lake, a crystalline expanse mirroring the imposing silhouettes of the Crestin mountains with a ring of bioluminescent willow-like trees. Their leaves, a soft, ethereal blue, pulsed with an inner light, casting an enchanting glow upon the water's surface. Beyond this luminous border, the terrain rose gradually, cloaked in a dense undergrowth of iridescent ferns, their fronds unfurling in shades of purple and gold. Towering over this verdant carpet were the iconic Aspen trees with smooth white trunks beset with silvery needles reflecting brightly across the lake below. As the trees ascended up the broad hillsides, the Aspen trees transitioned to a carpet of orange moss grass covering the mountain like a warm, comfortable blanket. Eventually, even the moss grass gave way to hard, sparse, rocky terrain, punctuated by hardy, lichen-covered shrubs that clung tenaciously to the mountainside.

The families who owned the few cabins around the lake, had owned them for generations, passing them down to the younger generations. There were approximately ten other families on the lake. All friendly, but also treasuring the peace and solitude this lake provided. Small beaches popping up at various locations around the lake, signaled there was a cabin hidden in the forest's camouflage. Each beach had just a simple dock tiptoeing into the lake. Most also had various boats tied to these docks.

Many years ago, Ode's mother fell seriously ill and had to stay in the hospital for several months. To help the family cope with their grandmother's illness, they spent a weekend together in the mountains. Little did they know, this weekend would provide them with unexpected solace. The older twins stepped up and supported the younger ones, assuring them they were there to help them through this challenging time. Ode also remained by his father's side, offering him strength and support. The trip to the cabin in the mountains held a special significance for his family. It served as a necessary retreat, allowing them to regroup and lean on each other during these difficult times.

Ode's mother stayed in the hospital for about two months. Then she got better. Both Ode's family and Felisa's family have longevity in their genes, with nearly all of their parents, uncles, aunts, and cousins still alive and still puttering around. The average life span of people is a wide range of from about 140 years old to about 230 years. Living to an age of 230 isn't the norm, but it isn't really that rare of an event either. There have been a few cases of people reaching 250 years old, but that is quite rare.

Every month, Ode and Felisa would come up to Crestin lake. It was always a good way for them to unwind and spend some family time together. As the children grew older, it was common for the kids to invite friends or significant others to the cabin when they visited. It had been a while since it was just the family and no one else. This weekend was important. More than ever, Ode needed his whole family behind him, helping to get whatever needs to be done for this upcoming disaster. He felt confident his children could offer a lot to help in this effort, but first, he needed to tell them the full story of what happened to him last week.

Once they all unpacked and got dinner started, most of the family went down to the lake to go for a swim. The lake stood at the foot of a bald faced mountain off in the distance. The mountains were stunning to look at and even more appealing to climb. At the top of these mountains, there were several peaks covered in snow. Typically, throughout the year, the runoff melt from the top of the mountains enters the Crestin lake on the far side.

Ode and Felisa first started coming here, right after they were married. Ode's father, grandfather and great-grandfather gave the cabin to Ode and Felisa as a wedding gift. He appreciated this incredible gift his family had given him. The cabin had been in Ode's family for countless generations, and each generation gifted the house to the oldest child of the oldest son or daughter. It had been a tradition in his family, which his family had been continuing for many generations. It was still a special refuge to have for his family to get away from all the complications of the job and life as a busy person. This location had a knack for slowing down not only his children, but also himself and his wife. Not exactly sure if it was just his imagination, but this cabin had always been a place where he could truly relax and find his center and a balance of purpose when he felt lost and unfocused.

In the past, he always relied on his inner voice when feeling lost, stressed about deadlines, or crises in his life. The challenges he has faced before pale in comparison to the one he is currently confronting. Now, his mind and emotions entangled him in a complex web of contradictions, resembling a life-sized spider web.

Everywhere he turned, he encountered resistance, and his doubts would cling to strands of insecurity. Fears would become entangled with sticky threads, pulling on his confidence and insecurities. He saw only a maze of emotions and contradictions, with no clear path out. Attempting to untangle one strand risked getting caught on another, making it feel inescapable, like a suffocating self-made prison.

However, his past has always shown him there was indeed a path to escape. Subtly woven into the web, almost invisible to the naked eye, was a single, shimmering strand. This strand represented a truth, a core belief, or perhaps a long-suppressed desire. Initially faint and easily mistaken for another strand, it held the key to navigating this intricate maze.

He brought in the last box from the AeroRover and put it beside all the other boxes that they brought up for the weekend. He said to Felisa, "This is the last of the items from the vehicle. Do you want me to help you make dinner?"

"No, I think I'm all set. I'll get it started and later, when the girls come back from the lake, they can take over and I'll go down for a swim."

"We can both work getting dinner started and then we can both go for a dip together," Ode said with a mischievous smile.

"Ok, it would help if you started peeling the vegetables and then cutting them into small pieces," Felisa said. "You know what? Let's skip the dinner prep and just go down to the lake now. It seems like we could both use a distraction."

"Before we go down, I want your input. When should we disclose the news to the kids about Ghia?" Ode asked.

"I've given it some thought, and I don't believe there will ever be a perfect time."

Felisa stopped what she was doing and came over to stand in front of Ode. "How about this as a plan? I think we should just enjoy our family and our meal. Once the younger kids have gone to sleep, you and I should talk to Dulvod and Helliod. This will shock and probably overwhelm them, but I think they will understand how big a deal this is. I know they will rise to meet the challenge.

Dulvod and Helliod are important because they are the ones that will help the triplets, Melliod, Kelvi, and Lumi to understand this. This is how our family works best and strongest. So why don't we find our swimsuits and go for a swim with our family?"

"Couldn't agree more!" Ode grinned as his eyes brightly lit up.

They both ran around a little crazy, searching for their swimsuits and changing into them wherever they found them. Once they got dressed, they ran out of the cabin, and they both sprinted down the path to the lake. Felisa was always one of the best runners, and she quickly sprinted past Ode as they crested the path leading to the beach in front of the lake.

All the kids were jumping on and off the dock that was floating out in the deeper part of the lake about 100 feet from the beach. Ode and Felisa swam out to the dock to meet their kids. Everyone swam and splashed around for the next several hours. By the time everyone when back to the cabin, they were all exhausted.

Ode and Felisa prepped the remaining parts of the dinner and Helliod made one of her famous *druvor* and *ananas* berry pie, which was definitely the family's favorite. Shortly after dinner, the triplets were all tired out from the activity of the lake earlier. Helliod and Felisa helped put some new bed sheets and blankets on the beds for them. They usually do this first thing when they come to the cabin. Tonight, they just never got around to it.

While Felisa and Helliod were taking care of the beds, Ode brought out an old bottle of aged whiskey that he had received from his great-grandfather many years ago. He poured four glasses and took one for himself and passed the other to Delvod.

"Dad, you only bring this drink out on special occasions or if there is a serious conversation to be had?" Delvod said.

"Yes. I suppose I usually do that. There is something I want to talk to you about, but I want to wait for your sister and mother." Ode was thinking to himself that Delvod should take a drink and enjoy his ignorance for the next few minutes, because after that, it would be pretty bad.

A short while later Felisa and Helliod came downstairs. Helliod eyed the two glasses of whiskey, and she groaned, knowing what the meaning was behind this.

Felisa got up and cut out four slices of the *druvor and ananas* berry pie. She easily carried all four plates, forks, and napkins over to everyone seated at the table in the other room.

Ode waited a few minutes for people to enjoy their pie before he started. With a deep breath as everyone finished up their pie, Ode told them what had happened to him on the trip to the Angbok area. He was going to gloss over the part where he got hurt, but he realized even though it might hurt them, it was important for them to know what happened and what Ghia did in return. He could see all of them taking the details in and, although they might seem a little surprised about it, they could see how healthy he was today when he was swimming. It appeared that they gave Ghia credit for my successful recovery.

When he finished the story about how he got hurt and how Ghia healed him, the next part of the story would be the hardest. "Now it was actually the sentience of the planet which was talking to me in my mind. It was very grateful with the new solution I applied to the planet, which corrected a long-standing problem we have been causing to the planet. Ghia asked for my help to do something. What it was asking me to do is very dangerous and will change everything that we know about on this planet."

He looked at both Helliod and Dulvod, and they were waiting for the next part of his story to continue. He again took a deep breath and said, "Ghia told me there is a very large asteroid heading toward Ghia and will end all life on the surface of the planet. The asteroid is extremely large and will make living on the surface of the planet impossible. This asteroid is due to arrive in ten months' time. Ghia has a plan to save all the animals and lead them underground to enormous caves it has prepared for them. Once Ghia places the animals there, Ghia will induce a special kind of hibernation to put the animals to sleep for a long time. Ghia wasn't sure how it would get all the humans to live underground and suspected they wouldn't wish to do this."

Dulvod said, "I suspect Ghia wanted to start from scratch with sentient lifeforms. I don't think it had any desire to save us or even telling us about it, except you showed it an act of kindness."

Ode looked at each of his children's faces and their eyes. He didn't see fear or disbelief, so he continued, "When I healed the land, Ghia knew it needed to save humans in the same way. Actually, I think I showed Ghia how to do something that it isn't capable of. Ghia is creating six huge caverns with sleeping beds for everyone. While the asteroid destroys the surface, we will need to be underground in several of these caverns. Once we are underground, Ghia would put all the people into a special type of hibernation which will make us sleep for a very long time. Ghia also said we will be in the pods in a suspended animation for however long it might take for nature to rebound. The time we might be underground may be as long as 500 years. It really depends on what kind of damage the asteroid does."

Ode looked at Helliod and Dulvod quickly to see if they had questions, but it seemed they wanted him to continue. "Ghia has asked me to be the spokesperson for this. Believe me, if I had the chance to hand this responsibility to anyone else, I absolutely would do this. The responsibility is enormous and I really need as much help as I can get. I don't know where these caverns are and Ghia said **IT** won't tell me their location until it is ready. So far, you three are the only other people who know this information. This information is extremely dangerous. We must be careful of who we tell this information to. It could cause widespread panic and massive disruption to our society."

Ode looked at Felisa and she nodded. Felisa asked, "So tell us what is going on right now with you? You must have a lot of questions."

Dulvod said, "My first reaction is I agree with you absolutely about who and when you tell people. We should carefully consider this. Certain members of the Continental Imperium members and some of the different regents will only save themselves. We need to get some proof of this information from the different scientists in the world. This will prevent the Defense Regency from coming in heavy-handed and just taking control. You said you don't know of the locations of these underground caverns?"

"Yes, Ghia said it didn't trust other people having this knowledge. These caverns could be hundreds of miles below the surface. Who knows? I don't know and actually I'm glad that I don't know."

Helliod asked in her sweetest voice, "Dad, are you sure you don't know the locations of these or are you just telling us this because you don't want us to know because it might endanger us?"

Ode chuckled at his daughter and said, "Nice try, kiddo. No, I absolutely don't know where these chambers are. Ghia said it would be in the thickest parts of the crust of the planet. I can get a general idea of what areas of the planet these are, but that would be a large area to pinpoint a cavern in the middle of the rock."

Dulvod asked, "Did Ghia say that we can take anything with us? I mean, if you think of all the information about our history, science, languages, culture, medicine, laws, and society structure should be something I hope we can preserve. It wouldn't make sense for us to lose all the knowledge which makes up our society. We should start creating a list and prioritizing this to get this ready. I think there might be one way to get ahead of this before the Regencies or the Continental Imperium mouth pieces bring their chaos into this difficult problem we have to solve. We should also talk to some of the leading schools that aren't Defense Regency affiliated and get them into action."

Helliod said, "There are a lot of community leaders and politicians that would be interested in this. I have several friends who are doing internships at the big companies who are responsible for creating content which the major digital feeds pick up. They might be able to plant a story about asteroid detection or something like that. Who knows, this might get a conversation going with some influential scientists or astronomers. I agree with Dulvod. The Imperium will kill any story it knows will come out. They will use this to their own advantage and bypass everyone else. If many people know about this, it will be harder to just make it go away."

Ode smiled at his wife and his children. They were so smart and doing exactly what he hoped they would do to solve the logistics of the issue. He said, "You're both right in your assessment of the situation. There are three things I think we need to do. First, we need to work with a group of scientists to prove the existence of the asteroid. Let them capture and get all the data they can and coordinate with other scientists in other parts of Ghia. Second, we can target certain newspapers and certain political leaders to bring this out in the open. We need to ensure that the Regencies or the Imperium officials won't influence any of the newspaper or political leaders we choose. And finally, take this to the schools. The schools will hold a huge sway on the people. They are also the ones who can create the lists of things we would need to preserve. Artwork might be possible, but the more stuff we put in, the less room we have for people."

Felisa said, "Helliod and Delvod, we are going to need your help with explaining this to the triplets. They won't understand it, but they trust you implicitly and will listen and try to understand this. We will also help them, but the way this family works best is when we trust each other. They trust you both a lot. I am sure they will want to tell their friends or other social circles, but until this is more common knowledge, we all need to be extra careful of who we share this information with. Dulvod, I fully expect you will tell your wife, Cherulina. Helliod, I also suspect you will want to tell your fiancé Kotlid. Let us know if you want any help to explain or discuss this information with them. Both of us will do whatever we can do to help."

Dulvod looked at his father and asked, "Dad, what was Ghia like?"

Ode laughed loudly at the question. "Well, it is strange. Ghia only communicated with me through my mind. It was very grateful for me fixing the part of the planet we had seriously hurt, but it didn't understand why

I would do something like that. I had put myself into serious physical risk to help the planet. Ghia was having a hard time understanding that. It's strange, but I think this sentience part of Ghia is a relatively new experience and it is still figuring its way out. In some respects, it is like dealing with a child. I'm just glad it fixed me correctly. I was seriously hurt and would have died if Ghia had not healed me."

Dulvod said, "Are you sure about that? I think you look a little shorter by about two inches!"

Ode smiled at his son while Felisa and Helliod broke into a fit of laughter.

The Next Day….

Ode woke at dawn. He crept out of bed so as not to wake Felisa. He collected some clothes and tiptoed downstairs as he headed to the kitchen to make a pot of *grawpa*. It's a standard staple for most people and is very similar to coffee. As he walked downstairs, he could also hear someone else was up at this early hour. Both Helliod and Dulvod were in the kitchen talking in lowered voices. He could only hear a couple of phrases. Helliod said, "… the Defense Regencies will find out about this, and they will fight it aggressively. I don't think it is a question of us telling them or not telling them. Eventually, they will find out. It's up to us to decide whether the controlling authorities will find out now or later."

Dulvod's voice was quick and a little tense as he replied to his sister, "Helliod, you know as well as I do, they will come in and force themselves into this and take control. To be honest, I trust *Dad* a hell of a lot more than those Imperium flunkies. I'm worried about Kotlid's family. His family goes back many generations of service to the regencies of law and order and has buried themselves deeply into the Defense Regency. When, not if, they learn about this, it might put a wedge between you and Kotlid. I'm thrilled to have him join our family. I just don't want this to cause problems between you two."

Helliod responded, "I honestly don't think I can tell him about this yet. He will be honor-bound to tell his family. We should avoid telling Kotlid about this for as long as possible, considering his family's political background. Wow! I can't believe I'm going to be starting a marriage based on a lie."

Before the conversation could go on longer, Ode stopped tip toeing and made some noise as he was heading into the kitchen. "You two are up early. Do you both feel up to taking the boat out on the lake this morning to watch the sunrise?"

"Good morning dad. Yeah, you kind of left us with an exploding bomb laid out on the table last night. Just be glad I didn't have you hauled off to the hospital to get a mental competency test," Dulvod smiled at his father and sister.

Helliod said, "Yeah, sleep wasn't that easy last night. I think taking the boat out into the middle of the lake is a perfect way to start today."

"Yeah, me too." Dulvod chimed in.

"Ok, let me gets some *grawpa* and then we can go. Let's leave your mother and brothers and sister to sleep."

With his cup in hand, the three of them left the house and walked down to the beach. There was a dock with a small boat tied up. Helliod and Dulvod untied the boat from the dock. Dulvod and Helliod jumped in the small boat as it silently departed from the lake's shore and made its way towards the center of the expansive lake, spanning several miles in width. Even with the darkness and the light of the two moons, the water was so clear you could see the bottom of the lake for quite a distance from the shore. As they moved to the middle of the lake, the depth of the lake dropped several hundred feet. The middle of the lake was approximately a little over a thousand feet deep. A glacier from one of the nearby mountains formed the lake many millions of years ago.

When they reached the center of the lake, the horizon was going from inky black to a light grayish color. While they waited for the sun to rise, all three of them were quiet and enjoying the silence.

Helliod was the first to break the silence, but this is exactly what he was hoping for. Helliod said, "Dad, I don't think I can tell Kotlid about this asteroid. I know if I asked him to stay quiet about this, he would honor me and honor you to keep quiet, but this would be at the cost of the honor of his own family. I don't think I can ask him to do that. Dulvod and I were discussing this earlier. Any involvement of the Imperium Ministries or Regencies will almost certainly start a lot of inner fighting among the different administration groups. Whoever is put in charge of solving this planetwide initiative will be an extremely important and influential person. I fear that there will be violence once people find out about this asteroid, and many people will get hurt, needlessly."

"Helliod, I didn't mean to say never tell him. Just don't tell him now. In three or six months, there will be more awareness around the planet of the coming event. Right now, we should really plan hard about how we are going to dump this awful news on the rest of society," Dulvod said as he looked out at the horizon.

Helliod replied, "I agree with you. His family has many generations of former Imperium officials. If I tell him about the imminent asteroid, he will want to tell his family to protect them, and they will insist that this go to the head of the Regency. Senior Commander Fulton sees everything as black and white. There is no gray area. She also does nothing halfway. His family means well, and they are truly not the problem with the Imperium Administration. The leaders and heads at the top of the political chain are constantly getting into these stupid series of moves of who is right and who is wrong and who is the strongest. I know Kotlid isn't like that, but he is deeply devoted to this family. It would be very unfair to ask him to conceal this from them. However, I can't really see any other way than being deceptive to him for at least three months. I still don't know what to do yet. Dad, did you ever keep a big secret from mom at one point in your marriage?"

Ode was a little surprised by the question. This one came out from left field, and he wasn't expecting it, but he could sense his daughter struggling to come to terms with what to do about being honest with her fiancé. He thought about her question and when he thought about it, he couldn't think of any secrets he kept from their mother. Nothing on this type of scale. He addressed his daughter, "honey, I wish I could tell you it is easy to keep a secret from your significant other. Your mother and I made a pledge to each other that we would always be truthful. That trust is a foundation you build your relationship with. It doesn't get any easier over time, but you have to have faith in their decisions."

Helliod asked, "So you always told mom about your secret work projects? We used to ask you about something at work and you just said you couldn't talk about it. Isn't that the same as lying?"

"No, it is different. I made a commitment to your mother and this family that I would be her husband and father to our children. Work has rarely sent me away on any trip that would be dangerous for me. The trip to the Angbok region was the first trip in a long time where my company was sending me into harm's way. I was explicitly told before I left work that day, not to tell any of you or my wife where I was going and what it was about. I ignored what my company told me because I already had a prior commitment to your mother in that I'll be husband and father to this family first. The company was putting me in harm's way, so I needed to tell your mother. We talked about it late into the night. Your mother was pretty upset with me and with my company. I told her I was sure I could fix the areas. She wanted to see if I could do that. It was important to me and important to our planet. She trusted me to go. You also have to understand if your mother could not get past me going to the Angbok area, I wouldn't have gone and would be looking for another job."

"That sounds like you're telling me to be honest with Kotlid?"

"Honestly, I'm not sure what the right answer is. I like Kotlid, and your mother does as well. He has a strong sense of being honest with his family, and it shows his devotion to them. There is no doubt about this. However, he will also feel honor bound to tell them. This will change all our lives over the next year. It is going to test a lot of relationships, I suspect."

Ode said, "Dulvod, you have been unnaturally quiet about this. Care to weigh in?"

"Yeah, my opinion keeps changing. My gut instinct is Kotlid shouldn't be told for at least three months, or at least until we can get some confirmation from other scientists about how real this calamity is going to be. I also like Kotlid, and he will be an excellent addition to our family. I don't know if we told him this information, if he could sit on it and stay silent for at least three months, but he might. We don't want to underestimate him."

Ode looked at Helliod and said, "Do you think if you tell Kotlid, he could stay quiet about this until after we got scientists involved and can corroborate the existence of the asteroid?"

After thinking about it for a moment or two, she looked at her father and said, "I suspect he would wait if

I asked. I just really feel awful asking him to choose. As Dulvod said, it would hurt him if we doubted his resolve. However, I know Kotlid's family cares about me in the same way our family feels about Kotlid. It wouldn't be fair for us to doubt them and their resolve. I don't think I could explain this to him in a way that he would understand how important it was to only tell the world once they confirmed it. Maybe if we could all talk to him, he could understand this better and make the right choice. My biggest fear is that when I go back to see him next week, he will know something is wrong and won't let it go until I tell him what is bothering me. It will be difficult and I'm not sure I can pull that off. I'm not very good at lying."

Ode hated having to have his daughter lie to her future husband. It doesn't set a good precedent. It has now become very important for him to reach out to the scientists he knows to look into this. "Hey why don't we go back to the cabin and start getting some breakfast for everyone. I was also thinking that maybe we could all go for a hike up the mountain today. This might be a good time to tell your brothers and sister about the asteroid. Or if you want to spend the day with them at the cabin, then your mother and I can go for a ride into town for some shopping. We will do whatever you want us to do. Let's head back and get breakfast started."

3 hours later …

After breakfast, they all agreed to go on a hike up the mountain. Once again, Ode told Melliod, Kelvi, and Lumi the story of what happened to him in the Angbok area. He explained to them how seriously wounded he was and he would have died had it not been for Ghia healing me. Lumi also thought Ghia got something wrong when he put me back together. His sons were becoming quite the *jokesters*.

Everyone helped with the discussion filling in each part and what the next steps would be like. His three youngest children were all seventeen years old. They were not identical triplets, unlike Dulvod and Helliod, who were identical twins. However, they were at an age where their autonomy was incredibly important.

Kelvi said, "I'm really surprised this hasn't already happened in Ghia's long history. I think this was something which was just bound to happen, eventually."

Kelvi looked like he thoroughly understood the information Ode told him. He wholeheartedly agreed that involving the scientists was absolutely crucial. Similar to Dulvod, Kelvi harbored a deep distrust towards both the Imperium and Regency politicians. While he had no qualms with the individuals in the Law and Order Regency or the Defense Regency, it was the politicians in higher positions that he found untrustworthy.

Melliod was fully aware of the seriousness of the situation. She had some ideas on how to engage the schools in the matter. At her school, several students were interested in expanding their curriculum by exploring various topics that could benefit their future studies. Melliod thought her friends could organize different research projects, or she could take the initiative to create astronomy clubs and connect them with renowned leaders in the field. This would not only encourage young minds to search for the asteroid but also involve the schools by collaborating with astronomers.

Lumi was the youngest among his three siblings, but only by a few minutes. He had always been a bit more introverted and tended to be quiet. However, the news about the asteroid posed a particular challenge for him in terms of processing and comprehending it.

Upon hearing about the situation, his face filled up with terror and fear. This asteroid would mark the end of the world. He repeatedly asked them if it was some kind of joke, clearly not finding any humor in it. In fact, he became quite angry with his older brother and sister.

They attempted to explain to him how Ghia would assist them in surviving this crisis. They mentioned Ghia would need to repair itself after the devastation caused by the asteroid. To ensure their safety during this time, everyone would enter special pods that would induce sleep. Lumi, however, remained highly doubtful about Ghia actually possessing a sentient part of itself.

Exasperated, Lumi said, "Planets don't know whether it is an asteroid or a bomb blowing it to bits. The planet is just rocks and dirt and not alive like we are."

"Lumi, what is nature then? Nature is the essence of life. All things that live on this planet are part of nature. Nature is in the wind and it surrounds us in millions of different ways. You and I are just as much a part of nature as the animals and the plants are. We can think, we can feel, and we are our own individual person, right? Ghia is just as alive as nature is. In fact, nature wouldn't exist unless Ghia existed. Ghia contains all the plants, animals, oceans, and everything that is alive. We are part of one of those animals, although a highly advanced version of an animal."

Kelvi expressed all of this with a strong conviction, maintaining a level and neutral tone. He didn't feel the need to raise his voice or convey any anger towards him. There was no trace of condescension, arrogance, or an attempt to portray himself as a superior or smarter sibling than Lumi. Kelvi stated his points with an undeniable conviction, akin to explaining that two plus two equals four and always will. He simply presented the facts, without embellishment. By paying attention to his delivery, it was evident that his conviction was unwavering.

It was impressive hearing how Kelvi presented this in a logical and neutral way. Ode made a note to himself that he could learn from the way Kelvi did this. He was very convincing in just the simplistic of ways.

Kelvi added, "Lumi, it's Ok to feel uncertain or afraid about the future and what will happen to us. I promise you," he said, gesturing to everyone around him, "as long as we remain a strong family, we will always be Ok. Our family is always there to support one another, and you can trust that none of us will ever leave you alone in this. It's alright to be scared, and to be honest, I'm a little scared too about what lies ahead for us. But I know that as long as I'm with my family, I'll always be Ok."

Dulvod echoed what Kelvi said, "Even though I'm the oldest by fourteen seconds," giving a quick look at Helliod, and smiling before he continued, "I'm scared out of my mind. I trust mom and dad though. They will help get us through this."

Lumi looked at everyone and said, "Ok. I trust you guys," and gave a quick look at his parents, "I know we will be Ok, yeah it's scary to think about it."

They all hugged each other.

Ode asked, "Are we going up the mountain or are we going down to the cabin?"

Everyone said at the same time, "Up!"

Ode was glad that they continued to go up to the top. He wasn't sure if they could ever do this again. Once again, Ode trudged up another mountain. Let's hope he wouldn't fall off the top of this one, he thought ironically.

Chapter 8
Swept Away

On the way home

WHILE THEY WERE FLYING BACK HOME from their trip to the mountains, Ode thought about whom he could trust to verify the asteroid coming to Ghia. It is imperative that the candidate be neutral in both Imperium and Regency affairs. More importantly, they understand how releasing this information would cause widespread panic.

Felisa was sitting next to him and was pensively looking out at the ground below. Ode noticed she was twirling the end of her long blonde hair in her fingers. While lost in thought and focusing on something she was trying to process, she engaged in twirling the end of her long hair in her fingers. He turned to her and said, "Polti!"

Felisa looked at him confused and said, "huh?"

"Poltibern Torkasu from AICS," Ode turned to look at his wife and continued, "He was the assistant to the head of Astrophysics for the Aratoro Institute of Cosmic

Sciences. Polti helped me to get through those classes at AICS. You remember, we used to go out to dinner with him and his girlfriend."

Polti, as his friends called him, later became a distinguished leading astrophysicist and planetary scientist. He started out just mapping some of the nearest galaxies, asteroids, comets, and nearby planetary systems. About ten years ago, he became known for his development of a new type of telescope using quantum mechanics.

Polti's revolutionary telescope not only could view distant objects, but it also provided an unprecedented level of detail. Unlike traditional telescopes, Polti's invention overcame the issue of diffraction limits. He achieved this by *quantumly* cloning the photons of the targeted area, enabling him to observe far-off spaces with enhanced light. The remarkable success of his Quantum Telescope allowed scientists to explore previously unseen regions of the galaxy.

Felisa replied, "Oh yes, I remember him. Very interesting guy. He was the one who developed the quantum telescope techniques we currently use, right?"

"Yes, that's exactly right. His expertise in astrophysics and planetary science would strongly persuade people about the incoming asteroid."

"He has been extremely busy since we have known him. I know the Imperium has been investing heavily in space travel and colonization on different planets. Wasn't he assigned to work on that project, building long-term generational spaceships that would travel for hundreds of years? Haven't they discussed this idea since our AICS days?" Felisa said wistfully.

Ode was very aware of this project Felisa was talking about. Despite its potential, this project always lacked funding and priority. Ironically, if one of those projects had been a top priority twenty years ago, it might be a very mature program, with probably hundreds of ships manufactured and an option for the population of Ghia.

Ode said, "Yes, I heard he got assigned to the project building the ships on Noth, but I don't believe they have made much progress on creating all the manned ships. The first ship is now completed, and they've moved on to the second. It's really a shame. Ghia could use a couple hundred of those spaceships right about now."

The two moons around Ghia, Noth, and Druna, have an atmosphere capable of people living there, but both of the moons depend on Ghia for almost all of its food and resources. Maybe they could live on the moons for an extra six months, but even that is a stretch. Everyone would starve.

"I read somewhere that Polti got assigned to work with the Science Regency, but I believe the project got put on hold for a while. However, he could be someone who could discreetly check on this asteroid coming to Ghia. He has the background and credibility we need to convince people I'm not a crackpot."

Felisa looked at Ode, caught his eye, and asked, "Ode, do you think you can trust him? He is heavily involved in several different projects sponsored by different Regencies under the Imperium. I read somewhere he was working closely with Senior Commander Fulton from the Defense Regency and with Juniv Koblatt from the Science Regency. Polti might not be the same person we used to know twenty years ago."

Ode started to turn and twist inwardly because of what Felisa had just said. In all the time he has been married, he got used to her incredible unflinching habit of asking questions from a different angle which others never saw. As he thought about it, he had to admit she was right. This was too important to trust one person.

He looked at Felisa and smiled, "You're right! I think Polti is a very reputable astrophysicist with a considerable amount of reputational clout, but it would be foolish to put all the eggs, or rather the entire population, in one basket. I liked what the kids said about involving the schools in the mix of this. Starting up some astronomy clubs would be a good way to get a lot of eyes looking into the sky searching for this asteroid. Ghia told me approximately where it was. Near the Lyra constellation. Maybe we could offer some kind of prize to find out if someone finds anything out there. Dulvod is going to contact some of his professors at his old school to see if they would be interested in it."

"I'm sure we'll find someone who will help spread the word of this calamity and help us prepare for it," Felisa said helpfully.

Felisa was looking out the window at the landscape down below. She twirled her hair in her fingers again. Ode could sense something was bothering her. He reached over and squeezed her hand and waited for her to be ready to voice what was bothering her.

It didn't take long. She looked at Ode with a pained expression on her face, "I don't think we gave Helliod the right advice. Kotlid is a nice young man. We both trust Helliod and Kotlid, and I think we should trust them in this. Helliod is bound to help this family in any way that she can help. Kotlid has proven his commitment to Helliod. We must trust in this." Felisa placed her hand on Ode's hand. Slowly, tenderly, and assertively, she said, "I don't want Helliod to start off a lifelong relationship with deception. You and I have always kept this separation between work and support of the family as different priorities. We agreed in the beginning that support of the family was always our highest priority. If you or I were going into any kind of unsafe situation, this just wouldn't work for us unless we both agreed on it. We have always talked about it beforehand and have been very deliberate in our decisions. I think Kotlid should be given a chance to make his own decision of such massive importance."

"This has been troubling me as well." Ode squeezed her hand and continued, "It felt like this was just the easy and convenient way to answer this. This is not how we have raised our children. You and I have always trusted each other's commitment to this family. We need to extend that same trust and faith in Helliod."

"I agree. Kotlid is perfect for Helliod, and they both bring out the best in each other."

"So, if we trust our daughter, then I think we need to make a leap of faith here. I trust Kotlid will understand the need to keep this as a low-profile thing for a time."

Felisa silently nodded yes.

Ode paused for a moment and said, "If we look at the rest of his family, I'm sure his brothers and parents aren't really any kind of concern. They all seem to have a similar *common sense* about them. However, he has several uncles that are deeply involved with the Imperium Policies. His uncle, Tomachlus, is someone who is in the upper hierarchy of the Defense Regency. My initial reaction is that we shouldn't trust Tomachlus, but I have to trust Kotlid on this."

"Ok, how do you want to proceed with this?"

"Let's set up a time to have dinner with Helliod and Kotlid this week. Either you or I could tell Helliod this is coming. I think this will take a lot of pressure off her. Kotlid is part of our family, and we can't let their relationship get sabotaged before it even begins. Agreed?"

"Absolutely!" Felisa said affirmatively.

Back at work …

The next morning, Ode left early to go to the H4A. Sadly, such a magnificent feat of engineering would be obliterated in the first few minutes of the asteroid impacting with Ghia. Such a tragic waste of effort and beauty.

The week started off as it normally does. Ode got all the required reports he needed to fill out. He knew he couldn't tell his commander the exact truth about falling off the mountain, but said it took him two trips up the mountain to get the test done. So far, he has heard no other mention of the crisis from ten days ago. Apparently, word has gotten around that we corrected it by using a weaker compound manually applied to the affected areas of instability. A lot of sensors got destroyed, so everyone just assumed the missing sensors would require a new site analysis of the area.

It didn't take long, but after a few days back at work, everything seemed to settle into a more normal routine of work. Ode did a little research on a couple of his college friends who went off into astrophysics or any other scientists he could contact to help with getting an independent verification of the asteroid. Ode needed to be very careful about how he approached these scientists. He wanted to make sure he could trust whomever he asked to verify the existence of the asteroid. He needed someone else who wasn't under any influence of the Continental Imperium. This would be an important qualification to determine.

His research turned up two astrophysicists who appeared to be very credible and well known in astronomy. He made plans with one, Simol Athebyne, for this Friday at a restaurant about forty minutes away from work.

Before the meeting with Simol, Ode set up a meeting with Polti via a holo link with his office on Noth. After the first five or ten minutes of catching up on work and events going on in their lives, Ode told him about the experience in the Angbok area on Prosun.

At first, Polti had all kinds of questions about how he could survive the fall from the mountain. At one point, he thought I was playing some kind of practical joke on him. Eventually, Polti could see Ode wasn't joking around and was serious about this.

If something was coming toward our planet, then we should start gathering data on this event as soon as possible. He gave Polti the approximate locations near the Lyra constellation. Polti said he could start looking into this right away.

The telescopes they use on Noth were far more powerful than anything on Ghia. By the time they had finished their conversation, Ode and Polti had come up with a list of specific data items needed. Some items they would need are things like the size of the object; how fast it was traveling; or if it was rotating. Other important pieces of data needed would be if the object is just one object or is it multiple objects; where will it start to enter Ghia's atmosphere? Ode signed off the video call feeling confident things were progressing well towards this impossible goal of shouldering this responsibility, which was unexpectedly upsetting his life.

A couple of days later, he was flying to the restaurant to meet with Simol Athebyne. Ode was thinking about how everything had just seemed to snap into place this week. Just this week, Felisa, Helliod, and Kotlid went to dinner to tell Kotlid of her father's experience in the Angbok area and how the asteroid is coming toward Ghia.

Kotlid was very upset by it at first, but he eventually understood the need for discretion in such a delicate situation. He volunteered to help with whatever needed to get everyone ready to go underground.

Ode also took some time to confide in a few trusted colleagues at work. One of them was Erig, a close friend and an exceptionally skilled scientist. Their collaborative work spanned many years, and Ode was confident that Erig would maintain the confidentiality of the information as long as needed. Having a companion in this endeavor was important to Ode, as he did not want to bear the weight of this significant event alone, aside from his family.

Ode arrived at the restaurant on time and spotted Simol near the door. The host seated them at a table in the far corner of the restaurant. After they gave their order to the server, Ode told Simol everything about the asteroid coming to Ghia in about nine months.

Simol listened quietly to what Ode was telling him. He seemed to absorb it all and only asked a few questions. He was very curious about how Ghia healed Ode. The whole concept of Ghia being a sentience part of the planet didn't seem to faze him at all.

Ode was a little surprised by this and asked, "So you seem to understand and be 'Ok' with the fact that our planet is a sentient being?"

"Surprised? Maybe, but not disbelieving. Nature isn't quite sentient, but what if it is? To me, Ghia being sentient is just a logical extension of what we have always insinuated when we anthropomorphize nature as sentient."

By the end of the meal with Simol, he was again feeling confident he was right on track with signing up one more person to help the planet and its population survive the catastrophe hurtling toward it. They were drinking *grawpa* and brainstorming about what data they might want to collect.

The server came over to the table and paused a moment before speaking until both Simol and Ode could give him their full attention.

"Sirs, I'm sorry to ask this, but my manager wants to speak to you both in the kitchen."

Ode looked at Simol and could see the confusion on his face. He seemed as confused as Ode was. He asked, "Is there something wrong?"

The server seemed a little nervous, but just said, "He asked me to bring you both into the kitchen, but he didn't specify why."

Neither of them knew what to make of this. They both shared a look of confusion about why the restaurant manager would want to speak to them. They both got up from their chairs and followed the server through the different parts of the restaurant to a side door near the kitchen. Once in the kitchen, they went directly to the back to where there was a small office, which Ode assumed this was the manager's office. It was a tiny office with barely enough room for more than three people standing shoulder to shoulder. The office had no windows and the door to the office had a small square window in the center. In front of the door was a man with a large build, wearing a black shirt with both sleeves rolled up on his forearms. Ode guessed that this must be the manager of the kitchen. The man's face was emotionless. When Simol and Ode approached the door, the server disappeared and the person in front of the door opened it, asking them to wait inside.

As they both walked inside the office, Ode felt something sting him on the back of his neck. He turned around quickly, just to catch the man with the black shirt bringing his hand quickly back from Simol's neck. Suddenly, a sense of panic came over Ode's face. He immediately felt a little wobbly and sat down quickly in the nearest chair. Simol did exactly the same thing, and they were both unconscious in moments.

The man walked over to Ode and found the keys to his AeroRover in one of his pockets. He also searched Simol's pockets for his keys as well. He then walked out of the office, turned, and locked the door. Next, he left the kitchen and went out to the front of the restaurant. Another person met him who was just as large as the man with the black shirt was. Then they searched the parking lot for both vehicles. While they were doing this, Ode and Simol were being taken out of the office and put on a separate transport vehicle. Once they found both the AeroRovers, they got in them and removed them from the restaurant parking area. They took the vehicles to some secret underground bunker that would be impossible to track.

Chapter 9
Liberation

Defense Regency Underground Bunker

Three months later …

THE ROOM IS DARK AND UTTERLY SILENT. Ode opened his eyes to the blackness of a room absent of any light. The velvety blackness was seamless, featureless, and lacked any orientation of up or down. The only sign of gravity he felt was his body lying on the mattress and his head on the pillow. With clockwork precision, as soon as his eyes opened, he began a daily ritual of a whisper count from one to twenty. One. Two. Three. At sixteen, as if on cue, the floor, and ceiling blushed with luminescence, turning the blackness into a drab gray. By twenty, as if taking a huge breath of air, the room exhaled light emanating from the moldings crafted into the ceiling and the floor. Velvety blackness transformed from nothingness to stoic beige plaster covering the walls.

The spartan, utilitarian function of the room seemed pervasive. It contained a bed just wide enough for one person to sleep comfortably. On each side of the bed, there was a stainless steel shelf, or table, built flawlessly into the wall. The seamless connection of the shelf to the wall hinted at coming from a large prefab factory. If these walls were being prefabricated, it would suggest these were being built on a large scale for thousands and thousands of rooms like this one. Just throw a bed in between the two shelves and you have a rudimentary bedroom.

There were two doors in the room. One door led to a small private bathroom with large blue and white tiles on the floor and walls. The vanity countertop was navy blue, with a bone white sink with stainless steel faucet and handles that were flawlessly molded into the countertop. The toilet and the shower were molded seamlessly into the walls and floor as well. Like the bedroom, the bathroom also had illuminated molding on the ceiling. The vanity contained a drawer which held any toiletries, soap, and other general items that you would find in a male bathroom. Oddly, there was no mirror anywhere. He wondered why they provided a razor and comb, but no mirror.

Another bedroom door led to a spacious common room with bland beige walls, also adorned with floor and ceiling lights. Throughout Ode and Simol's confinement, a locked door remained untouched at the far end of the common room. Simol's bedroom was a mirror image of Ode's room with the bed and a private bathroom. Again, everything about this confinement area reeked of prefabricated utility.

Ode, fueled by the promise of caffeine, launched himself out of bed and into the common room. The space boasted a table and chairs that looked strangely out of place in this sterile environment. Along the wall was a countertop stretching like a concrete road. Just beyond the end of the countertop was a refrigerator that hummed like a lonely monk. A sterile rectangular space carved into the countertop acted as a sink, which mirrored the bathroom's monotony. Above, open cabinets displayed their meager sets of glasses, plates, and bowls. Seamless and what one could expect from a prefabricated wall.

Ode surveyed the scene, a wry smile playing on his lips. "Home, sweet home," he muttered, and reached for the pot of grawpa that was sitting on the countertop. Every day, when the lights came on in the morning, a pot of grawpa magically appeared. The smell of the craved sweet brown morning caffeine boost reminded him of his life before being confined. Early morning having breakfast with his family before running off to work.

He took a seat at the small table. He stared at the only other door in their communal area. Neither of them have seen this door opened since being confined here. What or where this door led to was a mystery. Ode surmised there was a bigger mystery here other than where the door led. Like a heavy weight on his chest, he felt an impending doom, which continued to leach any strength or fight left in him. He felt responsible for Simol being here with him.

The night he met with Helliod and Kotlid seemed to be the obvious way the Imperium found out about the asteroid coming to Ghia. As much as he liked Kotlid, Ode didn't trust certain members of his family. Kotlid's parents come from a long lineage of notable and powerful people in the Law and Order Regency and also the Defense Regency. Somehow, the information about the asteroid coming to Ghia got out. In a typical Imperium fashion, their solution is to remove something they didn't want to deal with and just make it disappear. This way, it was no longer a threat to the unyielding unity of the Defense Regency. Regrettably, Simol got caught up in this as collateral damage.

Coming from the other room, Simol came and sat down with a cup of the grawpa that he had poured for himself. He mumbled sarcastically, "another day in paradise." As he was saying this, he used a small knife to scratch out another mark on a piece of plastic, which was their makeshift calendar to mark the days of their confinement.

Simol looked at Ode, and said, "ninety-eight by my count."

Ode glanced at it and nodding in agreement. Simol had done this every day when he woke up. It was the ritual they maintained to keep track of time. Other than the lights going dark at night, this is their only way of marking time.

Ode stared absent-mindedly into his half emptied cup of grawpa, when a sound came from the door that never opens. Both Ode and Simol looked at each other to check if they had actually heard something. A quick glance at Simol's face made it clear he had heard something as well. Neither of them were prepared for this. Their daily routine never changed, and this door has always been locked and closed. For a brief moment, Ode got caught in a juxtaposition of rapid, heart beating excitement and cloying, paralyzing trepidation. His innate curiosity held him in place, patiently waiting to see who was behind the door.

When the door swung open, any concern, or trepidation, he felt switched instantly to sheer joy. His wife, Felisa, stood in the doorway, flanked by his daughter Helliod and her fiancé Kotlid. Upon seeing Kotlid, Ode took a big breath, but remained silent. He wanted to find out all the facts before rushing to a judgement. Simol was looking at Ode to gauge what the next move would be.

Ode rushed into an embrace with his wife. Whatever his feeling was regarding Kotlid, he trusted his wife to do the correct thing. He turned to Simol and said, "This is my wife Felisa, my daughter Helliod, and her fiancé, Kotlid." Then, he said, "This is Simol Athebyne. Due to his presence at the restaurant with me, he got caught up in this mess. I'm dying to know what is happening outside."

Felisa said, "Ode, we don't have a lot of time right now. Kotlid has secured clearance for both of you to leave here, but we need to do this right now!"

"Right! Ok, let's go. We will follow you."

Ode and Simol followed Felisa and Kotlid out of a maze of corridors and different entryways. It appeared to be a complicated building built for holding thousands of people. They finally came to a set of elevator doors. There was only one button, and it pointed up. Kotlid reached in his pocket and produced a keycard. Bringing this card close to the button, the button lit up. A few moments later, the elevator doors parted, and they went inside. The elevator took them up to a ground floor. They passed through one more door and then they came out to a large parking lot full of vehicles.

The sun was shining brightly and Ode and Simol needed to shield their eyes from the bright orange glare. Kotlid took them to where his AeroRover was located. They all piled in and were quickly on their way, flying away from the facility.

Once they were several miles away from the facility, Ode gradually felt the weight around his chest lifting. The heavy shroud of confinement wrapping around him so tightly slowly faded away.

Kotlid and Felisa were in the front; Simol and Helliod were in the back of the vehicle with Ode. Felisa turned her head to both Ode and Simol. "Lumi and Kelvi retrieved your vehicles and they are waiting for us back at the cabin in the mountains. Many surprising events occurred during your absence."

"How many days have we been gone? Simol and I counted ninety-eight days, but we aren't completely sure. One minute we were in the restaurant's kitchen, and then we woke up in the cell."

Kotlid said, "It has been ninety-nine days since they took you from the restaurant. I'm sorry you had to endure that for so long. We have been trying to get you both released since they took you."

Felisa jumped in before Ode could respond to Kotlid. "First, you need to know what is happening right now. A huge divide exists between the Defense Regency and the

Science Regency. The Defense Regency is mobilizing the regional, political, and scientific leaders. Both sides disagreed on how to handle the asteroid approaching Ghia. Polti validated the information you gave him and found the asteroid coming toward Ghia. He betrayed you, Ode. He's the person responsible for you being confined in that underground bunker. Polti wanted you out of the way so you wouldn't contradict him. Polti claimed he was the person who accidentally found this danger to Ghia. It makes me sick and angry when I think about it."

Felisa took a deep breath and apologetically said, "Simol, I'm especially sorry for you getting dragged into this. You were just unlucky to be in the wrong place when Polti abducted Ode. We contacted your parents and sister, who are waiting for you when we land. If there is anyone else you want to be contacted and protected, just let Kotlid know. We will make sure to get them on any list to move underground when the time is right. We will all get through this."

Simol said, "Thank you. I appreciate that. My wife died many years ago and my sister and my parents are the only family I have left. Did you say they will be where we are going right now?"

"Yes, we told them we are going to bring you both back to our spot in the mountains. They are anxious to see you."

Felisa looked at Ode. "Unfortunately, Polti has the ear of many of the top leaders. Approximately 800,000 people have departed for Noth. A lot of basic services are breaking down because there aren't enough people left to do the normal everyday necessities we all rely on. Most of the people are working on those ships and they got conscripted to go to Noth."

"How many of those people will actually be able to get a seat on the ships they are building?" Ode asked.

"I heard there are maybe about 100,000 people with lots of money and power. They will most likely get a ticket on any ships they have ready. They are telling people that in six months, they can build at least twenty new ships to have the entire population migrate to another planet. Some people actually believe this."

"It took almost ten years to build that one ship. This sounds like a colossal lie,"

Felisa said, "If this wasn't such a serious matter, it would be comical. I hope we can find a way to get those people off Noth and go underground with us. I'm sure it will be extremely tough to break away from the forces stationed on Noth to keep all the conscripts in line and come back to Ghia. This effort to build these ships is called the Genesis Project."

Ode responded, "The Noth moon can't support even half of that many people, never mind 800,000. And do they believe six months is enough time to build these ships? That is insanity."

"Yeah, well, this is what most people feel about it. Another plan, called Operation Unity, is their Plan B option. They want to blow up the asteroid before it hits Ghia. About a month ago, they sent up almost a hundred missiles and bombs that are targeting the asteroid. The hope is they will blow it up so it won't be a threat to the planet. Almost the entire scientific community agrees with one thing. This plan won't work at all."

Kotlid interjected, "We should arrive at the Crestin mountains in about twenty minutes. My uncles got especially pressured by other leaders to evacuate tradesmen to Noth."

Kotlid stole a quick glance back at Helliod in the back seat and said, "Helliod did a masterful job of convincing my uncles and aunts that there is another way to save ourselves. She has convinced all of them and many other people who need to understand how serious this is."

Kotlid continued, "In the past month, many species of animals have disappeared from all over Ghia. Some people have spotted huge migrations of animals heading towards various places around Ghia. Then these giant herds of animals just vanished. I don't mean wandered off in the woods and then found a place to hibernate. I mean, they just vanished into thin air. Many people in some of the more rural areas were getting spooked about this. Again, Helliod was extremely convincing that Ghia was doing this and there was a plan for all the people as well. When she wants to, she can be quite convincing."

Ode couldn't see Kotlid's face, but he knew he was beaming and just absolutely and totally smitten with Helliod. Among all the news he heard today, this was the most touching. He made a note to himself to have a discussion with Kotlid about how happy he was to be proven so completely wrong.

Later that evening, he came to know the person who had discovered the whereabouts of Ode and Simol, who were being held captive. Surprisingly, it was Kotlid's uncle, Tomachlus, who had discovered their location. Armed with this crucial information, Tomachlus promptly signed the necessary documents to secure the release of Ode and Simol.

This was a moral lesson for Ode today. It just reinforced a critical character trait you just can't always say for certainty if someone will betray you or not. He was positive it was Kotlid and his uncle who orchestrated his captivity. It actually was the exact opposite. Both of them warranted trust, and it was an important commodity right now in these desperate times.

Chapter 10
The Big Pebble

Nine Months to Impact

Noth Moon

Polti

EARLIER, BEFORE HIS ABDUCTION, Ode made a terrible error in judgement when he trusted Polti to assist him. Ode had informed Polti about his prophetic conversation with Ghia. He had requested Polti's assistance in substantiating his assertion that an extinction-level event would occur in ten months. Ironically, Polti's immediate reaction to Ode was sadness and pity. It was clear to Polti that Ode had some kind of neurological breakdown. Polti told Ode he would look into it "the first chance he got". Polti used his well-polished charm and pledge of loyalty to convey hope and positivity.

At the time, he thought Ode wasn't an astrophysicist, and if memory served him, he was a horrible student.

Polti was working as a teacher's assistant when Ode attended AICS, or Aratoro Institute of Cosmic Sciences, many decades ago. He could remember some endless nights tutoring him to help him pass his astronomy classes. Now, Ode wants him to go chasing after a supposed runaway asteroid which will impact with Ghia. This would be an utter waste of time.

But what if he was right? Even though he decided it was all nonsense, it still intrigued him. One question he could not seem to escape rattling around in his brain was, "why hadn't we detected this years ago?"

After he finished his talk with Ode, he made a mental note to look, regardless of his skepticism. Polti's position on Noth gave him administrative control of the scheduling of all the telescopes. If he wanted, he could override any conflicts people might run into. He didn't need the high-powered telescopes, which were in high demand, but he just wanted something he could use to take a look. It was also because Polti didn't want anyone to think that he was searching for an errant asteroid in the Lyra constellation. The odds of something so far away being on a direct course to hit Ghia were astronomical.

A few days later

After a few days, Polti finally found some spare time to set up one of the many telescopes being used on Noth and began his search for the asteroid. The vastness of space is truly awe-inspiring. Quantum telescopes mostly collect data on objects that emit light, with the remarkable ability to capture even the faintest light from distant objects in the universe. By amplifying and reproducing these photons, the telescopes can unveil remarkable details. However, locating an asteroid that does not reflect or emit any light poses a significant challenge. It seamlessly merges into the dark void of space, making detection nearly impossible.

It took him two days on the telescope, and by sheer luck, he searched near the blue supergiant star known as Cerulastra. This asteroid was hiding behind the giant star, keeping it hidden for a very long time. The star's immense gravity has accelerated the asteroid, giving it a significant boost in speed and momentum. As a result, the asteroid will slingshot away from Cerulastra. Detecting this asteroid accurately would have been impossible if the asteroid had not been directly in front of the star.

Polti could calculate the trajectory and speed of the object. From his calculations, it became quite clear that this asteroid was on a direct course to impact on Ghia. He redid his calculations several times, but he kept reaching the same conclusion. In nine months, an asteroid will impact on Ghia. This will be an extinction event. The entire surface of the planet will be uninhabitable.

How did Ode know about this? Polti was certain he didn't use any of the telescopes on Noth. Nine months? This is consistent with the timeline of when Ode said he found about the asteroid several weeks earlier.

Confident in his results, Polti knew the next logical thing to do was to inform the Continental Imperium. A glimmer of sunshine crept into his mind like a silent thief. The information Ode told him could be used to his advantage. With a touch of irony, he immediately thought about naming this asteroid after himself. People could call it the Torkasu Extinction Asteroid, or TEA for short. He laughed when he thought of attaching his name to one of the biggest events to happen to the planet. Immediately, he shuddered at the thought of his name being associated with an event that would wipe out his planet and species. Ridiculous! He named the twenty mile wide asteroid the *Big Pebble*.

Chapter 11
Favor

Noth moon

Eight months till impact

POLTI COULD FEEL HIS NERVES getting the best of him. A tight knot of impending doom twisted in his stomach, leaving him in a perpetual state of uneasiness. Initially, he believed that his role as the harbinger of fate would elevate his importance. And it did, at least in the beginning. People, especially those in influential positions, eagerly listened to his every word. This only fueled his insatiable craving for attention and the feeling of superiority. Polti was highly skilled at manipulating people.

His mentor Simol Athebyne invented the quantum telescopes. The quantum telescope was like regular telescopes, but the technique Simol invented was to take any light from an object in space and multiply those light photons by several thousands of magnitude. Simol was adamant that more research and testing needed to be done before it could get released to the public.

Polti thought otherwise. He told the larger scientific and astronomical communities about this invented technique. He claimed full credit for it. Shortly after that, he lobbied several different sects of the Science Regency. Shortly after, they offered him a position in one of the research labs on Noth. Neither Simol nor anyone else associated with this research never disputed his claim.

Polti replayed the conversation he had with Ode. Ode said Ghia would place people underground. That is insanity. Some of the work Polti did here on Noth was to help with an enormous project of building a large spaceship to explore the solar system and beyond. The thinking behind this was that it would be a generational ship and be able to carry 150,000 passengers who were in space for several generations. This project had been going on and off for the last ten years. They had recently finished the first one. The Science Regency was pressuring him to start looking for passengers and start training for the crew for the spaceships. This might dramatically boost the funding for this project. If he could get the Continental Imperium behind this, he knew he could get them to put him in charge of building all these ships.

Polti knew that there were several habitable planets categorized within a range of twenty or thirty light years. It would take a couple of generations to travel distances like that.

This was undoubtedly the answer. Ghia would require an extensive period to recover from the catastrophic consequences of these asteroids' impact. It might take anywhere from 500 to 2000 years for the ecosystem to evolve and sustain basic single-celled organisms.

Continental Imperium

The Continental Imperium of Ghia operates under a unique governmental structure, combining elements of a ministerial system and a regency. At the helm are the Ministers, elected representatives from each continent who form the legislative body. These Ministers debate and pass laws, shaping the policies that govern the Imperium.

To ensure efficient execution of these policies, the Continental Imperium appoints a council of Regents. Each Regent oversees a specific area of governance, such as education, science, culture, defense, law and order, banking, economics and many more. This division of responsibilities allows for focused attention and expertise in each domain. The Regents work closely with the Ministers, implementing their decisions and providing expert advice. This dual structure, combining the democratic input of Ministers with the specialized knowledge of Regents, aims to create a balanced and effective administration for the Imperium.

Polti had to carefully consider and devise a strategic plan for informing the Continental Imperium. Interestingly, in a few weeks' time, individuals from the Science Regency and the Imperium Representatives from all six continents will gather on Noth. It was during this gathering that he would disclose his proposal. Entrusting anyone other than himself with this project would be foolish.

When the members of the Science Regency and Imperium Ministers first heard the news of this asteroid, they were shocked and couldn't believe it. The entire Continental Imperium argued for almost a month to decide what was the right thing to do for the planet. Wasting no time, Polti stepped forward and offered to take on the immense responsibility of constructing the spaceships to relocate the people of Ghia to a new, habitable planet. As Polti expected, they were extremely grateful to him for his courageous choice to take on this difficult mission.

There was a lack of consensus among the members of the Imperium Ministers and Regents regarding the construction of spaceships on Noth. The majority of the council supported the Science Regency, who proposed constructing dozens of generational ships to relocate Ghia's population. The Ministers voted on it and gave the Science Regency the green light to proceed with this enormous project. Almost a third of the Imperium advocated for the deployment of explosive missiles to the asteroid. Their aim was to detonate it or alter its path. The disagreements between the Justice Regents, Defense Regents, and the Science Regents escalated to such intensity and discord that they ultimately departed from Noth. They returned to Ghia intending to plan a strategy to launch missiles equipped with massive bombs capable of obliterating the asteroid.

This smaller faction of Ministers and Regents within the Imperium had considerable power, with many members occupying influential positions dedicated to maintaining peace and enforcing law and order. If there was any group capable of successfully launching missiles to destroy the asteroid, it was undoubtedly them. Polti took it upon himself to personally assure certain members that he would secure a place for them and their loved ones if the asteroid could not be halted or diverted from its collision course with Ghia.

Senior Commander Alginna Fulton was a highly influential and persuasive member of the Defense Regency. Within the Regencies, their primary responsibility was to manage all administrative tasks and provide specific policy direction for that Regency. However, in some cases, the workload became too overwhelming for one person to handle alone. In such instances, both the Regent and the Senior Commander worked together to oversee all aspects of the administrative function. These individuals held significant power, as they played a crucial role in day-to-day decision-making and had the authority to shape and guide various policies.

Polti found a private moment with her at the end of one of the final meetings shortly before she and the rest of her faction left Noth to go back to Ghia. Polti began, "Commander Fulton, I was wondering if there was something you could help me with when you go back to Ghia?"

Commander Fulton's face was a mixture of contradictions. Her smile was as inviting as a calm bath of water, but her eyes were like a gray, stormy sea. She said, "Ask me what you want me to do. I can't tell you if I can do something unless I know the details."

Polti said, "Straight to the point. I like that. Since time is of the essence in this matter, I'm concerned about a former mentor of mine, named Simol Athebyne."

Commander Fulton said, "Ah, I have heard the name before. I think he consults with a couple of the other regents. What exactly are you worried about?"

Simol said, "My fear is that he will want to debate every single detail of construction. He's very stubborn and I don't think we have the time for a long extended debate."

Commander Fulton answered, "I understand your concern. Don't worry—I'll handle it. He won't get in your way until after we've launched the missiles to divert the asteroid. The highest priority here is to establish a streamlined decision-making process."

"Thank you. I appreciate your help in managing this situation. I'll make sure we stay on track and keep everything moving forward smoothly."

It was a bonus for Polti that Ode was with Simol when he was abducted. Ultimately, three months later, it was Kotlid's uncle, Tomachlus Furgus, who worked for Commander Fulton, that discovered the location where Ode and Simol were being held.

Once Simol was out of his way, he could put all his efforts into building these ships. It was important to not let Simol come into this project and second guess or question every step Polti took. Many of the Ministers in the Continental Imperium and the Science Regency knew and respected Simol. It was important for Simol to get out of his way, at least until it was too late to change course.

If he honestly looked at it, he still harbored a lot of anger towards Simol from back in the time that Simol was mentoring him. Polti stole the idea of the invention of the quantum telescopes because Simol insisted on proper testing before announcing it. Polti didn't want to delay because he knew that the first person to announce a discovery could take all the credit and reward of the discovery. If you're late to announce a discovery or idea, you're still late. He learned this lesson the hard way with Simol. He would work furiously for days and weeks on an experiment. Simol fiercely argued every outcome or detail with him. Simol could uncover some inane trivial detail he didn't include in his proof, and Simol recorded his experiment as a failure.

It always irked him that Simol couldn't see the bigger picture of what Polti's idea was. Polti believed he deserved recognition for his idea, not for how he defended it. Unfortunately, it was Polti who didn't understand the bigger picture of the discipline required to be a successful engineer or scientist. It was important to challenge everything and find new ways to break your theories. If he was persistent and could endlessly challenge his thinking by trying to find each area where it failed, ultimately it would force him to think in new ways of approaching a problem.

Polti thought just simply coming up with a great idea or discovery is sufficient for him to gain the recognition and a certain amount of fame and fortune. This narrow view prevented him from recognizing the importance of critical evaluation. Conversely, Simol understood the value of subjecting theories to closer scrutiny by peers. Despite Simol's attempts to teach Polti this concept, Polti remained resistant and couldn't let go of his defensive mindset.

Construction

Backed by the Imperium's unwavering support, Polti devised a strategy to expedite the production of spaceships required for relocating the population to a new planet. He estimated they would need to build at least twenty new spaceships, at a minimum. The resources and the manpower to achieve this goal were almost impossible.

The Science Regency took almost ten years to build a massive ship that could carry 150,000 passengers. The construction of this enormous vessel faced many problems and delays over the past decade. It would be extremely difficult, if not impossible, to replicate this massive scale for twenty more ships.

Polti, consumed by the impending doom, wrestled with the design of the spaceships for the mass exodus. Scrapping existing blueprints, he pushed for his vision with relentless arguments, like a jackhammer pounding the same point. Initially, his passion captivated everyone. However, his repetitive arguments and refusal to consider alternatives wore thin. His voice turned into background noise, ignored even when he might have been right.

The crux of the conflict was the engine. Polti championed nuclear power for its abundance, but the radiation risks were too high. Senior engineers, fearing Polti might force his design, proposed a compromise. They have developed a technique for extracting hydrogen atoms from water and using them as a source of fuel. By super-heating it to a plasma state (like electrifying neon gas), they could achieve the necessary propulsion for the long journey, albeit without nuclear power.

Seven months to Impact

Passenger Manifest

Due to the tight schedule, Polti took on the responsibility of managing the passenger manifests, granting himself almost godlike power. He had the authority to determine which individuals would board the initial ships departing soon from the Noth moon.

Last week, Polti submitted the final manifests for the first eight ships that would depart later that week. He had to recalculate the final manifest to accommodate the change with the two ships leaving after the asteroid hit Ghia.

Polti divided the list into two categories. Most of the passengers were the manpower responsible for operating these massive spaceships. Everyone included in the ship manifest had a specific job assigned to them. Some passengers had the responsibility of handling the engines, while others were required to cultivate food in the hydroponics section. There were also individuals responsible for cooking and preparing meals, as well as numerous other labor positions essential for the efficient functioning of these ships. Polti categorized all the members of the Continental Imperium and Regents, along with their families, as executive passengers. It was the executives' responsibility to make critical decisions for both the vessel and the passengers. Essentially, they were only required to perform minor tasks.

Polti took on the role of the Chief Astronomic Officer, positioning himself as the third in command. The Captain and Vice-Captain held the first and second levels of authority on the vessel, but little did they know Polti had secretly installed a back door to the control systems. This allowed him to override their commands whenever necessary. Being intimately familiar with these ships and their destination, Polti believed it was crucial for him to keep complete control. His extensive knowledge of the design of each of the ships and the intended trajectory compelled him to hold on to this ultimate power.

Chapter 12
Quantum Dancing

Six Months to Impact

Crestin Mountain Cabin

Dawn

ODE OPENED HIS EYES TO a darkened room. For a brief second, he thought he was back in the underground bunker. Gratefully, he realized he was in his own bed and his wife was sleeping next to him. His nightmare of being confined for ninety-nine days was over.

Now, preparing his people for a massive migration weighed heavily on his mind. The situation had grown more critical because of population migration to the Noth moon. What type of provisions will they need underground? How will they preserve all of their history and the knowledge of their society? Questions kept bubbling up in his mind.

The more questions he came up with just highlighted the fact he needed Ghia's involvement in this planning. Selfishly, he felt disappointed that Ghia had not contacted him once during his confinement. Why hadn't Ghia reached out to him while he was stuck in that bunker? At one point, he questioned his recollection of what had happened to him in the Angbok region. Had he just been hallucinating? Ode knew his fall from the mountain was horrific, but it still felt unreal for him to believe Ghia healed all his wounds. A fall from such a devastating height would surely be fatal. How had he survived such a thing?

Nothing was going to be accomplished lying in bed. Ode got up quietly from the bed and put some comfortable clothes on. With a mug of hot grawpa in hand, he headed to the little beach by the lake. If he hurried, he could take the rowboat out to the middle of the lake to watch the sunrise.

It was still dark, but the sun would rise shortly. These times of stillness and quietude were special for Ode. In the pre-dawn stillness, his thoughts moved with unhurried grace like mist swirling over the mirror-like surface of the lake in front of him. His thoughts flowed freely, giving him the clarity to see the path he needed to follow. In the distance, the whisper of faint lavender and indigo calm him; however, the silhouette of the mountain stubbornly remained shrouded in black.

When Ode reached the small sandy beach that led to Crestin Lake, he noticed a long dock on the right side. Several watercraft were securely tied to the dock. A rowboat was resting peacefully on the calm, flat water. It was a simple vessel, equipped with two oars and a central bench. The open rowboat beckoned to all who ventured to this far end of the dock.

Ode slipped into the waiting rowboat, and it glided to the center of the lake; the water gurgling with each measured stroke. He had a front-row seat to the magical sight of the sun bursting out from behind the dark silhouette of the mountain. It was a spectacle that never failed to awe and inspire him.

Basking in the rising sun's warmth, Ode heard a familiar voice in his mind.

Ode?

Yes, Ghia. I'm so glad to talk to you again. I was afraid I was just imagining our discussion several months ago.

You know the answer to that isn't true. I have been very busy preparing spaces

for all the animals, plants, and your people to live underground.

Ghia, you said that for our species to survive, we will need to move underground into special areas so we will be safe from the asteroid. I don't know what I need to tell people about this. There will be a lot of questions!

Don't worry, my child, I will help you as much as I can. What questions do you anticipate encountering?

Well, the first question I can expect people will ask me is how will they get down to these underground caverns?

I am in the process of developing six distinct underground areas that will be available for all the people worldwide. The plan involves teleporting individuals from the surface into these underground caverns, which will take place gradually in multiple stages. To facilitate a smooth transition, I will teleport people from their beds while they are asleep. Each person will be placed in a cryogenic capsule, specially designed for their body. This will slow their body down to a level that will keep them safe, protected, and

nourished for as long as it takes to get the surface to be habitable for life.

What can they bring with them? This will probably be the most difficult hurdle for getting people to join us. What can I tell people who ask this question?

Ode, it is important for people to understand that all life will cease to exist on the surface. The asteroid will erase everything your people have built or created. Nothing will remain on the surface when this is over. It will not be possible for people to bring anything with them.

Ok, I agree with you that this is an all-or-nothing kind of thing. Why in multiple stages?

I want to do this in small groups, so I can preserve my energy for when the asteroid impacts the surface. The entire process will take about a month to transport everyone completely into the cryogenic capsules.

Ghia, can you estimate the duration we will spend underground in the capsules hibernating?

Ode, I'm afraid I can't provide an exact answer to your question. The extent of the damage caused by the asteroid's impact remains uncertain. Before the asteroid collides with the planet, I will need to reinforce the inner crust and tectonic plates. Once the asteroid enters the atmosphere, it will break up into hundreds of meteorites to rain down on the surface.

However, not all of them will fall simultaneously; some will become trapped in a gradual decaying orbit. This process may unfold over several days until the very last meteor succumbs to the planet's gravity.

During this period, I will enter a state of dormancy, akin to sleep. It will also take a significant amount of time for me to rebuild and replenish my energy, derived from Tol.

Ghia, if I were to take a guess. I would probably say anywhere from about a thousand to two thousand years. Would you consider this a reasonable estimate?

Yes, I do. It will take time to heal the planet, but when it is time for them to

leave the underground caverns, there will be a beautiful and vibrant planet awaiting them. I hope people will see this. I'll need your help to show people this future. The alternative is very dire.

Thank you. This will help with most of the questions people will ask. There is one question which I'm sure will come up. People will ask if this is the only option available to them. Many of the people are planning on building giant spaceships to travel to the nearest habitable planet. Is there another planet close enough to stay on while you're healing? Is this a viable option for people?

I have noticed many of your people are making trips to the Noth moon to help build giant spaceships. The nearest habitable planet capable of supporting life will take them centuries to reach. In the meantime, Noth can only support about 100,000 people living there. Nearly half of your population, almost one billion people, are currently planning to go there. This will be a mistake. This is truly the only solution.

When do you want me to alert everyone about your plan?

In a while. Ode, I'm going to teach you how to use some very special tools.

From out of nowhere, a bag about the size of a backpack floated across the lake and landed on the bottom of the small rowboat. Ghia spoke to Ode again.

In this bag there are fourteen different colored stones called quantum stones. You can only find these stones in special places within our galaxy. The moon, you call Druna, keeps these stones in abundance high up in the mountains.

Ode looked with curiosity inside the bag, all the while nodding his head, affirming he understood.

Your knowledge of science gives you an aptitude to learn and start to master the power of these special stones. Each stone resonates with a specific frequency. When touched, it will directly transmit its unique properties and potential abilities to your mind through quantum entanglement. Using quantum entanglement, each stone can affect the

quantum properties around it, or even those which are distant.

These stones hold immense power, each possessing both positive properties and negative properties. For example, the bright red stone has a capacity to heal and breathe life into a life form, but it also has the same power to inflict pain and take away life. Can you make a promise to me?

Yes, of course, I promise. Can I teach Felisa and my family how to use these? My wife and children have been organizing with several leaders around the planet. They are helping to get as many people involved with organizing the effort to move people underground.

Excellent! Yes, bring Felisa and your children down to the beach tomorrow morning. I can begin training them on how to interact with the stones.

Great! They have been dying to meet you.

Now let's begin. The first stone I would like you to learn is the **crimson** colored quantum stone. With this stone, you can

manipulate gravity, making objects weightless or incredibly heavy. You are right-handed, so take the stone in your right hand. Focus your mind on the object you wish to affect.

A small log of wood bubbled up to the surface of the lake and floated right next to the small rowboat.

Ode, I want you to focus on the piece of wood and see if you can feel the vibrations and movement of the particles inside this piece of wood. If you use your mind, you can almost hear them buzzing inside and around the piece of wood. Imagine nudging those particles to move faster and vibrate even more. When you feel you have increased them as high as you can make them go, visualize in your mind the piece of wood floating above the water.

It sounded like a crazy request, but he thought it wouldn't hurt to try. Ode focused on the piece of wood. It felt strange, but with the crimson stone in his hand, it felt as if he saw in his mind the subatomic particles inside the piece of wood. He imagined shaking the piece of wood, causing the movement and the vibrations of the particles in it to increase swiftly.

As the particles moved faster and the vibrations became greater, Ode noticed something strange. It was hard to describe, but it felt like the force of gravity was becoming weaker. The log itself was unchanged and still bobbing in the water next to the rowboat. Yet, Ode sensed the log was gathering up some pent-up motion that was just waiting to be let go.

When he felt the particles were vibrating and moving as fast as he could get them to move and vibrate, Ode visualized in his mind pushing the log up and making the log lift off the surface of the lake. Nothing happened at first and then he pushed harder with his mind and clenched the stone that much harder. The piece of wood jumped up out of the water like it got shot out of a cannon. It went up to about sixty feet above the water.

As the wood descended toward the water, Ode kept his intense focus on the piece of wood so he could gently keep the object still floating about a foot or so above the water.

Ode was giddy with excitement. If he hadn't seen it with his own eyes, he wouldn't have believed it.

Fantastic! Well done, Ode. Well done. Now put the stone in your left hand and see if you can focus on those same vibrations and moving particles and try to make them slow it down. When you feel

they are going as slow as you can make them, try to make the piece of wood flatter and thinner.

Ode switched the stone to his left hand, still keeping his focus on the piece of wood. Similar to the way he sped those particles up before, he put all his focus on making them slow down. It felt like the particles were almost slowed down to nothing. The piece of wood looked to be unchanged, but he used his mind to squeeze it like he was squeezing the water out of a sponge. Unbelievably, the piece of wood compressed to a flat platter.

Ode, that was fantastic! Great job, you're getting the hang of this. I'm very impressed.

Ode continued focusing on the platter of wood and increased the particles and let them move in its most natural speed and vibration. Magically, the wood stretched itself back into the normal shape it is supposed to have.

Ode, that was fantastic. Very well done. I'm proud of you. You have a lot of skill using that stones. I wasn't sure if your species could use these stones effectively, but you have proved me wrong on that by a long shot.

Thank you. I'm just as amazed as you are that this worked. As a scientist, I wouldn't think this was possible.

Ode, this is just the start of learning about these stones. Anyone possessing these stones has incredible power to wield. You can now understand the need to be careful of the temperament of the people you will teach to use these stones. Let's move on to the next one. In the bag, take out the yellow stone and hold it in your right hand.

Over the next several hours, Ghia showed Ode how to tap into and use the power stored in different colored stones. All the stones had a similar way to tap into its energy. It was a combination of increasing the particle speeds, vibrations, or the spin of each particle. Each of the stones had its own trick to access the stored energy.

Ode learned that the **yellow** stone was about the physical movement of the object. He could toss the piece of wood rapidly around the lake or he could slow the speed of the piece of wood. Ode then learned about the power of the **pink** stone. It seemed similar to the Aegis formula, because it could strengthen an object or weaken an object. If he imagined breaking the piece of wood in half, it resulted in two pieces of wood floating on the water. Next, Ode imagined he was applying glue to the two pieces to make it one piece of wood again. When he finished, the log floating in the water appeared seamlessly whole, as if never broken.

Ghia also taught Ode how to move objects instantaneously from one place to another using the **brown** stone. The brown stone was a little trickier to use. Ode looked down and saw the oar resting on the bottom of the small rowboat. Focusing on the wooden oar, Ode used the brown stone to try teleporting it to the dock where the rowboat was moored that morning.

While he was holding the stone, he could see all the particles moving and spinning all around the oar. It was strange when he focused on a spinning particle. It seemed to disappear and then reappear along the same trajectory. Ode imagined pushing the oar into those spinning particles just before they disappeared. When the spinning particles reappeared, the oar had vanished. The oar was resting on the dock by the beach.

Next, he imagined the oar coming back to him. Ghia warned him to be careful to only imagine just the oar itself and not the dock. Otherwise, he might bring part of the dock with the oar. It was trickier, but he could successfully bring the oar back to the boat.

Ode found himself overwhelmed by the incredible sights he was witnessing today. His mind was racing, trying to comprehend the endless possibilities that these quantum stones held. It was astonishing to think that he could instantaneously transport matter from one place to another. He sat in the boat, at a loss for words, taking a moment to absorb everything he had learned so far.

Ghia, if it is ok with you, I want to try to teleport my notebook from the cabin. I would like to record a list of the properties of each stone. This way I can show Felisa and the kids more about how each stone works.

Yes, of course.

Ode teleported the digital notebook tablet into his hands, similar to what he had done with the rowboat oar. Displayed on the tablet was a table with a list of each quantum stone and the positive and negative property associated with it. For the next ten minutes, Ghia told Ode what each stone's primary power was. This would be a good way for him and his family to learn about each quantum stone.

STONE	POSITIVE ABILITY	NEGATIVE ABILITY
BLUE	Gain Knowledge	Lose Knowledge
RED	Body Healing	Body Death
GREEN	Nature Healing	Nature Death
YELLOW	Strengthen	Weaken
PINK	Speed Up	Speed Down
GREY	Time Forward	Time Back
VIOLET	Truth	Untrue
CRIMSON	Heavier	Lighter
BROWN	Object To	Object From
ORANGE	Teleport To	Teleport From
OLIVE	Compel	Comply
LILAC	Give Protection	Remove Protection
WHITE	Amplify	
BLACK	Nullify	

Now, the last stone I want to teach you is the **orange** stone. This stone is similar to the **brown** stone.

The way to manipulate this stone is to imagine there is a bubble surrounding us of all the quantum particles. If you look closely, you will also see that each particle spins in a clockwise or counter-clockwise direction. As these particles spin, you should be able to see them blink in and out of existence.

Your goal is to cause these particles to move and spin faster around you. Once you feel they are moving and spinning as fast as you can get them to spin, imagine an exact location you can see in your mind. It must be some place where you have an absolute recall of all the details in that specific location.

Once you feel you have the location firmly in your mind, lean into the blinking particles. If you do this right, you will teleport yourself to that exact place. Wanna try to teleport from the rowboat to the beach?

Sure, I'll give it a try.

Ode imagined the particles surrounding him moving and spinning all around him. As the particles were moving and spinning faster and faster, he imagined he was standing on the edge of the beach. Once he had this pictured in his head, he watched the particles blinking in and out of sight. It was a strange feeling, but he leaned into the particles and in an instant he was on the beach. Ode couldn't believe how easily this worked.

Outstanding!! Well done, my son. Now, this might be a little trickier. Use the stone again to teleport back to the boat, but this time imagine you're sitting in the boat versus standing in the boat.

Ok, here goes nothing.

Ode imagined himself sitting in the stern of the boat with the bag of quantum stones in front of him. Once he got the particles moving as fast as possible, he leaned into the spinning particles. In an instant, he was back on the boat and sitting where he had been before.

Ode, that is fantastic. You can see what I meant when I told you about imagining yourself sitting down. If you had not, you would have been standing in the boat when you arrived. Ode, why don't we stop here today? You're getting a good handle on how to use these stones.

Ode didn't want to say anything to Ghia, but he was getting tired. The initial surge of excitement and adrenaline he experienced was gradually subsiding.

I agree. I'm feeling unusually tired after using these stones. Is that natural?

Yes, it is. Using the stones for longer periods will help you build up more stamina, but it's also important to know when to stop. Let me push you over to the dock.

Will the brown stone work with something that is alive when it gets transported?

Very good question. The brown stone lets you move the inanimate object from one place to another. The brown stone can't work with a life form. If you're to transport yourself or someone else with the powers of the stone, then you must use the orange stone. This is an important point, to remember about the abilities of the brown and the orange stone. For example, if you had tried to teleport the rowboat back to the dock using the brown stone, you might teleport the boat, but it would leave you here in the middle of the lake.

Ode could feel the boat moving toward the shore.

I'll bring my family down here tomorrow morning at dawn.

After saying goodbye to Ghia, Ode walked back up to the cabin where his family was awake and just finishing up their breakfast. He walked over to give Felisa a good morning kiss and whispered, "You won't believe what Ghia was showing me this morning."

Felisa looked at him. She noticed the bag containing all the stones and asked, "Is that a gift from Ghia?"

"Yes, it is." He turned to his family and said, "I have just spent the morning working with Ghia. It has shown me some amazing and powerful tools in this bag. Tomorrow morning, Ghia would like to teach all of you how to use these tools properly."

Each of his children was listening with their full, undivided attention to everything he was saying.

Ode then described the powers of the stones he knew about from his work with Ghia today. The crimson stone was to make objects lighter or heavier. Next, he explained how the yellow stone moves an object either slowly or rapidly in a direction you specify. The pink stone's purpose was to make something stronger or weaker. He explained how he did this with the piece of wood. Then he explained how the brown stone can teleport an object away from you or toward you. Finally, he described the orange stone and how it could teleport someone from one place to the next.

A rare thing happened while he described his encounter with Ghia. All his children were totally speechless. He and Felisa shared a secret, all-knowing smile. Everyone simultaneously broke the silence, peppering him with questions.

"What about the other stones?"

"How do they work?"

"Can you use two stones at the same time?"

"Can we use the stones to break up and divert the asteroid coming at us?"

"If more than one person uses the same stone, does that make the power twice as strong?"

"How far away can you teleport something?"

These were all excellent questions. Ode raised his hand to slow everyone down, and he said, "Fantastic questions, but I don't have answers for these. Why don't we start a list of questions we can ask Ghia tomorrow morning? Did I mention we were supposed to be on the beach at dawn?"

Each of his children groaned at once. They were hoping to sleep in.

Ode quickly finished the breakfast Felisa had prepared. He stood up and looked at everyone and said, "Using those stones was really exhausting. I don't know about everyone else, but I need to get some sleep for a few hours."

Chapter 13

Teaching

Five Months to Impact

The next morning

ODE'S EXCITEMENT WAS PALPABLE. Sleep was a thin veil of unconsciousness, balancing the need for sleep and his excitement at the unfolding day ahead of him. Today, the quantum stones would reveal their secrets, not just to him, but to his entire family. Can they embrace the sentience of their planet? Or would it scare them? Would his family have the same reaction that he did? Would they trust it?

He slipped out of bed, his bare feet whispered across the cold, rough wooden floor. Felisa felt the absence of her husband next to her as she opened her eyes. She whispered good morning to him. Ode came over to kiss her softly and whispered good morning to her as well.

Felisa, sensing Ode's nervousness and excited energy, said, "I'll get the kids awake. Last night, it felt like everyone was eager to meet Ghia. I don't expect more than just the cursory complaining. I'm thrilled about this as well. This is a novel experience for Ghia also, right?"

"This marks Ghia's initial interaction with humans, I think. Ghia could have interacted with us before all this happened. I just don't think it really had a reason or desire to talk to us. My photosynthesis experiment surprised it. Ghia was curious about the motives behind risking one's life to heal the planet."

In about twenty minutes, everyone was ready to go. Ode held the bag of colored quantum stones over his shoulder. Leading the group, consisting of Felisa, Dulvod, Helliod, Kotlid, Lumi, Kelvi, and Melliod, Ode made his way down the sandy path to the small beach. The sand felt warm beneath their feet as they approached the lake. No one spoke! With an unspoken agreement, the group tried to preserve the morning stillness while they walked to the beach.

When they reached the beach, the lake glistened with the scattered brilliance of a jewel, yet its stillness was comforting to Ode. The morning sun struggled against the horizon to rise higher in the sky. The orange sun painted the sky with a different color of the rainbow for each moment that passed. As it rose above the horizon, the lake reflected the full breadth of the colors on display in the sky.

Ode?

Yes, Ghia. Good morning.

There is a blue stone in the bag you brought with you this morning. Take it out and give it to Felisa. This is how I'll be able to communicate with everyone at the same time.

Ode reached into the bag and said to Felisa, "Ghia asked me to give you the blue stone so you can communicate with it."

When Felisa put the stone in her hand, she remarked, "It feels pleasantly cool in my hand."

After a moment holding the blue polished stone, she smiled. Felisa turned to her son, Dulvod, and handed him the shiny blue stone. As each person held the stone, Ode can hear their voices and Ghia's voice in his mind as well. It was a strange sensation to be talking to his son or daughter without actually saying anything. Lumi was the very last person to hold the blue stone.

A wooden log, as thick as a man's thigh, instantly appeared in front of Ode.

Ode, I would like you to illustrate how you made this piece of wood float on top of

the lake yesterday. Tell everyone exactly what you did and felt to make the log rise above the lake.

Ode turned to the group to face everyone. He really didn't need to turn towards the group, as they were all watching him. He reached into the bag and brought out the deep red, highly polished crimson stone. Speaking directly to his family, Ode said:

Yesterday, I took the rowboat out to the middle of the lake to watch the sunrise. Suddenly, a small log floated next to the rowboat. Ghia requested I hold the crimson stone in my dominant hand and use its power to lift the wood from the water, using only my mind. The stone can manipulate all the particles surrounding the log and change them.

Kelvi spoke aloud to ask a question, not realizing everyone could hear him speak in their minds. "Dad, I know you and Lumi are the scientists of this family, but what do you mean when you say 'particle'? Do you mean a speck of dust or dirt? Or, are you talking about those sub-atomic things they keep trying to experiment with?"

Actually, Kelvi, that's a great question. When it comes to atoms, we know they consist of electrons, protons, and neutrons. However, did you ever consider what makes up protons and neutrons? This is where quantum physics comes into play.

The atom's nucleus tightly packs protons and neutrons together. We see, upon closer examination, that protons and neutrons consist of many particles in constant motion, vibration, and spin. It is these particles that we seek to manipulate. And that's precisely where these stones come into play - they will enable us to achieve that. Does that help, Kelvi?

"Yes, dad, that helps," Kelvi said aloud again.

Ok, now back to yesterday. The first thing I did was to relax both my mind and body. It took several seconds, but I just controlled my breathing and let my body fully relax. I cleared my mind of any thoughts and just focused on the wooden log in front of me. It seems unbelievable, but when I sensed myself relax, I could start to perceive the particles moving and vibrating around and inside the log. Next, I tried to imagine I could nudge the particles to move and vibrate faster.

When you sense you're achieving the highest level of movement and vibration in the particles, then you can try to push the piece of wood up with your mind. Be careful with how much force you apply to the wooden log. When I did this, I pushed it too much. As a result, it shot up very high above the lake. It takes a little practice, but you will get the hang of how much force to apply to something. Once you get more practice with this, you will have more precise control of the height the object will go up or go down.

Ode turned and focused on the piece of wood in front of him. His mind and body relaxed, immediately sensing particle movement and vibrations. He encouraged the particles to move faster and faster. Ode pushed the wood up softly and it rose about a foot off the ground. Again, he pushed it up and the wooden log rose off the ground and floated up to a height that was at eye level with everyone standing in front of him. Finally, he let the log float softly down to the ground.

Ode smiled at the amazed expressions on everyone's faces. He noticed Lumi's face wasn't showing a look of amazement, but something else. Was it confusion? Fear? Confusion, he could understand. If it's fear, then he and Felisa would need to address this. Ode thought back to several months ago when he told his family about the existence of Ghia's sentience. That alone was shocking, but he also told his family about how the devastating asteroid in deep space will impact with Ghia in five months. Everyone was stunned at first, but they also accepted it quickly. Lumi had a more difficult time accepting it. Helliod and Dulvod played a crucial role in comforting Lumi by treating him like a sibling instead of a parent. He made a note to himself to talk to Felisa about Lumi's reaction.

Ode asked out loud, "Who wants to try?"

Surprisingly, it was Kotlid who volunteered first to use the crimson stone. Ode heard Ghia giving instructions to Kotlid in his mind. All expression drained from his face. Kotlid's eyes narrowed, and his brow furrowed. His body relaxed, and he closed his eyes as he tried to imagine the millions of atoms and their subatomic buddies which made up the wood vibrating and spinning in a complex dance.

He saw Kotlid's lips move slightly, as if he was whispering to the wood, "faster, go faster…" His face displayed an insurmountable concoction of sheer determination and self-confidence. Kotlid also inherited a lot of his family's powerful *force of will,* which they had gained over generations of service to the Imperium. When confronted with this powerful concoction, the subatomic particles responded by moving faster, generating more heat and force.

The wooden log vibrated slightly and then, like a windblown feather, the wood becoming lighter, as if it was losing its connection to Ghia. He opened his eyes and saw the wood hovering a few inches above the ground.

Kotlid smiled and lifted his hand, guiding the wood with his mind.

Complete disbelief rendered them speechless. Once their brains had processed it for a second or two, everyone asked at the same time to use the crimson stone. However, Ode couldn't help but notice that Lumi was the only one who didn't join in. He mentally reminded himself once again to speak to Felisa about this matter as soon as possible.

Over the next twenty minutes, most of the group got to use the shiny crimson stone, except Melliod and Lumi. Dulvod tried to lift the wooden log into the air. He focused and concentrated for several minutes, but he couldn't lift the wooden log from the ground. He tried using the stone in each hand, but there was no change to the log in front of him.

It was evident that everyone was really hoping something magical would happen and that Dulvod would be successful. Ghia interjected and said to everyone in the group.

Every stone's reaction is unique for every person. These stones are just tools to enhance some of the quantum properties and the quantum forces we interact with in our everyday reality. Each quantum property vibrates and spins in a certain

direction and a certain speed. Some people possess impressive ability in using these stones. Sometimes it just takes practice. Don't regard this as a failure. Using some stones may come easily for some of you, while others may struggle to use particular ones.

Why don't we move on the yellow colored stone? Ode, can YOU show the usage of the yellow stone the way you did on the lake yesterday?

Ode reached in the bag and took out the brightly colored yellow stone. He held the stone in his right hand. He intensely concentrated on the wood, sensing the particles swirling within. Ode attempted to do what he had done with Ghia the previous day. Upon feeling all the particles around the log, he used his mind to push it away from him. The log moved across the beach. But, not really, as far as he thought it would go. Yesterday, he could push the log away from him while it was floating in the water. On the beach, he struggled with the log's friction on the sand. Connected to the particles in the log, he pushed it forward once more.

Ode said, "When you can feel and sense the object's particles moving and vibrating, push the log using your mind, like magnets repelling each other. Then, to make the log come back to you, think of it like a magnet attracting a piece of metal. Here the magnet would be the quantum stone. Lumi, would you like to give this a try?"

The unexpected question from his father caught Lumi off guard, leaving him momentarily without an answer. However, Ode perceived a flicker of something else in the subtle shift of Lumi's expression. Fear.

Lumi's reluctance was unmistakable in the way he hesitated and shifted his weight from foot to foot. Lumi didn't really know exactly where to start. He also felt very self-conscious, with everyone now focused on him. Finally, after several seconds of struggling internally, he looked at his father. He said, "I'll try it. I'm still not really sure how I can sense or feel an object. I mean, it's just a piece of wood."

He reached out to his father's hand, offering the yellow stone. Lumi held the stone in his right hand. He shut his eyes, feigning activity, but truly stalling because of his uncertainty.

Lumi? It's just me talking to you privately. No one else can hear what we are saying to each other. Let's do this together Ok?

Uh, yeah sure. I'm looking at the log in front of me, but I don't understand how I'm supposed to feel or sense the wooden log. I know at one point this wood was part of a tree and was part of nature. It isn't part of a tree anymore, so isn't it dead, right? I mean, just an object without life?

Lumi, everything around us is comprised of atoms that you can only see when you use powerful microscopes. There are billions upon billions of these atoms in this wooden log. Those atoms are all moving around the object. Parts of these atoms have even smaller pieces which make up this one atom.

Right. I remember we learned about atoms in school. So when you say movement, you're talking about the electrons circling the nucleus of neutrons and protons in the center, right?

Exactly! Those electrons flying around the nucleus in the middle are moving quickly. In addition, they are vibrating and spinning in a particular direction. You can use this stone and your mind to influence electron movement, vibrations, and spinning. In simpler terms, this highly technical explanation boils down to these tiny particles that are constantly moving, vibrating, and spinning. These quantum

stones allow you to have a certain influence on the movement of those particles. Lumi, I know you can do this. If I didn't think you could, I wouldn't have asked you to give this a try.

Ok, I'll try it.

Lumi kept his eyes closed and tried to relax as much as he could. It was hard to relax when everyone around you was expecting something momentous to happen. He slowed his breathing down and imagined feeling anything moving in the log. It slowly felt like he could sense something moving. It reminded him of a pet he had a long time ago. If he hugged the animal, he would hear and sense the animal's heartbeat and the life coursing through it. The memory of holding his pet and sensing the animal's heartbeat helped him to let his senses extend out to the wooden log. Slowly, he detected movement in and around the wood on the ground. He patiently waited until he could perceive the movement and vibrations occurring inside the round piece of wood. When he thought it wouldn't go any faster, he opened his eyes and Lumi pushed the wooden log as hard as he could.

The wooden log moved so quickly it was hard to follow. The log moved so fast it seemed shot from a cannon. It flew across the beach and into the lake. The small piece of wood continued moving across the lake, leaving a wake of water behind it. The log finally stopped somewhere in the middle of the lake.

Everyone, including Lumi, was stunned. Everyone applauded him!

Lumi, I knew you could do this. Well done. That was amazing. Now, let's see if we can bring this back to you. Try to feel the wood in the middle of the lake and pull the log to you. Pull gently, just enough to move through water and stop in front of you.

Lumi's searched in the lake to sense the piece of wood. Finding it was easy because of the rapid movement of the atoms; it stood out like a beacon to him. He complied with Ghia's request, giving a powerful pull to the floating log. That pull brought it back to the beach, but only to the edge. Lumi pulled the log lightly and watched it move across the sandy beach to stop in front of him.

Once again, everyone applauded. They were all amazed by what Lumi had just shown them. Everyone congratulated him all at once. Ode was beaming with relief. Lumi showed he had a strong ability to use these stones. He wasn't sure what happened, but it appeared Lumi had broken through some fear or trepidation he was having with Ghia and the quantum stones.

Over the next several hours, Ode showed everyone how to use the pink stone to weaken or strengthen an object. Ode showed how he could break the log in half and then to fuse it back again. They all broke and fused the log back and forth many times. The poor log got broken and fused together over and over. Everyone seemed to accomplish the task without difficulty.

Kotlid asked Ghia if slowing particles and vibrations would allow objects to be permeable. If I weakened a wall or door, could I pass through it and then restore it?

That is an excellent question. With practice, the answer is yes, you can. If you do this incorrectly, there is a danger of ending up in the middle of the object. For right now, don't try this unless I'm with you. I can correct it if something goes wrong.

Over the next couple of hours, Ode showed everyone how to use the brown stone and the orange stone. Amazingly, everyone seemed to figure out exactly how to nudge and push objects and themselves into those spinning particles and teleport them to another location.

Ode also explained a couple of the differences between the orange quantum stone and the brown quantum stone. Ode repeated the cautions Ghia had given him about transporting just the object and nothing else.

He also explained the difference between the brown stone being only able to teleport an object and not people or living things.

Over the next two hours, everyone used the shiny brown stone and the polished orange stone. It was kind of comical to watch people and objects suddenly disappear and pop up in different locations.

They played a game to see if anyone could move the oar to the other side of the lake, about a mile away. In the end, Melliod won and Lumi and Kelvi were close behind her. Ode was excited to see everyone effectively use the stones.

Everyone practiced with the different colored stones they had learned. Melliod and Lumi went back to the crimson stone and tried to use it effectively. They tried to see who could lift the rowboat out of the water highest. Melliod just barely beat Lumi.

Felisa came over to Ode after she tried to use the stone. Her smile was radiant. She whispered to Ode, "I can't believe how tiring it is to use these stones."

Ode smiled back and said, "These stones are incredible, aren't they? But, yes, I agree. I'm getting quite tired as well."

It became clear that everyone was getting exhausted from using the quantum stones all day. They decided to stop for the day. The thought of a warm and satisfying meal drew them back to the comfort of the cabin. Waking up so early and working hard made them tremendously hungry. After eating, most of the group went back to bed while Kotlid, Helliod, and Felisa went down to the lake to go for a swim.

Chapter 14

Fire

Dawn

THE NEXT MORNING, ODE WOKE up early to the soft stillness of the pre-dawn morning. He got out of bed and thought it would be nice to visit the lake once again and witness the sunrise. As he dressed in comfortable attire, the faint aroma of freshly brewed grawpa floated in the air.

Silently, Ode descended the stairs, the sound of his footsteps barely audible. In the kitchen, he discovered Helliod and Lumi sitting at the worn-out table, their voices hushed as they engaged in conversation.

Eagerly, Ode poured himself a cup of the warm *grawpa*, the aroma of the rich beverage enveloping him. With a hopeful smile, he suggested they go down to the lake to watch the sunrise. Their eyes met, and both Helliod and Lumi's faces lit up with delight. Lumi playfully remarked, "We have been down here waiting for you! We know how people at your age need a lot of sleep."

They left the cabin, making sure not to wake the rest of the family still sleeping. The darkness still enveloped the cabin in the stillness of the morning. Tol's light patiently awaited its grand appearance. The path to the lake was lined with a gentle, soft blue glow emitted by tiny bioluminescent lumensbloom flowers.

As they reached the beach, the air felt crisp, carrying a slight nip, yet utterly invigorating. The sweet scent of aerisprig filled the surrounding air, as their bright red feathery branches swayed in the gentle Ghian breeze. Ode breathed in the freshness of the morning air. The scents of all the plants triggered fond memories of being on this beach throughout his childhood.

As they walked to the end of the dock, they noticed a hint of dew on its surface. Despite this, they all agreed that it was worth it to secure a front-row seat for the spectacle that awaited them.

As promised, Tol emerged on the horizon, painting the sky in a magnificent spectacle of vibrant colors. Each hue of the spectrum took center stage, showcasing its brilliance and illuminating everything in sight. The dazzling display created a symphony of shades, captivating the eyes with a kaleidoscope of beauty. As the solo auditions of each fantastic color ended, the colors harmoniously united, reaching a crescendo that burst forth into a cascade of colored confetti, gently descending upon everything, creating a sensory feast for the eyes.

Lumi whispered, "Wow! That was fantastic."

Ode and Helliod wordlessly nodded in agreement.

"Do you think Ghia will want to teach us more about the quantum stones?" Lumi asked.

Ode looked at Lumi and saw him beaming, like he was about to do something exciting. He said, "Yesterday, you got pretty good at moving objects around. Both you and Melliod are getting very proficient with the quantum stones."

"At first, it felt impossible to get something to move, but once you concentrate on making the particles speed up or slow down, it's a piece of cake," Lumi explained.

Ode smiled affectionately at his son, noticing that his earlier concern about Lumi being afraid of Ghia or the quantum stones had disappeared. Playfully, he remarked, "Looks like someone's getting the hang of it!" which earned a beaming smile from Lumi in response.

Ode said, "I don't know if Ghia wants to teach us more skills using the quantum stones, maybe? I figure

Ghia will tell us when it wants to teach us some more. I imagine being in charge of an entire planet must keep **IT** pretty busy."

As Ode finished saying this, three bags of quantum stones magically appeared behind them.

Good morning, my children!

When Ghia spoke to them in their minds, they did not feel surprised. Each of them looked at each other, ensuring that Ghia had addressed all of them.

Ode said out loud for the sake of everyone hearing this, "Good morning, Ghia!"

Lumi and Helliod also said good morning.

Behind you there is a bag full of quantum stones for each of you. I have also created a bag of quantum stones for everyone else in the cabin. They are all sitting on the countertop in the kitchen. As we practiced yesterday, we focused on five specific colored quantum stones. They were the crimson, yellow, pink, brown, and orange colored stones.

"Did we use them correctly?" Ode inquired.

The three of you manipulated the stones we worked with yesterday perfectly. However, I think your ability with the pink

stone could be far greater if you tried to do something slightly different. This may help us all in the end.

Ode could see Lumi and Helliod both smiling. Yearning for progress, they were eager to improve.

When you held the pink stone yesterday, you attempted to make the particles move faster and faster. When you sensed the particles were going as fast as possible, you then used your mind to push the piece of wood. All three of you used your dominant hand.

Today I would like you to use your non-dominant hand this time. I suspect you'll see that you can make the particles move two or three times faster than you did yesterday. This increased movement of the particles generates a tremendous amount of heat.

This stone can tap into the energy of that heat. Each quantum stone has an immense capacity to store power. You may notice the stone warming up, but

there's no need to be concerned. It won't cause any discomfort or burn you.

Now, while holding the stone in your non-dominant hand, use your dominant hand to touch something that is combustible, like a small piece of wood. Once you touch the object, the stone will instantly release all that energy and ignite the wood into flames.

Lumi whispered, "Wicked!"

In front of all three of them, a small pile of tiny twigs magically materialized.

Ode said, "Ghia, this sounds like we would be creating a laser beam. Will we get hurt if we touch something to make it start on fire?"

You will find that you can exert a significant amount of control over how this energy is released. Yesterday it was used to move the object. Today, the goal isn't to move the object but to capture that energy into the quantum stone.

As you hold the stone, you'll notice a gentle warmth spreading through it. Rest

assured, it won't cause any harm or discomfort. When you feel that you've absorbed all the energy you can, reach out and touch the pile of twigs before you. If your attempt is successful, the twigs will immediately absorb the stored energy from the stone. This rapid transfer of energy will ignite the twigs, causing them to burst into flames.

"Can I try?" Lumi asked.

Helliod and Ode exchanged a secret smile as they observed Lumi's eagerness. They were genuinely pleased that he wanted to be the first to go. Despite his doubts, Ode had to trust in Ghia, hoping it wouldn't put them in danger. He constantly reminded himself that he was communicating with the very essence of the planet itself. After all, Ghia had already saved his life once before when he had fallen off the mountain. Ode was certain, without any doubt, that Ghia possessed the power to mend any harm that might befall Lumi in case their plan went awry.

Lumi reached into the bag of quantum stones and felt the smooth, polished surface of a vibrant pink stone. While holding the stone in his left hand, he attempted to sense and feel the particles in the pile of twigs, perceiving their movement in and around the small sticks. Lumi tried to recall the memory of how he could sense and feel the life force of his pet. He thought this would spur the ability to sense and feel the particles in the twigs moving. This time, he couldn't feel or sense anything moving in and around the twigs.

Instantly, Lumi recognized what he was doing wrong. He was focusing on all the twigs in the pile. He slowed his breathing down and let his body and mind relax. Now this time, Lumi just focused on only one twig and not the whole pile.

This made a dramatic difference. He was now sensing all the movement and vibrations of all the particles that make up this single twig. He urged and nudged the particles to move and vibrate faster and faster. Lumi noticed how the movement and vibrations were many magnitudes higher and faster.

While he coaxed the atoms to vibrate, spin and move as fast as possible all around the twig, a slight bead of perspiration appeared on his brow.

At first, Lumi thought it was because of his intense concentration. His entire face was a sheen of sweat and it was then that Lumi understood why. He was holding back the intense heat of all the energy he was creating by feeling and sensing the particles in the stick. Lumi reached down and lightly touched one twig, releasing all the contained energy down the arm that wasn't holding the stone. The stored energy escaped through his finger when he touched the twig.

Initially, there was no response. Lumi was confident he felt the surge of power leaving his hand when he touched the small stick. He felt sure he did this correctly. There was no other explanation for the sudden surge of energy he felt leave his hand when he touched the small stick. Slowly but surely, tiny flames began to flicker and dance upon the surface of the small piece of wood, gradually spreading their fiery glow to the adjacent twigs.

Lumi, not realizing that he was even holding his breath, exhaled, and took in a deep breath as he whispered, "Wicked!"

Lumi that was outstanding! I thought I could sense this power in you yesterday.

Ode and Helliod looked at each other with a devilish grin. They both reached into their bags of stones and pulled out the shiny pink stone.

Two small piles of twigs appeared in front of Ode and Helliod. They both followed the example Lumi had just set for them. In a matter of moments, both had their small pile of sticks on fire.

Ode, I want you to try something different this time. After your fall from the mountain, leaving you severely injured, I

used my healing powers to restore you to your former self. Though you rarely discuss it, there is something extraordinary about the birthmark on your neck. When you were born, a powerful bolt of lightning struck the tree just outside the house, where your mother was in labor. The air crackled with static electricity, and a surge of energy coursed through the midwife. It was at that precise moment, as you took your first breath, that the birthmark appeared on your neck. This detail is significant, as it suggests an additional ability you can access with the pink stone.

The pile of twigs in front of Ode vanished, replaced by a diminutive square sheet of steel, merely a couple of inches in diameter.

As Helliod and Lumi ignited the branches, they felt hotter and their body temperature increased slightly, akin to being trapped in an oppressively hot room. They expelled this energy when they touched the small twig.

However, Ode, your body temperature remained constant and did not increase. The birthmark on your neck has a remarkable ability to concentrate all the energy particles you emit into a single beam of purple light with significantly more energy. It functions like quantum photosynthesis, where energy gets transferred through a coherence event. This violet light is powerful enough to slice through almost any object. Want to give this a try?

"Are you kidding me? Of course, I would love to try this," Ode said excitedly.

He grinned at Lumi and Helliod and said, "Lasers! Piece of cake, right?"

Ode focused all his energy on the piece of steel in front of him. He narrowed his total focus onto an imaginary dot in the center of the metal sheet. Clearing his mind and relaxing his body to receive the sensation of the particles moving faster and faster. He kept doing this until he felt a great sensation of warmth coming from his neck. He let it build a little bit longer until he felt he had to release it.

He pointed his finger at the piece of metal about six inches above it, and an incredibly bright violet light emanated from his finger to land in the exact spot he had focused on. When the light hit the metal, it smoked for a brief second, and then it bore its way through the metal to hit the sand beneath it.

Ode slowly moved his finger from the center of the sheet towards the edge, feeling a strange sensation as he did so. Intuitively, he knew he needed to keep the laser beam going to expel all the energy from his body. The thought of stopping abruptly made him fear he might hurt himself. After reaching the edge, he brought his finger back down to the other side, ensuring that the laser beam remained active. Ode took his finger again from the dot in the center to the side of the piece of metal that was ninety degrees from his first cut. One piece of metal dropped away from the other piece of metal. It was truly an extraordinary experience to witness a laser beam emanating from his finger.

Well done, my son! Well done, indeed!

Lumi and Helliod sat there, completely awe-struck. Equally surprised, Ode couldn't believe what they were seeing either.

You made sure you expelled all the energy out of your body before you stopped. This is very important. With practice, you will find out exactly how much to take in and how you can safely

release any excess. If you had needed to release anything, it would have been perfectly fine to release in the lake.

"That feels amazing! I can't believe that happened."

Why don't we end this for right now? I'm thrilled and proud of what you have accomplished here this morning. Later this afternoon, we can get everyone together in your living room in the cabin. There are some additional properties of the quantum stones that you were practicing on the other day.

"Sounds great! I'm feeling quite a bit more tired after this workout today. Let me know and I'll gather everyone in the front room. Is that Ok?" Ode said, wanting to make sure he heard Ghia's instructions properly.

I will talk to you later today.

Chapter 15

Ice

Later that afternoon

HELLIOD AND KOTLID PREPARED a delicious lunch consisting of a variety of vegetables and freshly grilled fish caught from the lake. Meanwhile, Felisa and Melliod baked a mouthwatering pie made with sweet fruits and topped with a tangy cream. As everyone finished their meal, Ode told them Ghia wanted to gather everyone in the living room of the cabin.

Observing his family and Kotlid, Ode saw them settling into the comfortable chairs of the spacious room. A subtle twinkle sparkled in each person's eyes, revealing their excitement for another lesson on the intriguing quantum stones.

He still felt awkward and unnatural when communicating with Ghia in his mind. Ode assumed everything he said to Ghia was also heard by everyone else. To be certain, he proposed everyone to speak audibly when communicating with Ghia. Ode thought by doing this, it would give Ghia the option to speak privately with someone, allowing them to express themselves without feeling self-conscious about what they said.

Ghia, can I ask you a question? In private?

Certainly.

He noticed yesterday that at one point Lumi was having a private conversation with Ghia. The reason Ode had a hunch was the sudden transformation of Lumi's facial expression. What worried him the most was how fear and confusion were written all over Lumi's face. Over the years, he became attuned to the subtle signs that indicated his son was feeling this way. He saw it for a second or two when he first gave Lumi the stone. Then, almost immediately, he could see the fear and confusion wash away and turn into confidence and determination. The conversation between Ghia and Lumi apparently helped him to overcome any uncertainty of using the stone.

> *Yesterday when I handed the yellow stone to Lumi, he looked like he was afraid and uncertain. His face changed after a minute. I could see a burst of confidence light up in him. Did you speak privately with Lumi?*

Yes, we did. Lumi said he felt confused about exactly what he was supposed to do. Lumi was just feeling self-conscious of failing to perform the task in front of his family. Talking to him seemed to help give him some confidence. Lumi is a very special boy. I sense some amazing potential in him.

Thank you.

Ghia then addressed the whole family gathered in the cozy living room.

Good afternoon. Today, I want to talk to you about the quantum properties of the pink stone. The water in the lake outside is quite refreshing when you go for a swim. One reason you can swim in the lake is because the water is currently in a liquid state. How fast the particles move, vibrate, and spin in each atom of water controls the state of the water. This is true for any type of matter. If you raise the temperature of an object, in this case water, then it will boil and then eventually dissipate into steam. If you bring the temperature of water down to a certain point, water will turn into ice. The way to

accomplish this is by increasing or decreasing the movement of the particles in the water. All matter that exists can change into different states.

Felisa, would you like to see if you can turn this glass of water into ice?

A glass of water materialized on the coffee table in front of Felisa. Ode has grown accustomed to Ghia's surprising feats.

Felisa inquired, "Ghia, when I'm trying to make the particles go faster or go slower, are we also saying that I'm also slowing or decreasing the vibrations and the spins of the particles as well?"

Yes, that is exactly what I'm asking you to do.

"Ok, I'll give it my best. Here goes nothing."

Felisa put the pink stone into her left hand and focused on the glass of water. Nothing happened at first. As everyone looked at the water in the glass, you could tell that something was happening. The surface of the water appeared a little cloudy and finally took on a dull white color. In several seconds, Felisa made the once translucent glass of water into a solid, cloudy white piece of ice.

Well done, Felisa. Could you sense the resistance of the particles as they got slower and slower?

"As a matter of fact, I did sense it was taking more effort to get them to the slowest point possible. Why is that?"

Water at this temperature and air pressure will always want to be liquid water. The particles want to be in an equilibrium with their surroundings. If this room temperature was extremely cold and you had a glass of water, the movement of the particles would want to go slower to become ice. Would someone like to turn the ice back into a water form?

Almost instantly, Melliod asked if she could try to do this. Melliod's heart raced with anticipation as she excitedly absorbed every word of the discussion. Felisa smiled proudly and handed her daughter the polished pink stone.

The surface of the water appeared to get watery looking and slightly shiny. The ice was definitely changing to a liquid form, but it didn't happen right away. It took about ten seconds for all the ice in the glass to transform back into liquid. Melliod looked very pleased at what she had done. To check the temperature, she dipped her finger in the water and discovered that it was at a comfortable room temperature.

Fantastic! How did that feel?

"Wow! I hope I did that correctly. It felt like once I got the particles to move just the slightest bit faster, the particles went faster on their own. Did I do that correctly?"

Yes. You did that perfectly. Who else would like to try?

Kelvi was first to ask, "Can I try it?"

Ode turned to Felisa and said, "Once Kelvi gets the hang of this, he and Melli will be playing pranks on all of us."

"Without a doubt!"

The rest of the afternoon, everyone had time to practice turning water into different states of liquid, ice, and steam.

Chapter 16

Storage Lockers

The next morning …

ODE AND HIS SEVENTEEN YEAR OLD SON Kelvi prepared a large breakfast for everyone. After everyone finished eating, Melliod and Dulvod cleared the breakfast table and cleaned the dishes, while everyone went out into the living room to relax.

Lumi asked, "Dad, do you think Ghia will want to teach us more about using the quantum stones today?"

Before Ode could respond, Ghia spoke to everyone telepathically, asking them to go down to the lake for some more training on the quantum stones.

Lumi and Dulvod shared a smile of delight. In a loud voice, Lumi exclaimed, "Yes! This is exactly what I've been hoping would happen today."

About ten minutes later, they were all assembled on the beach. When they arrived at the beach, there was a strange box on the sand. The box was tall. It was about a foot taller than the tallest among them, which was Kotlid. The width of the box was about half as wide as it was tall. The color of the box was a swirling mix of white and green. Distinguishing the color was challenging. It appeared green from one angle and milky white from another.

Ode had spent years researching and experimenting with various materials at the H4A, constantly striving to find innovations in material science. He remembered working with something that looked similar to what he saw in front of him. This material had unprecedented strength and exceptional resistance to extreme temperatures. While it resembled the Aegis compound, it didn't share the same bonding ability characteristic of the latest formula of the Aegis epoxy.

As Ode examined the material, its unique properties amazed him. Its thinness, comparable to a delicate piece of glass, belied its incredible strength. It was as if someone had discovered a way to compress immense power into the tiniest of forms.

Ode wasn't sure how these green and white boxes fit into the over-all plan, but he trusted Ghia. Like everyone else, he waited for Ghia to describe what their responsibility would be with these boxes.

Good morning my children! Tol is blessing us with a beautiful, sunny day. For the last couple of days, we have been learning how to use different colored quantum stones. These stones will help prepare the caverns with individual capsules for every person on the planet. Under the thickest parts of the planet, six very large caverns have been created. Each continent will have one of these deep underground caverns.

When the asteroid impacts the planet, it will be devastating to the surface. No living thing will survive this. It will be necessary for you to prepare these caverns so they will be ready to hold special cryogenic capsules. These capsules will hold all the people of Ghia. Today, what I want to teach you is how to prepare each capsule.

The box in front of you is a highly compressed storage container for five different capsules. Each capsule will hold one person, and it will automatically bring the occupant into a state of suspended animation. The capsules are like special beds designed for long-term stasis. This stasis state is very much like taking a long sleep.

In this suspended state, your bodies will stay inside these capsules for an extensive amount of time. It will take many years for the planet's surface to heal and become safe enough for people to live on the surface again. While people are asleep at night, they will get transported into their individual capsule. The process will occur in phases. There will be no discomfort or pain for anyone.

Here is where all of you can help. Each cavern will contain several hundred green and white boxes like the one in front of you now. Today I would like to have you practice trying to expand these

boxes into the five cryogenic capsules which it contains. Ode, what do you call the leader or the person in charge of organizing large projects?

Ode scratched his chin and thought for a second and said, "We call those *Captains*. Yes, I think *Captain* is the appropriate term we would use. All the *captains* of a project take instructions from the **chief**. Ghia, you are most definitely the **chief** here. We will prepare the caverns for the people to be transported into. We are also the ones to answer questions people might have. This way, the **chief** can focus entirely on the more important issues with no unnecessary disruptions. Isn't this the reason we are learning how to use the quantum stones?"

That is correct and a good analogy. You will all be my captains for each of these enormous caverns.

Felisa smiled thoughtfully, admiring the calm and confidence of her husband. Ode took her hand at her side and gave it a reassuring squeeze. It was the hidden code they shared. This was going to be a difficult and daunting task, but together they would get through it.

Now, this box in front of you only contains five capsules. This is just for practice. When the time comes to expand these storage lockers in the caverns, there will

be substantially more than just five capsules.

So far, when you have been using the quantum stones, we have only used one stone at a time. Today, we will use the yellow stone, as well as the white and the lilac colored quantum stones. If you remember, the yellow stone helped you to push an object away from you. We used the wooden log on the beach to push it into the water of the lake. The yellow stone also let you pull the object to you. This is essentially the basic mechanism we will use today. However, these green and white storage lockers going into the caverns will contain thousands of individual capsules. If you combine the yellow stone and the white stone together, it will amplify the power of the yellow stone.

Each cavern is in the shape of an extremely large torus, or doughnut-like shape. All the capsules will get stacked efficiently all around the diameter of the tubular portion of the torus. To give you an idea, picture yourself standing within the tubular section of the torus. Storage lockers will get stacked on top of each other on your left and right. Storage lockers on the ceiling get placed side by side. Each storage locker can now be ready to get expanded into rows of capsules which will follow the circular shape of the torus.

In the center of the torus-shaped cavern, there will be a vast reservoir of specially created liquid. This liquid will start the hibernation process and will flow through all the capsules.

Soon, each enormous cavern will have all the boxes placed inside and ready to be expanded. I know this is an enormous task, but it's crucial that we prepare the caves before the asteroid hits the planet.

"Ghia, I'm sorry to interrupt. How many capsules are you thinking of having in each cavern?" With a gaze towards his family, he added, "We are all fully committed to this. If we have to expand five capsules at a time for almost two billion people, this will take a lot more time than we have."

You're correct. This object in front of you is for testing and familiarizing yourself with expanding these capsules. Within each cavern, there are between 750 to 1000 storage lockers stacked on top of each other. Each storage locker will then be able to get expanded into a single row of cryogenic capsules that will follow the circumference of the torus. Some of these rows of capsules could contain as much as 350,000 individual cryogenic capsules. This should adequately house the nearly two billion surface inhabitants. There are unfortunately 850,000 people still working on the Noth moon. If they choose to come back to the surface, we will have a spot for them. It is up to them if they want to stay on Noth.

Melliod nervously said, "No pressure, right?"

This task is daunting and will be difficult. However, I have complete faith in what you can accomplish with the quantum stones. Each of you has the innate ability

to use them interacting and connecting with everything around you.

Kotlid asked, "Ghia, is there a possibility of bring other into this group to help us complete this task?"

There is a possibility of adding additional people to be captains for this task. If you want additional people to help us with this task, we can easily train them on how to use the quantum stones. Just remember that this is an all-or-nothing type of task with serious consequences. Anyone you get to help in this effort must be someone you trust completely.

"Ghia, do you know when the asteroid will impact the planet?" Felisa asked.

The last approximation showed arrival in approximately three months, assuming correct calculation. Time is slightly different for planets. Planets measure time by revolutions around Tol.

These capsules will use the yellow stone to expand them out to multiple capsules. In addition, put the white stone at the base of the box. The white stone will glow a brilliant white to signify the stone is amplifying the power of the yellow stone. Dulvod, would you like to give this a try?

"Absolutely!" Dulvod said excitedly as he reached into the bag of quantum stones that he brought from the cabin.

The material used to make this box is incredibly dense and highly compressed. Try to feel the movement of particles in the box. It will take a little longer to make the particles move or vibrate faster because there is so much material compressed. Once you get the particles moving and vibrating as fast as you're able to, then try to increase the spin of the electrons moving around the particles.

If you spin them to the right or in a clockwise rotation, the green and white box will expand into individual capsules contained within the box. If you spin them to the left or counterclockwise, the capsules will collapse and shrink into the green and white box. Be patient! It will

take more time to see the capsules expand from the box.

Ode added, "Do you remember when we went to that science fair last year? We watched the performer spin a plate on top of a stick. Once the plate was spinning fast enough, it could stand on its own. This is how I envision what we do with spinning the particles in a direction. Ghia, is this the correct way to look at it, or did I get it totally wrong?"

Ode you're correct. This is a good way to envision it. Once the electrons are spinning as fast as you can get them, you will start seeing the green and white box expand into individual capsules connected to each other.

Take a deep breath, stay calm, and focus on gradually accelerating the motion and spin of the particles. Once you start them moving faster, the particles will have a momentum which will affect the other particles that are condensed.

Dulvod gripped the yellow stone in his left hand and focused on the green and white box in front of him. It was difficult to feel any movement from the box at all. He noticed the white stone slowly glow brighter and brighter white. Like a piece of fabric with a small tear, he imagined widening and opening the tear larger and larger. Pushing the atoms to move or vibrate faster did not bring the desired change, but forcing the electrons to spin faster did. At first it was hard to see, but the box expanded out. Dulvod maintained his focus on the spinning electrons until he got them spinning as fast as he thought he would be able to.

The white stone at the base of the box glowed as the green and white storage locker box expanded into five compartments. Each capsule resembles an elongated teardrop, its surface a seamless fusion of iridescent green and a milky white. The material appears both lightweight and impenetrable, a paradoxical blend of fragility and resilience.

The inside of each capsule had hundreds of tiny bioluminescent filaments, near invisible to the naked eye, extending from the walls, monitoring every vital sign. They carefully wove a web, ensuring precise regulation of each body's vital signs, striking a perfect balance between preservation and slowing. Next to the occupant's head rested a neural crown interface adorned with filaments. When donned, it would interface with the quantum consciousness of the person inside. The transparent material on the outside of the sleeping chamber merged seamlessly with the rest of the capsule. Each capsule was identical to the one next to it.

Dulvod that was excellent. When you expanded the capsules from the original box, you found that spinning the electrons faster made it easier to pull each of the capsules out of the compressed container. Who else wants to try?

Ghia compressed the five compartments back into the original green and white box. The white stone stopped glowing and was again its normal bone white color.

Melliod jumped up and exclaimed, "I would like to give this a try! I mean, if Dulvod could do this, then it must be easy-peasy, right?" and she winked at her older brother.

All of them got a turn at trying to expand and compress the stasis compartments in and out of the green and white storage locker.

Now, the white stone will amplify the power of the quantum stone and, as you saw, the white stone glowed a brilliant white while it was being used. The next stone I would like for you to try is the lilac colored quantum stone. The lilac stone

will protect the capsules from anything coming into contact with these cryogenic capsules. You will see a slight purple haze create a protective bubble around the capsules. This protective bubble is very strong, but it isn't infallible. If it was, then I would have just put a protective bubble around the entire planet. The asteroid coming here has too much momentum and mass to withstand the assault it will cause. Who wants to try next?

For the rest of the day, they all had a turn at expanding and then compressing the capsules back into the green and white box. Not surprising, but it appeared Melliod could expand the capsules in a significantly less amount of time than her brothers and sister. She could do this in about half the time it took everyone else.

After dinner

Felisa and Ode luxuriated on the rear deck, basking in the serene atmosphere enveloping them amidst the majestic Crestin mountain and lake. The gentle breeze whispered through the towering Aspens as if inhaling deeply, their luminous leaves shimmering with a soft silver glow. The ground around the cabin was adorned with a tapestry of bioluminescent lumensbloom flowers, casting a soft blue glow, while the moonshadow moss radiated a delicate orange hue, having absorbed the abundant daylight. The air carried a fragrance of trees and blossoms, mingling harmoniously with the tranquil serenity of twilight.

The soft trilling of Ode's eidolon sounded from the little device he placed on the table next to him. The noise broke the fragile tranquility into pieces each time the sound came from the device. Ode looked at the name of the person contacting him and immediately recognized it as his manager at the Hulton facility. He quickly glanced at Felisa. He could see her disappointment in having their peace being rudely interrupted. She knew as well as he did, this was going to be inevitable.

He had been away from work for almost four months now. Many of the people living on Ghia got conscripted into helping to build the gigantic generational ships on Noth. Ode believed that the individuals who remained on Ghia were either knowledgeable about the secret plan to go underground, or they had influential connections within the Imperium that allowed them to stay on Ghia. Ode knew he would eventually have to go back to work.

He felt sure that not everyone at his office was convinced that the missiles or the new ships were going to save the planet. Ode wanted to go back and at least offer an alternative to the people he has worked with for a long time. He suspected many of them could use the quantum stones proficiently. Most importantly, they were very pragmatic people and would be helpful to have working on these issues.

Ode pressed the "Accept" button and a holographic image of Bodar O'Dell's face appeared slightly above the table the eidolon rested on.

"Good evening Bodar."

"Ode, I know you had some problems with the Imperium officials and could not come to the office, but I need you to come to work tomorrow."

Ode felt Felisa stiffen, sitting next to him. She was thinking exactly the same thing he was. *Bodar knew about his detention for over three months!*

"Sure, I'll come into the office tomorrow. Is there a problem with the Angbok area, or do you want to do more testing out there? I thought almost all resources were working on creating the colossal ships on Noth. What project did you want me to work on?"

"We are getting a lot of data back from the missiles we sent to the asteroid. I don't trust what these flunkies are telling me about the data they are getting back. Some say the asteroid has been totally obliterated. I think they are just telling us what we want to hear. I want you to come down here and find out what the truth is."

"I have to run a couple of errands for my daughter, but I'll be in after I finish them. Ok?" Ode said. This was an absolute lie. He was angry that his boss had so casually said, *"you had some problems with the Imperium officials"*. It was childish, but it was his small way of venting his frustration and anger toward Bodar.

Bodar hesitated a second, but with a cheery, *"I'm your buddy"*, cheshire like grin said, "Sure. Contact me when you get in."

Ode quickly disconnected the call. He knew Felisa didn't miss the fact that Bodar and others at his office knew where he and Simol were the whole time, when they had confined him in that underground bunker.

"Errands for your daughter, huh? At least we can have a nice breakfast with the family tomorrow morning," Felisa said, smiling.

Chapter 17
Hidden Truths

Countdown: 5 Months till Impact

Dawn

ODE WOKE UP BEFORE DAWN and quietly got out of bed. He rose with the fluid ease of someone who liked to get up early to face the day. He carefully made his way downstairs, the rough-hewn wooden floorboards of the cabin sighing softly beneath his bare feet. There was still some stale *grawpa* left from last night. Not precisely his first choice, but it will suffice.

Stepping outside, a wave of cool air washed over him, carrying a mixture of early morning dew, sweet air of the Aspen trees and the lumensbloom flowers. A refreshing blend that cleansed his lungs with each inhale. Nestled in and around the trees and flowers was a living lampshade of orange moongrass, each blade faintly glowing with the remnants of yesterday's vibrant sunset.

Ode sat at the edge of the dock, watching the little tendrils of mist rising from the lake. The air held a hushed reverence, as if the world was holding its breath in anticipation of the coming light.

It still troubled him at the unfairness of getting confined for three months. During those three months, separated from everyone and everything, his boss, Bodar O-Dell, knew exactly where he was. He felt horrible that Simol got dragged into this mess.

During their confinement, Ode discovered Simol had an unwavering faith that everything would work out in the way and manner it was supposed to play out. Ode found this quality to be both admirable and inspiring.

Ode believed that if Bodar knew his location, Senior Commander Fulton likely did as well. She wouldn't do this just on a whim, which meant this went all the way up to the members of the Continental Imperium. He still couldn't grasp the compelling motive behind his confinement. Polti wanted to keep him out of the way so there would be no one who could refute his claim of finding the asteroid heading to Ghia. Polti had the reputation and professional clout to squash anything Ode said about finding it. Why go to the extreme of putting him in a bunker for three months?

Suddenly, it hit him. Bodar and Commander Fulton wanted to hide the fact that building these generational spaceships wouldn't work. If people were aware of the centuries-long journey to the nearest planet, they would question the effort being put into the shipbuilding. It wasn't even clear to anyone yet what this habitable planet was. So, in the meantime, they were just going to stuff as many people as possible on Noth. Everyone knew Noth was a small moon and couldn't support them all.

Wait, is this the only reason, though? Ode wondered as he stared at the smoky mist coming off the surface of the water. No, it had to be more than just that. Constructing those ships was a foolish and a simplistic response to the threat of complete annihilation. Simol had a highly respected reputation among other astrophysicists in the Science Regency.

Like a slap in the face, he realized the people behind this were not trying to confine him, but their goal was to confine Simol. Simol wasn't in the wrong place at the wrong time; it was Ode who was in the wrong place. Simol knew the astrophysics of building a ship to the nearest habitable planet wasn't possible. He had much more reputational and professional clout than Polti. The members of the Continental Imperium and other higher echelon bodies would listen to him rather than Polti. If anything, it was a bonus to confine both of us.

Simol is still in danger and needs to be alerted to this. Simol needs to disappear so they can't get him again. As the asteroid's date approaches, they may still attempt to silence him.

Ode rose swiftly from the dock and hurried back to the cabin. It was still early morning, but he needed to contact Simol as soon as possible. He just hoped he wasn't too late. He found his silver eidolon and searched for the information he had stored in the device to contact Simol. Calling Simol, Ode received no response. He tried again with the same result.

Felisa heard him downstairs and entered the kitchen. Seeing the panicked look on Ode's face, Felisa asked, "Ode, honey, what's going on? You look very distressed right now."

"I'll explain in just a minute. Do you still have the contact information for Simol's sister or his parent's?"

"Hold on a second." Quickly, she left the kitchen and went into the next room to get her digital pad. She came back in the kitchen and gave him the contact information for both his sister and his parents.

Handing the pad to Ode, she listened carefully as Ode explained, "Felisa: I don't think Simol was just someone who was in the wrong place at the wrong time. It was exactly the opposite. They were after Simol, not me."

"Why do you think it was Simol they were after?"

"Simol's reputation threatened the shipbuilding effort for a distant, habitable planet. Because Simol is a highly respected astrophysicist in this field of study, he would have a lot more clout and respect than Polti."

"I think you're right. It would take a few weeks for Polti to organize something so dramatic."

"Simol is probably one of only a few scientists who could refute the claim of traveling to a habitable planet. I need to contact him as soon as possible."

Hearing the anxiety in his voice, she said quickly, "You called his house, right? Maybe he already left for work and wasn't near his eidolon. You don't think Polti or some of the other Defense Regency people will try to silence him again?"

"I can't be sure of that. They might try to get to him again. I need to warn him about this as soon as possible," Ode seemed panicked and fearful.

"You were heading into the office after breakfast, right?"

"Yes, that was the plan."

Felisa could tell Ode was getting really worked up and frustrated about this situation. "Work isn't expecting you until later, after you run all those elaborate errands for your daughter, right?" Felisa said with a mischievous grin. "Go up and get ready for work and I'll make you a cold smoothie with druvor and ananas dewdrops drink and some Susta-bars you can take with you. You go to Simol's house and see if he is there. If he's not there, then keep trying to reach him on his eidolon. While you're doing that, I'll try to contact his sister and his parents to see if they have any information about where he is right now. I'll call you as soon as I have any information," she said as she packed his food.

"Is it okay if I ask Simol to stay with us temporarily? I think he would be a good person to learn how to use the quantum stones."

"Absolutely. He can stay with us in the spare bedroom upstairs."

Ode kissed his wife and whispered, "thank you." He rushed upstairs to get ready for work.

Absently, Ode thought about what things might have changed since he was last in the office almost four months ago. While he was showering, he decided it would probably be best not to get into any kind of confrontation with Bodar. Or anyone else at the office, for that matter.

He ruefully anticipated today would be full of surprises. Just before he left, it occurred to him he might need to use the quantum stones today. Specifically, the blue stone, which is the way he and his family communicate with Ghia. He grabbed the backpack with all the stones and put it inside his AeroRover.

Getting into the vehicle, Ode set the coordinates to Simol's house. Simol lived in a town called Ryeferen, which was in the same town where the Aratoro Institute of Cosmic Sciences, or AICS, was. Polti and Ode both attended this school, doing their undergraduate work. Simol split his time between teaching astrophysics at AICS and also working at an Imperium Research Organization.

Ode was angry at himself for not spotting the source of his confinement all along. During their time in confinement, Ode disclosed to Simol that he had been in contact with Polti a few days before their meeting. Surprisingly, he learned Polti used to work under Simol in one of his research labs. As the chief scientist at the lab, Simol was responsible for the discovery of the quantum telescope technology. Simol was the scientist who pioneered this area of astrophysics, not Polti. He stole the idea, and a lot of the research Simol and his team had created.

Simol never lodged a formal complaint against the Scientific Regency Council that regulates intellectual property. He confronted Polti and extracted a commitment from him to give credit to the other members of the research team who tested and created the Quantum Telescope. Simol was a scientist at heart and just wanted his work to be an advancement in the field.

Ode could feel his stomach churning as his anxiety increased. He picked up his eidolon and tried to contact Simol again. Why wasn't Simol answering? Did Polti and his henchmen already kidnap him? It was still early, but most people were awake by now and either getting ready for work or eating breakfast. He was still about twenty minutes from Simol's residence. Hopefully, Felisa will have better luck contacting Simol's parents or his sister.

Just as he was thinking this, his eidolon chimed. It was Felisa calling. He accepted the call, and a holographic image of Felisa's face appeared in front of him.

"Hi, did you have any luck getting a hold of Simol's sister or parents?"

"His parents were unreachable, but I spoke with Simol's sister. She said he's going into AICS today and he would most likely be there all day. She also told me his classroom was number 410 in the Zwicker building. Remember, Ode, this is the place we used to meet after some of your classes or labs. I didn't know it was called the 'Zwicker' building. We always just referred to it as building Z."

"Ok, thanks. I think I remember the address," Ode said as he quickly changed his destination on the AeroRovers navigation system to the new address. This address was familiar to him because in the past he had various types of materials required for his unique experiments shipped there.

"I should be there in about fifteen minutes. I just remembered something Simol told me while we were confined in the underground bunker. Polti used to work for Simol at the lab where the quantum telescope got invented. He also told me the quantum telescope technology we use today was first invented by him, not Polti. There are countless reasons for Polti to capture and silence Simol."

"Didn't Simol file a complaint with the Science Regency? This surely would have escalated up to the Continental Imperium. I'm sure they would have been able to find out who actually created and did the research on this technology. The only name I ever heard associated with the quantum telescopes was Poltibern Torkasu."

"No, Simol never filed a complaint. He told me he confronted Polti at an AICS party. Everyone was talking about Polti's quantum telescope, but Simol wasn't interested in recognition or notoriety for his invention. However, Simol had one condition for his silence. He made Polti agree to recognize and credit the team of researchers and other scientists who helped to make this technology a reality. If Polti failed to do this, Simol promised him he would publicly expose him for being a fraud."

Felisa smiled and said, "Hmm, not caring about fame and fortune sounds exactly like someone I know."

"Who me? Maybe a little. We are both scientists and love the science much more than being famous. If I was younger, maybe. I'm getting close to the campus, so I'll call you a little bit later if I find Simol. Bye, love."

Chapter 18
Building "Z"

Building "Z"

OFF IN THE DISTANCE, ODE could see several buildings and areas that looked familiar to him. This area holds a special meaning because this wasn't just a place of fond school memories, but it was also where Ode met Felisa. She was working on her degree in one of the medical sciences. Almost 98% of the graduates in the medical sciences, typically ended up on Noth. Anyone studying for advanced medical degrees usually did part of this work on Noth. It also contained vast facilities and laboratories for medical research.

Felisa went to Noth for a couple of years to finish her education in biomedical medicine. They both decided after they got married that starting a family would take the higher precedent than any of their career aspirations. Now, neither of them had any regrets.

Ode navigated to the Zwicker building and landed in the area for vehicles. Going into the building, he went up to the fourth floor and found classroom number 410. As he got closer, his chest tightened with a renewed sense of anxiety and fear of who he was going to find in this classroom. He hoped Simol was Ok. Ode would feel horrible and guilty if Simol got kidnapped again.

As he got closer, he could hear someone talking, but Ode didn't recognize this as Simol's voice. Arriving at the classroom door, he could see that the person in front of the class wasn't Simol. Ode felt crushed.

Now what? Most of the faculty offices were on the second floor. Maybe he got here before Simol's class was supposed to start. This might be plausible since it was still early. Maybe Simol was in his office. He made the trip all the way out here. It would be foolish for him not to at least check if he was in his office.

He went down to the second floor of the building. There was a long hallway of offices on both the left and the right. About halfway down the corridor, he found Simol's office, and his door was closed. He felt a little foolish, but he knocked on the door. The sound of his knocking on the door echoed down the hall. He heard some noise in the office after a moment. It sounded like a chair squeaking and someone walking over to the door. The person opening the door surprised Ode. It wasn't

Simol. The person looked to be about the age of his son, Dulvod, when he was a student in college.

Ode mumbled, "Sorry. I was looking for someone else." He quickly turned and started to walk back down the hallway.

"Ode!"

He turned around and saw Simol standing next to the young man, who had opened the door of the office.

Instant relief flooded back into Ode. "Simol, I'm so glad to see you! Do you have a few minutes to talk?"

"Certainly! Would you mind if we took a walk outside to the courtyard? It's a lovely day, and it would be nice to get out of the office." Simol turned to the young student who was following this conversation intently. "Jaxton, repeat your experiment with those two additional chemicals and I'm sure you will get the results you're looking for, Ok?" Simol said, making sure his student understood.

"Thank you, Professor. I'll do that."

Both Simol and Ode walked down one flight of stairs and went outside into a large square courtyard located in the center of the building. The different classrooms and offices of the Zwicker building surrounded the courtyard like a Roman Colosseum. Each window was a portal to gaze out at the gladiators of students and professors, all seeking to slake their thirst for knowledge, as if it were a vast arena of intellect.

There were several tables and chairs littered around the center of the courtyard. Scattered in different parts of the courtyard were many lush, colorful plants of all sorts. There was a path that followed the perimeter of the courtyard.

Once they stepped outside, Simol guided Ode towards the path that traced the perimeter of the courtyard. Planted on both sides of the path, there were several rows of delicate flowers standing at waist height. These beautiful blossoms resembled large, deep bowls, glowing in an iridescent, neon-like shade of blue. Thousands of vibrant red, yellow, and pink petals filled each of these blue bowls. Mingling among these larger flowers were smaller round white flowers edged with green leaves. As Ode walked through this enchanting scene, a brisk citrus scent filled the air, leaving him with a refreshing sensation. Walking around this courtyard path was an indulgence for the senses.

Simol, surprised by Ode's unexpected presence, inquired, "Ode, I wasn't expecting to see you today. Is there something I can assist you with?"

"Yes, there is. I'm sorry I didn't realize this earlier," Ode said as they walked along the perimeter of the courtyard. Trying to keep his voice at a low volume, Ode continued, "You're in a dangerous situation, my friend. Do you remember when we were flying back from the bunker, my wife mentioned Polti was the person who got the both of us confined?"

"Yes, I do. At the time, I was still trying to adjust to being released from captivity."

"Actually, confining me was just a bonus to Polti. Polti wasn't looking for me. He was looking for you!"

Simol said, "I don't think Polti could organize something like this himself."

Ode sarcastically said, "I'm sure this issue goes all the way up to the Continental Imperium. Over the last ten years, the Imperium and specifically, the Science Regency, have been funding but never really finishing the project to build the ten interplanetary spaceships. In the past ten years, they have barely been able to complete one of these spaceships on Noth."

Simol said more to himself rather than Ode, "So that is why everyone is leaving for Noth."

Ode said, "The impending asteroid gives them the reason to ramp up the construction of those spaceships exponentially. I doubt they are planning on building enough ships for the entire population. They are probably working furiously to build enough ships for only the rich and most powerful to get on one of those spaceships."

Simol just nodded.

Ode continued, "Each of those ships will also need to have enough room to carry and support all the laborers, servants, and support passengers to keep them in luxury for the long journey. Polti just gave them the perfect excuse to build them."

Before Ode could continue, Simol interjected, "Building those ships is a total waste of time. They would need several hundred of those huge generational ships to save the almost two billion people on Ghia. It will take centuries, if not millennia, to reach the first semi habitable planet."

"Exactly! Simol, you're probably one of the few scientists who has the reputational clout and respect of the Continental Imperium. They might hear your opinion, but they have already gone too far and invested too much into this operation right now. Do you remember when I told you that Ghia has a plan for us to withstand this asteroid coming to the planet?"

"Of course. You were waiting for more details from Ghia about where and when we could go underground. Did Ghia contact you with more information about this?"

"Yes. Ghia's plan is to put all the humans on the surface into cryogenic stasis pods. These stasis pods will be located deep underneath the thickest parts of the planet."

Ode and Simol kept walking around the courtyard silently. Finally, Ode anxiously said, "Simol, if they could capture you before, then there is no reason they can't do this again. My family is staying in the Crestin mountains at a cabin we own on Crestin Lake. Can you come up and stay with my family? I'm afraid they might try to capture you again."

Simol hesitated for a second to digest what Ode had just said. He asked, "Do you really think they will try to confine me again?"

"Yes, I do. Ghia is creating these spaces underground and all the stasis pods, but we can help to organize and layout the stasis pods in each underground cavern. Once we are underground and in the individual cryogenic capsules, Ghia will need a long time to heal. This could be centuries for the land to heal and become viable again."

Simol looked at Ode to make sure he heard this correctly. "Centuries?"

"Yes, centuries. It all depends on how much damage the asteroid does to the surface. I expect everything above ground will get destroyed. This is where I could use your help. We can't save everything, but we need to make plans for what items we can preserve, like our science, history, education, philosophy, religion, languages, and many other valuable parts of our society that we should try to preserve. We have limited storage space. Ghia will also protect all the items that get put into this special storage area while we are in stasis."

Simol's pace slowed, and a furrow appeared on his brow. "I'm still playing catch up in my day job," he admitted, his voice sounding tired with weariness. "Two more classes to go this week, then I'm clear. Jaxton can handle the rest. It's the perfect chance to give him a bigger role." He halted abruptly, his eyes widening in sudden realization. Ode noticed the sharp change in his expression. "Wait," Simol said, his voice edged with urgency, "is there some kind of … list? Of people going underground?"

"So, Ghia's plan is to put everyone on the surface into these stasis pods while they're asleep. Ghia hasn't given me a specific date yet, but it's going to happen in stages. Think of what an enormous task this is. Ghia will have to teleport hundreds of millions of people at once," Ode said, his voice filled with a mix of awe and admiration. He continued, "The good news is, Ghia will ensure that no one gets left behind. If anyone's still up top when it's time, they'll automatically get teleported to these underground caverns into the cryogenic pods."

Ode paused, considering his next words. "Sadly, Ghia can't teleport the people who are on Noth. If anyone who is currently on Noth can get to the planet surface before the asteroid impacts with Ghia, they will also get put into a stasis pod. My son-in-law's family is discreetly working to get people off of Noth."

Simol halted his steps and gazed sadly at the trail adorned with vibrant flowers. He said, "It saddens me to realize that all these exquisite creations we are privileged to witness every day will soon get destroyed. Yet, I suppose we must place our faith in Ghia, kind of like a cosmic gardener who tends its crops. Ghia will guide us through this phase of devastation, knowing that eventually, they will get rejuvenated in a distant future, just as the seasons bring life back to barren fields."

They both started walking to the end of the path around the courtyard. Simol said, "I think you're right about Polti. Getting rid of both of us has made life for Polti much easier. Ok, I'll stay with you and your family up in the Crestin mountains. Give me two days and I'll tie up all the things I need to do before going underground," Simol said with a smile.

"This is fantastic news! I can't wait to show you the incredible quantum stones Ghia has provided us with. They will play a crucial role in our efforts to help rescue the people of Ghia."

Chapter 19
H4A

Later at work

ODE LANDED IN THE REAR parking area he normally used. He walked into the building and thought it would be best to hunt down his boss, Bodar, first. He really didn't want to talk to him. Ode felt betrayed by Bodar. Since he had worked here for the last twenty years and had worked for Bodar for seven of those years. Bodar knew Ode was being kept in confinement for three months. Why didn't Bodar get him released, or at least tell his family something?

Ode could feel himself going down a dangerous dead-end with this thinking. So, he decided this morning to just "not react" or get caught up in the past. Ode was grateful to be free from his confinement in that underground bunker. He also knew he would accomplish nothing by confronting Bodar about it.

Ode went straight to Bodar's office and knocked. He heard a sharp gruff snap, "Come in."

When Ode opened the door, he saw Bodar sitting behind his desk. "Hi Bodar, what did you want me to help with today?"

Bodar stood up with a big smile and shook his hand. The smile actually looked authentic. "Glad to have you back in the office. It's been a tough couple of months since you've been away."

Oh, really? Ode didn't let his anger come to the surface. It was just too easy to flare up at Bodar's insulting comment right now. In a calm, measured voice, he said, "What can I do to help?"

Sitting down, Bodar addressed the issue, stating, "We're currently facing some complications with the 'astro' team. They can't seem to reach a consensus on the data we are getting back from the special EKP missiles deployed to the asteroid."

"EKP missiles? What are those?"

He went on to explain, "All continents have banned this type of missile. The EKP missiles are Electromagnetic Kinetic Pulse missiles. These EKP missiles possess distinct features that set them apart from other missile types. Its detonation involves the utilization of quantum quarks to create massive electromagnetic pulses of energy, like a nuclear explosion, but with far greater force."

"As you may know," Bodar continued, "Their ban is a result of the immense potential for the destruction they possess. However, simply prohibiting something doesn't guarantee its disappearance. It's common knowledge that each continent safeguards a reserve of these missiles, ensuring their preparedness in the face of intercontinental threats. Each leader on the Continental Imperium plays by the standard operating procedure of mutually assured destruction."

"Sure, I'll head over in a few minutes. I have to get something from my office and then I'll check in with them."

"Thanks, Ode. In the next couple of weeks, I might have to travel to Noth to attend some high-level meetings. A lot of the Commanders and Regents are slowly taking up a permanent residence on Noth. They can't trust doing this via holo-vid-call. All travel between Ghia and Noth is going to start getting restricted."

Ode bit his lip to maintain a neutral composure and conceal his thoughts. He speculated that Bodar's journey to Noth indicated that he had secured a coveted spot as a passenger on one of the generation ships under construction.

Bodar continued, "All travel will need a special clearance approved by a Regent or one of the Imperium Ministers. Luckily, Senior Commander Fulton is here frequently, which gives us greater access to get the approvals we need."

Ode quickly thought sarcastically, "It gives you greater access, but definitely not anyone else."

Bodar continued, "They want me to present some data that the astrophysics people here are gathering. The problem is we have two different groups that aren't in agreement. One group swears by Poltibern Torkasu's claim the asteroid will still impact with Ghia in twelve months."

Ode took a sharp intake of breath, but didn't show or give away anything to Bodar. Twelve months? Ghia assured him the asteroid would be here in less than six months.

Bodar, oblivious, continued, "The other group is saying that the missiles have completely negated the risk of the asteroid impacting with Ghia at all. I would appreciate it if you could make some sense of what the heck the actual story is about this."

"Sure, I'll head over there."

Once Ode was out of Bodar's office, he let out an enormous sigh. Now that Polti is saying it's twelve months away is criminal. How could Polti be off by six months? How could he be so naïve? This is going to be a big problem. Should he call him and tell him he is so deadly wrong? At the moment, his mind was spinning. Right now, he couldn't do anything about this.

Ode went back to his office and looked around to see if there was anything here in his office he would want to keep and bring back home today. He chuckled a little as he realized there wasn't anything in his office he really needed or wanted. There was one picture of his family on his desk that he conceded he would like to keep. Other than that, there was nothing else.

He walked out of the office to go over to the location where Bodar said the astrophysicists were hammering out the details of what the current data was telling them. As he walked over to where the astrophysicists were located, he thought, "Felisa is gonna love this story tonight."

Later that night …

After dinner, Felisa and Ode were relaxing on the back deck of the cabin. Watching the sunset was a nightly ritual for them. It was always a special time for them to share what the day had given them.

It surprised Felisa that Bodar had miscalculated the time of impact with Ghia by such a large margin. She said,

"Why do you think Polti is telling Bodar it's twelve months away and not six months to impact?"

"I think Bodar is just playing a game with me. Maybe it's his way of giving me back the three months of time he took away from me by putting me in that underground bunker. My meeting with him today was strange. I'm positive he's aware that I know he had a part or full knowledge of where I was being confined."

"While you were away, I spoke to him to ask if he knew where you were. I could tell he was lying to me when he said he didn't have any information about your whereabouts. Bodar is a horrible liar, by the way," Felisa dryly said.

Ode chuckled a little at Felisa's comment. "Yes, that is true. I decided today that I'll not be going back into the office."

His wife said, "Good. It really just makes little sense to waste the time going there."

"This crisis will require our full attention. I can't waste any time doing something which doesn't help us complete the mission that Ghia has entrusted to us. I spoke to a few of my colleagues about the plan Ghia has for all of us. I trust these coworkers and friends. I also asked them to recruit any other people who might help us. I know they will be discreet."

Felisa quietly said, "Ode, can I ask you a question? I think I have a slight understanding of this, but can you explain to me exactly what is going to happen when the impact hits Ghia?"

Ode paused for a second and said, "The answer to that question is a long one, but I agree with you. These details of what will happen need to be reinforced so that people will have the unvarnished truth of this crisis."

Ode described to Felisa what he and other scientists felt would occur if a potential extinction level event caused by the impact of such a large asteroid. He started by telling her that most of the details he was about to tell her were based on hypotheses. Since this event has never happened before, it was possible for some details to change.

Once the asteroid strikes Ghia, it will impact the entire planet; not just the specific part of the planet that was impacted. Will anything be able to survive after the impact of the asteroid? It's still unclear as to the answer to this, but the only probable course of action will be to save the planet will be to store, save, and preserve all living things on the planet. Then to reintroduce them later in time. In a sense, it is like restoring a backup to your computer when you need to start over.

When the asteroid hits the planet's atmosphere, it might break into a couple of smaller chunks. Regardless, it will still have the same effect by creating one or more gigantic craters, possibly one hundred to one hundred and fifty miles wide. In the first week, gigantic tsunamis will hit every coastal area on the planet. These bodies of water will undoubtably shift and move to different locations around the planet. New areas of land may develop, or existing lands will get flooded.

The heat generated by the impact will be intense. Cities and forests could ignite devastating anything living on the surface. Forest fires and burned cities could release ash and cinders into the atmosphere. The ash and dust propelled into the atmosphere would completely block out any light from Tol. Ghia could experience a prolonged period of darkness because of dust and debris thrown up into the atmosphere. The sunlight will get blocked. The temperature in the oceans would likely increase, causing nearly all the aquatic life to die. This impact winter could last for as long as one hundred years, hindering plant growth and disrupting food chains. All resources necessary for life would need to be built up again before any feasibility of reintroducing seeds or plant life.

Slowly, the delicate balance to establish a self-sustaining ecosystem could take anywhere from one hundred to five hundred years. This should involve careful selection and nurturing of plants, potentially using greenhouses or controlled environments. New prey or pollinators will progressively improve the chances of a viable chain of life taking hold.

Over the next 500 to 1000 years, there is a possibility of reintroducing simpler animal life forms, such as insects and small vertebrates. They would play a crucial role in rebuilding the food chain and aiding plant growth through pollination and seed dispersal. Establishing a more diverse and established ecosystem should get reintroduced slowly, one step at a time. After a 1000 or more years, the environment will stabilize, food sources should become plentiful, and we could manage diseases and predators, gradually reintroducing larger mammals, including humans.

Felisa listened intently with a look of desperation on her face. Ode continued, "Evolution patterns of animal or plant dominance might be the exact opposite to what it was before it impacted with Ghia. A lot depends on a roll of the dice of what species went extinct or claimed dominance prior to the asteroid's impact. Numbers matter to who wins or loses the battle to dominate."

When Ode finished explaining all this to Felisa, he looked at his wife. Small tears were rolling down her cheeks. Ode understood why she felt so sad about this looming destruction. He squeezed her hand and said, "Yes, I also feel very sad about this. So much life and vitality on this planet, only to be erased by the universe's fickle nature."

Chapter 20
Twins

Two Months To Impact

Items Going into Storage

ODE AND HIS FAMILY HAVE BEEN very busy over the last eight months. In some of Ode's earlier discussions with Ghia, he asked if there was a way to preserve parts of their society so that after they emerged onto the surface, they would have all the knowledge they had gained over the last several thousand years. It wouldn't make sense starting from scratch. Future generations would have this information available and they could move forward as a society rather than starting all over at the beginning. Ode understood that underground space was at a premium, so it was vital to make sure anything they were going to preserve would have to be the essentials and not just the "nice to have" items. Sadly, this meant many pieces of art, sculptures, or anything that wouldn't help them survive when they woke up, was most likely not going to be preserved.

Felisa, Simol, Dulvod, Kotlid, and Tomachlus all reached out to many different knowledge experts in the academic and cultural parts of Ghian society. Many of these knowledge experts were on different continents, so it was vital to make sure the makeup of the members of this group had the diversity needed to know things which would be vital to survive once they emerged from suspended animation.

Getting input from people who would know what would be essential in different environments proven to be difficult. Once they felt like they had reached a critical mass, then it was time to create a long list of the items they would need to survive once they emerged, and then to preserve these items for the future generations to build from. It had taken thousands of years to attain all the knowledge and it would be a shame to not attempt to make this available for the future generations.

Sadly, there were going to be many items which wouldn't be able to get preserved. All the paintings and sculptures each continent contained wouldn't get preserved. There just wasn't space. If the group saved a specific painting or sculpture, rather than keeping one more power generator, it made little sense. At first, it felt like everyone was trying to unravel a large, tangled ball of yarn. Every person in the meeting was wrestling with a tangled mess, their fingers fumbling and frustrated. But once they found the starting point, slowly the ball of yarn unraveled, the process becomes smooth and almost rhythmic, each person pulling out a strand and contributing to the growing solution. Once they reached this point, it became a lot easier to trim down the list. Since space was so limited, it was essential to maximize the efficiency of the space available within this special cavern.

It was sobering to realize that the size of the cavern, and the constraints of limited space, were daunting. Ghia told Ode the amount of space available would likely be like one of their biggest stadiums on the continent of Altira. Although this stadium was quite large, it would probably only be as large as one of the six caverns Ghia was creating for all the people.

They created a final list that was well thought out and as complete as possible. It would be impossible to store every part of their culture. They could store many of the items digitally. These digital archives would contain a tremendous amount of data. Digital copies of historical documents, scientific journals, medicine, engineering manuals, and educational materials in various languages. Other items stored digitally would focus on how things worked rather than specific models. For example, detailed descriptions of how to make an AeroRover and the designs that were used to produce them. Storing a fleet of AeroRovers into storage wouldn't make sense. Surviving didn't specifically require entertainment like movies, music, or literature, but if you could digitally store it without compromising space for something more important, then why not attempt to preserve it?

While the amount of data being stored digitally was enormous, it wouldn't take up a lot of space. They would store information in etched crystals, which could last thousands of years. Any documentation of the structure of the Continental Imperium and law systems would be essential once they got stabilized as a society. Foundational documents like constitutions, legal codes, and historical accounts of past administrations, both successes and failures, were important to preserve.

While digital storage would hold vast amounts of information, it was equally important to consider various physical items for their survival once they got revived: those things which would be an immediate necessity after they were awake and had emerged on the surface. The most important items that the group deemed necessary were medical necessities, engineering items to produce power, water filtration systems to make the water safe for everyone, an initial stockpile of food, and clothing for different environments.

After identifying the items for an immediate need, they created another list for longer term survival. The items on this list would help them become more self-sufficient. Once they became more self-sufficient, the larger society of people would stabilize and everyday life will eventually become easier.

The group created a priority-based list of items in the short term and items in the long term. In the short term and the long-term forecast of society emerging from the underground, everyone would need shelter, food, and safety. Building shelter for everyone would take a while to create, but it would be possible to create crude shelters for large groups of people and depending on what climate they were in. People located nearer to the north or south poles of Ghia would require shelter, which would protect them from the cold. It would also be necessary for people to have clothing available to protect them from the environment depending on the climate. Shelter would also require basic hand tools, metalworking equipment such as forges and lathes, and several 3D printers.

Some of these items would require power in order to run. Storing some of these items would also require power sources. They will need to generate energy almost immediately. Items like generators, solar panels, wind turbines, and knowledge on building sustainable energy sources would help. Various construction materials and metals such as steel, copper, wood, and other essential building materials would also be helpful.

Once crude shelters were available, it would be necessary to create areas of the land to grow food on so they could be self-sufficient. They planned to leave basic nutrients in a freeze-dried form, which would suffice for the first couple of months, but it would also be necessary for them to hunt and fish as an additional source of food for them. For the longer outlook, Ghia had created a vast seed bank with a wide variety of plant life. It would become important to prioritize staple crops, vegetables, fruits, and medicinal plants. The need to plant and grow enough food for everyone would require large farms. People would need basic hand tools to prepare the ground for planting crops.

For safety, medical supplies such as antibiotics, basic medical equipment, surgical tools, and long-lasting medications needed to be available initially. It was unclear on how safe water resources would be available after they were awake. It was important to have engineering materials essential for water purification systems, well-drilling equipment, and knowledge of safe water collection.

Twin Asteroids

While these preparations were going on, Ghia saw a shadow behind the asteroid called the Big Pebble. At first, Ghia thought the darkness following the large asteroid was a shadow. As it got closer, Ghia realized it was, in fact, two different asteroids approximately the same size. Ghia looked a little closer and saw that it wasn't just one asteroid hurtling to Ghia, but there were two asteroids roughly about the same size coming to the planet. Ghia was prepared for one asteroid and couldn't withstand the impacts of two asteroids. Ghia knew it must be prepared to absorb as much of the impact as possible.

A new wrinkle in the problem came when Ghia looked at the asteroids after the missiles had impacted and blown up the larger asteroid. The first asteroid broke into four large pieces and it had deflected these pieces to bypass Ghia altogether. It was good news that the initial asteroid broke up and deflected and wouldn't hit Ghia, but it was now heading directly for Noth. It would destroy everything and everyone on the surface of the moon.

More disturbing was when Ghia projected the new landfall of the second asteroid, Big Pebble 2, was going to impact with Ghia in different places on the surface. Not where they had expected them to hit the surface. Of all the six caverns being built, the cavern on the Irsun continent would be in danger of being breached from the Big Pebble 2.

Of the six caverns Ghia had already created, five of them were still going to be safe after the asteroid impacts the surface. These five caverns were in the thickest and strongest parts of the planet. Now with the new data of the large Big Pebble 2 asteroid striking Ghia in different areas, the precise impact areas needed to be recalculated. Thankfully, five of the caverns Ghia built over the last ten months are still safe. The thick parts of the planet's crust would continue to protect these five areas. However, one area on the Irsun continent, the Irsun Station, will suffer an almost direct impact above this cavern. The thick planet crust above the Irsun Station could not provide sufficient protection for this cavern. Irsun Station will get demolished and not be safe for the people of Ghia.

This is unexpected, but not terribly surprising. The Irsun continent was the specific continent that the Hulton 4A organization has been using as its testing area for decades. Recently, the continent became overly saturated with missiles and explosions. The thickest parts of the planet's crust had experienced significant weakening, and Ghia knew the cavern wouldn't survive the impact at this new location.

Ode and his family had finished preparing the Irsun cavern. The suspension capsules were ready and just waiting for people to be transported directly into them. Time was short, but with help, it would still be possible to accomplish this. It normally took Ghia a minimum of two weeks to fully carve out and supply a cavern large enough for the 150,000 people.

Ghia would need to get some help to create a new cavern. Ode, Lumi, and Helliod had the ability to manifest lasers which helped carve and sculpt any new cavern. The location of the new cavern would get created in the southern portion of the Sumira continent. This would be the second cavern Ghia had created on the Sumira continent.

Once they formed the new cavern, they transferred all the vacant hibernation pods from Irsun Station to Sumira Station 2. It was a shame that Felisa, Melliod, and Dulvod had done a great job expanding the hibernation pods in the Irsun Station. Time would be tight, but Ghia felt confident it could deflate all the hibernation pods and then transport them into the new Sumira Station 2. After transporting all the capsules into the new cavern, the green and white boxes would get fully expanded again.

Once everyone was safe in the hibernation capsules, Ghia would then put Ode and his associates into long-term stasis. He wanted all of them to go into the capsules earlier, but each of them insisted they only go into the hibernation pods once everyone else on the planet was secure.

Despite not fully understanding motherhood, Ghia could recognize Felisa's formidable nature as a mother. She was firm, relentless, and vocally expressed her refusal to consider putting them in early. She adamantly insisted that they would go in last, a sentiment echoed by each of her children. Ghia chuckled at the memory of her unwavering and compelling tone. Ghia realized Felisa was attempting to wield her influence in a manner comparable to how she would manipulate the olive quantum stone. Felisa was trying to compel or force Ghia to obey her. Chuckling even more now, Ghia realized Felisa didn't need the stone to be compelling. Ghia pondered how Ode and his children possessed all the necessary qualities without relying on the quantum stones. They had the innate ability to harness the power available, manipulating the movement, vibrations, and spin of particles. It was truly fascinating.

Chapter 21
End Phase

One Month Left To Impact – Noth Moon

As THE LOOMING ASTEROID DREW closer, a chilling sense of dread took hold of Polti. Alongside the other leaders, he callously realized that there wouldn't be enough spaceships for everyone. If there were no unforeseen issues or complications, Polti felt reasonably confident that they could complete ten spaceships, provided that each ship passed all the tests and systems checks before the asteroid struck Ghia. However, Ghia wouldn't be a viable source for additional materials after the impact. While the destruction on the surface of Ghia wouldn't be instantaneous, the asteroid strike would render the planet's surface uninhabitable within a week at most. It was a desperate race against time, a struggle for survival with seemingly impossible odds.

Out of the ten spaceships, only eight successfully passed all the rigorous tests and inspections they underwent. The remaining two vessels failed because of the incorrect installation of an engine part sourced directly from Ghia. Thus, it became necessary for someone to go to Ghia and make sure they obtained the correct parts and brought them back to Noth. Assuming that the required resources and workforce were already in place, it would be possible to finish the unfinished vessels on Noth. Although this setback would cause a delay of approximately two weeks for those two ships, the team considered it a minor but essential setback.

The engine parts were very specialized. Since they were dealing with the extreme heat of hydrogen in a plasmatic state, the engine parts needed to be coated with a special chemical which could protect these parts from the heat. Ironically, the same plant where Ode worked produced the chemicals needed to protect these engine parts. Polti would need to send someone down to the surface of Ghia and go to the Hulton 4A plant to get these parts specially coated.

Call with Commander Fulton

Last night, Polti received an unidentified caller to his eidolon. When he answered the holo-call, it was Senior Commander Fulton.

"Nice to see you again, Commander," Polti said, as confidently as he could muster.

Almost like clock-work, military precision, she called him at the beginning of every month to get updates from him on the progress of building the ships. Commander Fulton isn't someone to cross swords with. She was a ruthless analytic tactician and logistical wizard. He felt a strange juxtaposition of both fear and admiration for her ability to make things happen with lightning speed.

"Nice to see you as well. What is the latest situation report on the construction of the new space ships? Are we still going to have ten vessels completed before the asteroid is due to impact with Ghia?"

Polti knew this was a trap for him. She already knew the answer to the question before she asked it. If he gave her anything less than the truth, she would perceive this as insubordination. Honesty with Commander Fulton was always the best, and the only, way to communicate with her.

Polti said, "We have recently completed all the tests and systems checks on the existing ten ships we have finished constructing. Two of those ships failed a critical test of the engines at maximum propulsion. The failure happened because somehow we neglected to coat two very specialized parts in the engine array with a special chemical to withstand the extreme heat and stress the engines endure."

"Where are those parts usually sourced from?"

"Actually, the workers at the Hulton 4A plant usually treat those parts with a variation of the Aegis chemical."

"Send me the exact specifications for the chemicals and the process they need to follow. I'll get the manager in charge of that chemical process to make this a top priority. His name is Bodar Odell. I trust him to make sure this gets the proper attention. However, Polti, I want you to come down to Ghia to oversee this process. Don't worry, you will still leave with the rest of the ships. The work down here would only take a day or two to complete. Once the parts are done being treated with the Aegis chemical, I'll travel back with you to Noth. How long will it delay the complete construction of those other two ships?"

"All the materials and the manpower are currently available here on Noth. Getting the parts installed correctly and then tested would delay these two ships for a minimum of two weeks," Polti said.

"Okay, I'll see you when you come down to Ghia. Also, I'll send you a list of additional names you will need to reserve space for on the passenger manifest. These are dear friends of my late husband. I just wouldn't feel right if I couldn't provide room for them."

"Sure thing, Commander. If it isn't too much trouble, could you please send me a final list of all the passengers you want me to allocate space for? I want to ensure that I have correctly accounted for everyone you have informed me about."

"I'll send this to you in a few minutes. Thanks."

Polti ended the holo-call. The cold sweat on his forehead and the knots in his stomach got even tighter, wrapping him up in a blanket of nausea that made his head hurt. *Why does she want me to specifically to go down to Ghia?*

Polti was expecting her monthly call. Besides providing progress updates, the commander typically asked him to revise the list of her family and relatives whom she wanted Polti to ensure spots on the spaceships. Typically, with each monthly status update call, she would add an additional ten or twenty people to her list of spots he needed to reserve for her. Commander Fulton currently had 125 family members Polti was holding space for.

Polti was a survivor, so he padded the passenger spaces for all the members of the Imperium and different continental regents. He dramatically told each member how difficult it was to reserve space for fifty passengers on board these ships. If they needed more than fifty spots, he could do this by bleeding off five or ten spaces reserved for other Ministers of the Imperium. At some point, he will need to disappoint some Ministers by not reserving the specified space for the passengers.

Commander Fulton was the most feared and the most powerful member, so she wasn't to be disappointed. This gave him tremendous bargaining power with all the Imperium Ministers who wanted more than the fifty spaces he promised he would reserve for them. It also told him who was the strongest and who was the weakest politically of all the Ministers of the Continental Imperium.

The weight of the anxiety and stress he had been carrying for the past nine months was taking its toll on him. Every night, the feeling that he was fleeing from something haunted him or that he could never complete these ships. And now, adding to his burdens, he had to go to Ghia to oversee and guide the technicians in their work. It had been years since he last visited Ghia. Polti never regretted his decision to live on Noth. As the night descended and his dreams began their nightly torment, he couldn't help but wonder why she insisted on sending him there.

Chapter 22
Party Crasher

48 Hours to Impact

POLTI IS ANGRY AND IRRITATED. His patience for the work being completed on the two special engine parts needed for the spaceship on Noth was wearing thin. The people in the H4A facility finished the parts yesterday.

Several weeks before he came down to Ghia, a restriction on all vessels leaving or arriving on Ghia had to have special clearances. Luckily, Commander Fulton made this possible by arranging his clearance to land on Ghia. Now he had to wait for Commander Fulton to join him on the passage back to Noth. Commander Fulton had all the clearances and credentials they would need to leave Ghia, so he had little choice but to wait for her.

He was pacing back and forth, waiting for her to contact him. His pacing was creating a path in the soft carpeting of the modest temporary quarters they gave him when he arrived on Ghia. Commander Fulton was supposed to contact him an hour ago. She was always punctual and had a natural tendency to never be late. Finally, his eidolon alerted him of an incoming call. He saw it was from Commander Fulton, and he quickly accepted the call.

"Good afternoon, Commander," Polti said.

Without exchanging the usual conversation pleasantries, she barked, "Polti, I'm going to be unavoidably delayed leaving for Noth. Last night I secured a transport ship for the additional passengers I want on board those spaceships. They should already be there by now. I want you to take the two special parts back to Noth and get them installed as soon as possible. I have a situation I must correct before I can travel to Noth."

Polti held back a tsunami of rage and calmly said, "Commander, are you sure this is wise? There is very little time left to leave Ghia." He regretted saying this and knew it was a mistake to question her.

Commander Fulton glared at Polti with her piercing gray eyes. In a low, forced voice, she said, "That isn't your concern now, is it? You will need to deliver those parts to Noth as soon as possible."

"Yes, Commander. If you're only going to be delayed a short time, I can wait."

Polti knew he was pushing the envelope with Commander Fulton. He was hoping to sound accommodating, but many knew that she was difficult to read through her body language. She hesitated a two full seconds before answering him.

"Polti, you have your orders. Those engine parts are the priority right now," she snapped at him.

"Very well, Commander." Polti said and disconnected the call.

Polti sat back, surprised. This wasn't the reaction he was expecting. The more he thought about this turn of events, the more perplexed he was. He should be glad to finally be getting off the planet and be safely inside his space ship on Noth. That ship was going to leave in fifteen hours, whether either of them were on the ship. Why this sudden change in plans? She must have an ulterior motive for doing this. It didn't matter. He was now free to head up to Noth as soon as possible.

As soon as he thought this, he realized there was a problem. Commander Fulton had all the clearances that he would need for a departure to Noth. It was highly unlikely he could leave Ghia without those clearances and credentials.

Commander Fulton's temporary quarters were in the more expansive and luxurious apartments located ten floors above him. For him to leave Ghia, he had to go to her quarters and get these clearances directly from her. He couldn't think of any other method to achieve this.

Polti got in the lift and pressed the button for the fifty-third floor. He half expected the upper floors would have restricted access, but the elevator took him up with no issues. Her apartment was at the far end of a long hall. Judging by the hallway's length, he would likely pass other apartments. There were none that he could see. So, he surmised, this entire wing was her apartment.

As he neared the end of the hall, he picked up on the loud voices emanating from behind her door. There was one voice that was unmistakable. Polti instantly remembered a holo-conference he was required to attend in the first few months after he informed the Imperium of the large asteroid approaching Ghia. The purpose of the meeting was to determine how much effort and resources were required to build the spaceships. Tomachlus Furgus, a subordinate to Commander Fulton, possessed a unique inflection and a gravelly voice. He proposed prioritizing the construction of missiles to divert or obliterate the asteroid. The atmosphere grew tense when Juniv Koblatt, the science regent, insinuated that the idea was foolish and dismissed it as a mere waste of time.

Polti paused a couple of seconds to see if he could hear the discussion going on inside. He heard phrases like, "must leave tonight" and "Noth will get wiped out".

As soon as he heard this, he understood Commander Fulton's ulterior motive. Something had changed about the trajectory of the Big Pebble that he wasn't aware of. He pushed the button to announce himself to Commander Fulton's apartment. A small screen inset into the surface of the door, lit up and said, "Do Not Disturb". Polti pushed the button a second time to announce his presence to the Commander. The voices stopped, and the door abruptly opened and Tomachlus Fergus stood in front of him.

"I'm here to speak with Commander Fulton. It is of vital importance!"

"She's busy. What's this about?"

Before he could respond, Commander Fulton bellowed from behind Tomachlus to let him enter. Tomachlus fixed his gaze upon him, his eyes cold and piercing like steel. The intensity of his stare created an atmosphere devoid of any visible body language, much like a black hole that swallows everything, even light itself. Polti had an unnerving feeling that Tomachlus still had unfinished business with him. Polti didn't want to wait to find out whether or not this was true. He quickly entered the apartment.

Commander Fulton was clearly unsettled by her discussion with Tomachlus. He was expecting her to be furious with him for breaking protocol and coming to her unannounced. Strangely, she looked displaced and unsure of her surroundings. Polti could feel Tomachlus coming up behind him and Tomachlus quickly said, "Commander, the time to leave is now. We can't wait any longer. There won't be another opportunity for Ode to transfer people to the Altira cavern."

Startled, Commander Fulton shook her head slightly, like she was trying to wake up from a bad dream. She looked at Polti and said, "I thought I gave you an order to return to Noth with those engine parts."

"I can't leave Ghia without the correct clearances you have to get to Noth. What is he talking about? Time to leave to go where?" Polti paused for a second, not really expecting an answer. He continued and said, "The only place anyone can go to is to Noth. In twenty-four hours, this planet will be uninhabitable for anything living on it."

Tomachlus chuckled and said, "Precisely!"

Polti spun around quickly and spat, "You're a fool!"

Without any warning, Tomachlus' left arm came up quickly and with a quick jab, punched Polti in the face. Not really a "take down" or "knock out" punch, but it had the desired effect of surprising Polti and making him think twice before saying anything disrespectful.

Commander Fulton watched this happen, and it somehow broke her out of her unfocused state of mind.

She needed to act right now. Tomachlus is right. There is no time for these childish playground antics. She looked at Tomachlus and said, "Ok. Enough of that. How much time do we have and where do we need to be? I need time to tell everyone who is on Noth to leave ASAP. Anyone not in one of those eight spaceships needs to leave any way they can and go to Druna. If they make it there, they might survive. Polti, can those two ships still operate to make their way to Druna under half thrust?"

Polti scratched his head and said, "Yes."

"Commander, how much time do you need? It will take about an hour to travel to the transfer location in the Crestin mountains," Tomachlus said.

"I need about half an hour to contact any of the Continental Imperium that are still on Noth and Ghia to get them to mobilize everyone to get on those spaceships and leave immediately. I'll need to use the holo-conference hardware in the conference room on the top floor. This is the only way I can reach all the Ministers and Regents at once. Some of the other calls I can make on the way to Crestin."

Polti was watching this play out before him, but he still couldn't understand what either of them was talking about. Polti asked, "What is located in the Crestin mountains?"

Tomachlus looked at Commander Fulton and she nodded approval for him to explain further to Polti. "The Big Pebble isn't just one asteroid, it's actually two asteroids. Another asteroid of a similar size was hiding in the shadow of the first one, so it didn't show up on our telescopes. When we sent missiles up to the Big Pebble, they broke it into four smaller asteroids and deflected them sufficiently so they will not hit Ghia. However, those four large pieces are now on a direct course to impact with Noth."

"So, both Noth and Ghia are going to get hit by these asteroids?"

"Yes. Sadly, anyone on Noth has approximately twenty hours to evacuate from the moon and either blast off in the massive spaceships they have constructed which are space worthy and also any other vehicle that can get them away from Noth. They need to get as many people that they can fit into those ships and leave Noth, immediately."

"Those ships can only hold a maximum of around 70,000 people. Maybe they could increase that number to 90,000. They just don't have the food and supplies for everyone," Polti snapped at him. An uncomfortable pause occurred. Instinctively, Polti waited for the second punch in the face, but Tomachlus chose not to react. Polti felt on treacherous ground here and he would need to be more conscious of what Tomachlus could and would do if Polti became a hindrance to him.

"Currently, there are almost a billion people on Noth who have been drafted into service for the purpose of building these ships. Originally, we planned for at least twenty ships. There are currently only eight ships that are completely constructed, which can leave Noth. If those other two ships can make their way to Druna, then they should do that as soon as possible. At the very least, we need to tell everyone on Noth to get as many people as possible into any ship available and just not be near or on Noth in twenty hours. With every inch of every spaceship being occupied by the people on Noth, maybe 600,000 people will have a chance to live. The other 400,000 won't have a chance when the asteroid impacts with Noth."

Tomachlus continued, "The plan from the beginning was to get all the animals, plants, and humans who are on the surface of Ghia to move into six gigantic caverns which Ghia has built underneath the planet's crust. These caverns right now contain nearly two billion suspended animation capsules that will allow a person to be put into a state of cryogenic sleep for many years while Ghia heals itself. It will take many years to achieve this, but this is the plan Ode and others have been working on for the last nine months."

He stopped and looked directly at Polti and said, "Polti, you should already know the details of this plan since you were the first person Ode told outside of his family. He told you all about the asteroid coming toward Ghia. He told you this nine months ago, right?"

Polti felt his face burning, his slightly swollen cheek amplifying the sensation of dull pain as his blood rushed to his face. "No, Ode never told me the plan," he defended himself, his voice growing higher pitched. "He only mentioned that he 'thought' there might be an asteroid approaching Ghia. Pointing to the sky in any direction is easy. Anyone can do that. And, if you search long enough in that direction, you'll eventually find something. But I am an astrophysicist, unlike Ode," Polti practically screeched the last part.

"Ode? Is this the same Ode you specifically asked me to put into the underground bunker for three months? You lied to me. You mentioned Simol Athebyne, not Ode!" Commander Fulton scolded Polti.

Commander Fulton's disappointment was evident as she realized Polti had used her and the members of the Imperium to inflate his own importance.

She glared at him and hissed, "Polti, you're a fool! This Ode person is going to save everyone on this planet, and you wanted me to hide him in a bunker for three months. Tomachlus, feel free to punch Polti if he shows any disrespect again."

"Over the past six weeks, Ghia has been emitting precise waves of quantum energy at midnight every day. These energy waves have been sweeping across the planet during the night, teleporting large groups of people while they sleep and placing them into hibernation capsules. Remarkably, Ghia had relocated nearly ninety-five percent of the population into these underground caverns. You may have noticed a gradual decrease in the number of people in cities and towns in recent weeks.

"Why do we need to go to the Crestin mountains to get moved to these caverns? Won't Ghia just transport people at midnight?" Polti asked.

"One cavern had to be recreated. Ghia has been working with Ode and his family nonstop for the last two weeks to prepare a new cavern and get all the special pods in place. Ghia had to stop teleporting people temporarily while this new cavern was being created. We are trying to make up for lost time. They will start again in two hours to teleport people again. There are about a half dozen gathering areas around the planet where Ode's family will use the orange quantum stone to teleport people into that final cavern. This will happen every two hours for as long as possible, but time is running extremely short. We are going to go to a large central park in the town center of

Crestin. My nephew, Kotlid, will be at the location I'm taking you to."

Commander Fulton said bitterly, "Polti, whatever issues you have with Simol or Ode, you need to leave them behind. If you want to come with us, you can. If not, then I'll give you the clearances and wish you the best of luck. If you're going with us, you must follow the instructions they give you. If you resist at all, I won't stop Tomachlus next time he wants to hit you." She looked at Tomachlus with a sly grin.

Commander Fulton got up and went into the other room to make the calls to the Imperium. Polti went into the kitchen to get some ice for his eye socket that was getting swollen.

Tomachlus looked down at his timepiece and sat down on the couch.

Chapter 23

Impact

Four Hours Until Impact

OVER THE PAST MONTH, TIME seemed to fly by as Ode and his group of helpers pitched in to help create this new cavern in the southern portion of the Altira continent. They named this new cavern Altira Bravo to distinguish it from the other cavern on the Altira continent, which Ghia had created several months prior. The new cavern mirrored the shape of other caverns, forming a large torus located several thousand feet underneath the planet's surface. They organized all the cryogenic capsules inside the cavern, forming a complete circle around the torus, and they stacked additional rows vertically along the toroid shape. At the center of the torus, in the center of the donut shaped cavern, a sizable pool brimmed with a specially infused nutrient liquid called *viridian-soma.* Several hoses connected this pool to each row of stacked capsules, creating a closed loop system. The plan was that *viridian-soma* continuously circulated, keeping everyone in a state of suspended animation, allowing Ghia to work on healing the planet's surface.

Walkways were constructed all around the cavern to ensure easy access to each cryo chamber. These walkways, both on the ceiling and on the floor, featured long plant boxes filled with the bioluminescent lumensbloom. This plant species emitted a soft, comforting glow in an iridescent blue hue. To supply these plant boxes with nourishment, they rigged an additional hose from the central pool of viridian-soma located at the torus' core. The plant boxes were equipped with motion sensors that emitted a gentle blue glow when no movement was detected. However, as soon as the plant boxes detected motion, a stronger and brighter bioluminescent blue light illuminated the walkway. If no activity occurred for approximately twenty minutes, the glow would slowly fade back to its faint blue hue.

The message informing everyone left on the planet told people to assemble in specific locations around the planet. Felisa, Simol, Kotlid, and anyone else who was adept at using the orange quantum stone would then teleport these large groups of people into the Altira Beta cavern. Teleporting a large group of people was a challenging task, but they could accomplish it by maintaining a physical connection between individuals through hand-holding.

Once these large groups arrived, Ghia would then take over. The task of putting each person into an empty cryogenic capsule was a delicate operation. Ghia taught each of them how to accomplish this, but it was very time consuming and posed a lot of risks if done incorrectly. It was much more efficient for Ghia to perform this last task.

For the last two weeks, Ode, Lumi, and Helliod were assisting Ghia to create this gigantic cavern. Using their ability with the pink quantum stone to create laser beams to carve and smooth the walls of rough stone into indents within the wall for each of the cryo chambers. Ghia did the tough part by creating the cavern by teleporting large sections of the cavern out to the surface. The effort required for this was physically draining on all of them. They diligently worked at this almost nonstop. Ghia would sense the physical drain they were all experiencing and would force them to stop and rest.

Near the end of the two weeks, they had completed the new cavern. Then, they expanded all the cryogenic pods, stacking them vertically and horizontally around the circumference of the torus. The middle of the torus contained a pool filled with the bluish-green viridian-soma, all connected up to the rows of individual hibernation pods. Everything was complete.

Ode could connect with Kotlid, Felisa, and Simol using the blue stone. This was the only way to communicate with anyone else who was assisting in this effort and scattered around the planet, whether on the surface or inside one of the other caverns.

In his last communication, Ghia reported that approximately 1.2 billion people on the surface were safely inside their stasis pods. Ghia said this was approximately 1.2 billion people. The last people to go into the cryogenic capsules would be all the people who were helping Ode and his family and friends who have been helping to assist getting the remaining people on the surface into the cryo pods. Ghia would teleport all these people to the Altira Bravo cavern and place them in their own stasis pods.

One of the last groups to teleport into the assembly area was Tomachlus and about forty other people. Tomachlus said this was the last group of people on this continent. In this group were Polti and Commander Fulton.

Simol noticed an unusual member of the group that had just teleported in with Tomachlus. Ode also noticed the same thing, but Simol beat him to the punch by telepathically inquiring if Ode also saw this.

I thought Polti and Commander Fulton were safely tucked away in one of the spaceships ready to blast off from Noth. The chunks of asteroid the missile blew up were on a direct course with Noth.

Ode responded to Simol and also connected Tomachlus into the conversation thread.

Tomachlus, is that the last group from Crestin? How did Polti get involved in coming down here? I thought he was already in one of the spaceships and surely would have launched by now. The impact on Noth is imminent, from what Ghia has told me.

Tomachlus responded.

I was in the middle of a conversation with Commander Fulton when Polti burst into the room unexpectedly. I was just explaining to her the urgency of the situation - if she wanted to go to Noth, she could give it a try, but time was running out. The first asteroid was on schedule to hit Noth soon. I suggested she join us underground, considering her exceptional strategic skills would be incredibly valuable in our efforts to rebuild civilization once the planet is healed and the surface becomes habitable again. However, Polti rudely interrupted our meeting and demanded to know our plans. His behavior was disrespectful, so I had to take disciplinary action.

Tomachlus sent over a video image of him jabbing Polti in the nose when he called him a fool. Simol and Ode were laughing at the image Tomachlus sent to them.

Commander Fulton decided to join our cause and remain on Ghia. She approached Polti and presented two options: either he could attempt to escape to Noth and abandon Ghia, or he could choose to join us in our underground operations. At that moment, it felt like the right course of action. Commander Fulton cautioned Polti that he must adhere to strict discipline, warning him she would resort to force if necessary to ensure compliance. Knowing her formidable fighting skills, I wouldn't dare challenge her. Polti agreed to these terms, and now we eagerly await Ghia's teleportation of our final group into the cryogenic pods.

Ode reached out to Felisa and Kotlid, added them into this telepathic party line.

Felisa and Kotlid are now joining us in this group chat. Felisa, can you give us an update on the status of what is happening in the other caverns? The last group of about forty people from the Crestin location have just arrived. We are waiting for Ghia to transport them into their individual capsules. Once that happens, it will be our turn next to go into our own cryo pods.

Felisa said.

As far as I know, Melliod, Dulvod, and the rest of our team will arrive soon. Ghia briefly sent me a query to see if I was ready to go to the Altira Bravo cavern where you're located. Ghia said it would be teleporting me and the rest of the team soon. I think the Big Pebble 2 is almost here, so I hope we have completed everything necessary for us to survive this onslaught.

Ghia mentally spoke to everyone connected to this current conversation.

Prepare to receive the last group of people to be teleported to the cavern named Altira Bravo. This is the final group of any remaining humans on the surface. Additionally, this will also include all those who have been assisting in this gargantuan task. Your help has made a difference.

As expected, the four sizable fragments of asteroids have now collided with Noth.

The impact predominantly occurred in the southern regions of the moon. Most residents on Noth currently live in the central areas, which are experiencing nighttime. Hopefully, these regions get spared a direct impact. The fragments have caused extensive displacement of the moon's surface, throwing it into the atmosphere. Consequently, the fragments will soon obscure the entire surface of Noth. Additionally, there have been multiple secondary explosions in the settlements, where numerous warehouses and factories are situated. It is suspected that anyone in those areas wouldn't be able to survive the massive devastation.

Before the debris got thrown into the atmosphere and obscured everything, there was evidence that many ships left Noth.

The orbit of Noth appears to remain stable and the force of the asteroid

impact will not change its normal orbital path.

The asteroid you call Big Pebble 2 is very close to impacting the surface of the planet. Teleporting the last group to this cavern now.

Simol and Ode looked over at the platform. Ghia was teleporting all the people who were helping us from all over the planet. Slowly, over the next few minutes, groups of people started to show up in the cavern. Ghia stationed each group in one of the other caverns or at a common location where **IT** teleported the rest of the population into their stasis pods.

The last group of about ten people teleported into the cavern. Among this group were Tomachlus, Polti and Senior Commander Fulton. This was the last of the population on the planet.

Currently, there are about forty people scattered around the main section of the cavern. Ode expected Ghia would be teleporting this last remaining group into the stasis pods soon now.

While the extraordinary ability to teleport individuals from one location to another was gradually becoming more common to witness, it was still a remarkable occurrence. As this group of people waiting for Ghia to transport them into their capsules, nothing happened. They waited there for five minutes, and still, nothing happened. Ode and Felisa exchanged questioning looks, unsure of what was causing the delay. Ghia was usually quick with this process.

As five minutes turned into ten minutes, Ode tried to reach out to Ghia.

Ode! Sorry. Not. Able. To finish.

Ghia? Ghia? Are you OK?

Above everyone in the cavern, they heard a deep, low frequency grumbling sound reverberating around the cavern. The floor of the cavern trembled, and the sounds of tremendous explosions boomed overhead. It was deafening and debilitating. Ode reached out again plaintively in his mind to Ghia. Fear gripped him tightly with the deafening silence.

The torus shape of the cavern was the perfect echo chamber for each staccato burst of booming and explosions from the surface. The noise from every explosion would circle around the cavern many times before it would slowly decrease in volume. The deafening roar reverberating through the cavern, accompanied by the trembling ground beneath their feet, transported Ode back to his vivid memories of standing atop the majestic Angbok mountain.

Over time, the staccato sounds of devastation gradually diminished on the surface. Despite the difficulty of ignoring these sounds, everyone gathered closely to provide comfort to one another. It didn't require verbalization; the knowledge that their previous lives on the planet's surface had been completely wiped away was evident in everyone's eyes. All they had left was each other, their sole source of support during this trying period.

The Big Pebble 2 has finally arrived and was delivering its promised devastation and damage to the surface of Ghia.

Chapter 24
Silence

Aftermath

SLOWLY, THE REVERBERATING SOUNDS echoing around the cavern slowed and finally stopped. Ode looked at his family and friends. A paralyzing fear gripped him. His mind raced. Images of destruction and impending doom paralyzed him. Everyone in the crowded the cavern fixed their gaze on Ode, searching for some clue of what to do next. What happened to Ghia? What if the damage to the planet was too much? Question after question kept him paralyzed while his brain was still processing what had just happened.

Tomachlus looked at Ode and saw the fear clouding the expression on his face. From his training, Tomachlus knew instantly when someone was battling fear or confusion. In those instances, a decision had to be made before order disappears and chaos takes over. Tomachlus could clearly see something was wrong with Ghia. He reasoned Ghia was dealing with *Big Pebble 2* landing on the surface right now and **IT** wouldn't be available. Whether it was instinct or training, he got everyone in the center of the cavern where the enormous pool of viridian-soma was located.

"Everyone! Can I have your attention?" Tomachlus said, using his firm and commanding Defense Regency voice. It was short, direct, and it wasn't to be questioned. "Everyone, move to the center of the cavern now." He glanced at the different groups scattered around the cavern. "Everyone, listen up! Please move into the center with everyone else."

Once everyone moved into the center, he said, "I'm not sure what is happening right now, but I trust Ghia will let us know when **IT** can start teleporting again. You all heard the loud explosions. The *Big Pebble 2* has arrived, and this cavern is still intact. I suspect Ghia is awfully busy right now, contending with the damage happening on the surface. We are hundreds of miles below the surface of the planet, and we are still safe. This is probably just a temporary delay."

Ode was grateful for Tomachlus jumping in and giving everyone some direction. Ode was extremely worried about Ghia right now. Ghia had said, "*Not able to finish*". What did this mean? Will Ghia still be able to teleport the last forty people into the cryogenic capsules?

Or did it mean *Big Pebble 2* had destroyed the planet beyond fixing?

Ode walked over to Tomachlus. He caught his gaze and gave him a curt smile to signify his gratitude for taking control of the situation when Ode hesitated.

Raising his voice, Ode addressed everyone in the cavern. "I know this isn't exactly what we were expecting. As you can all hear, the explosion and noises from the surface are much less right now. We're safe here. I know Ghia will let us know when **IT** can put us all in the cryogenic pods. I suspect this is only temporary. We have food and water here in the cavern to last for a while."

Ode looked at Dulvod and his wife, Cherulina, "Could both of you help to bring out some of the food and drinks which are stored in the outer ring into the cavern?"

Commander Fulton looked at Dulvod saying, "Let me help you with that. I can probably mix something together for all of us to eat."

Tomachlus smirked and said, "MRE Chili?"

The MRE's that Tomachlus was referring were the acronym for *Meal–Ready to Eat*. She looked dead-pan at Tomachlus and replied, "Of course. I have told you many times that this is the perfect food. It has everything you need to function properly. MRE Chili has gotten me through some pretty tight spaces over the years."

"Ok, but I want it mild heat. The last time you gave me your spicy version, it wrecked me for days."

Commander Fulton and Cherulina got up and followed Dulvod to the outer ring of the cavern where the food was being stored.

Felisa and Simol came over towards Ode to discuss what was happening. Ode could tell by the questioning look that they had not heard the last thing Ghia had told him before it went silent.

They walked over to a private spot that was private enough so no one would hear their whispered voices. Ode relayed what he heard Ghia say to him. Ode said, "Simol, I heard about four explosions. The first two were the loudest, and they occurred closely together. The other two happened probably about thirty seconds after the first two. Would you agree this sounds like *Big Pebble 2* broke into approximately four large meteorites? The first two were deafening, but I would guess they hit this continent and the other two most likely impacted west of this cavern. I hope it impacts with the ocean, but if they don't, then they could hit the Irsun continent."

Noticing the puzzled expression on Felisa's face, Ode took it upon himself to clarify the situation. "The Big Pebble 2, although initially classified as an asteroid, becomes a meteorite once it enters Ghia's atmosphere and collides with the planet," he explained.

Felisa smiled at her husband, signaling for him to continue his conversation with Simol. Ode turned his attention to Simol and inquired, "What are your thoughts on the fate of Big Pebble 2?"

Simol nodded in agreement. "Yes, I agree with your assessment that the meteorites impacted Altira, although probably to the west of where this cavern is situated. It's difficult to speculate on the exact locations where the other two meteorites landed on Ghia, but I share your belief that they most likely struck somewhere between Altira and Irsun. If one of them hit the ocean, it could have vaporized a significant amount of water, which would then enter the atmosphere. While a portion of that water vapor would likely turn into rainfall, some of it might linger as a greenhouse gas. Ghia had expected this, which is why we had to rebuild this cavern. My guess is that the other two meteorites landed remarkably close to the Irsun continent."

"I hope those last two meteorites didn't impact on Irsun. If they did," Ode said while his face grimaced with pain, "an impact on any part of Irsun would be devastating to Ghia. The tectonic plate is extremely brittle from all the years of testing that H4A has done to it. Ghia mentioned to me when I was in the Angbok area that planets can sometimes go into a hibernation like state. It rarely happens, but it can happen when a planet is under extreme stress."

Felisa, who had said nothing yet, asked, "Did Ghia say how long this might be? We have supplies here for at least three to four weeks, but the only way for us to survive longer than that is to put ourselves into the cryogenic pods."

Ode interjected, "To be honest, I don't feel comfortable doing that myself without Ghia being present. If I made a mistake, then it could cost someone's life. I think we should wait a little while to see if Ghia comes back to us."

"Yes, I think you're right. Hopefully, this will just be a temporary delay," Felisa said.

Chapter 25
Redemption

Three months later

ODE STOOD BEFORE THE WALL of shelves, his eyes drawn to the vibrant tapestry of many colors. The various plants, bathed in the soft glow of the artificial amber light emanating from the bottom of each shelf. Each leaf was a miniature solar panel, absorbing the photons that cascaded from the pink stone's quantum weave. The green stone, a silent partner in this botanical symphony, accelerated the plants' growth, as if it were a conductor urging the molecules to dance faster.

The air was thick with the scent of chlorophyll, a fresh soil-like aroma filled Ode's senses. He could almost hear the tiny symphony of growth, a rhythmic dance of molecules absorbing photons and converting them into life. The plants seemed to sway gently, as if responding to an invisible melody.

Ode reached out and touched a leaf, feeling its soft, velvety texture. Underneath, he could sense the vibrant energy coursing through the plant, a testament to the power of his creation. The sight of these thriving plants filled him with a sense of wonder and accomplishment. Ode knew he was witnessing something unique. He had harnessed the power of the quantum realm to create a living, breathing ecosystem, a testament to human ingenuity.

Ode experienced a deep feeling of belonging, as though he had discovered his spiritual home among the lush and vibrant surroundings. Finding himself surrounded by a tranquil sanctuary, Ode realized the plants provided a comforting and calming effect for his soul.

Every day, Ode used the blue stone to reach out to Ghia. He also tried to amplify his call by adding the white stone into the mix. It was very unsettling when he didn't receive a reply. His last conversation with Ghia left Ode with an overwhelming feeling of concern for Ghia's wellbeing. It was strange, though. **IT** was the planet. Without the planet, Ode, and the rest of the life on Ghia would perish. However, waiting for Ghia to initiate contact with him, or anyone else, was not a productive approach. They needed to survive and his wall garden was just one way that he was trying to accomplish this.

In the past few months, Ode and his family had been teaching everyone else how to use the quantum stones. Each person had a unique ability associated with these stones. Ode, for instance, used the green stone alongside the pink stone to expedite the growth of plants and vegetables they relied on for sustenance. By harnessing the power of the pink stone, Ode could simulate the orange light emitted by Tol. Then, Ode enhanced the photosynthesis process, significantly reducing the time it took for the plants to grow from days to mere hours.

Ode took a step back to admire the array of greens, blues, and oranges on his wall. As he immersed himself in his creation, he suddenly felt Felisa's presence nearby. It wasn't a result of any audible noise or sound that she made; rather, it was an unspoken connection that he could sense internally. This ability to perceive when his wife or children were in close proximity or even at a distance was a newfound talent that had emerged with his use of the blue quantum stone.

The first time Ghia introduced the blue stone to Ode, it was for communicating with him in his mind. It was necessary for Ode to hold the smooth blue quantum stone. Once he held the blue stone, it allowed Ghia to connect to him telepathically. In some strange way, Ghia could tune in on the person who held the blue stone. This allowed Ghia to target communication directly. This was sort of how he sensed Felisa coming down the constantly curving hallway, filled with individual cryogenic pods.

The ability to sense the relative location of someone familiar to you, happened almost by accident. They found that as people became familiar with the blue stone, it had the unusual ability to let people perceive a sense of relative proximity of others who were around them. As more people used the stone, this ability to sense the proximity of someone near to them, allowed them to detect the unique signature of that person. This is how Ode knew it was Felisa coming toward him. He was familiar with her unique signature.

Others in the group started to attain many unique skills. Senior Commander Fulton had a remarkable skill at manipulating matter with the crimson-colored stone. She possessed an unusual mastery over it. Her abilities went beyond simply shaping objects; she had the uncanny talent to alter the composition of matter itself.

Within the first week, she astounded everyone by extracting fibrous material from pockets of limestone on the cavern's walls. She took the limestone material and also any reusable or transmutable matter from the storage containers which held their stock of food. She took all this material and converted it into warm and comfortable beds and blankets for people to sleep on. By reshaping certain rocks, she even fashioned pots and pans for cooking. It became clear that she could convert any material within the cavern into almost anything imaginable.

She had the incredible knack for transforming any of the scattered objects in the cavern into something useful. Even with little bits of dust or taking particles of water from the air, she could transform into useful kinds of matter. While Tomachlus also had the ability to manipulate matter, Senior Commander Fulton's proficiency with the crimson stone was unparalleled.

Senior Commander Fulton decided to drop her title and preferred to be called Alginna or Ginny. Her move signaled a major change in her personality. With the burden of managing large teams lifted, she became more laid-back, friendly, and enjoyable to be around. Most people had no problem with her new role except for Tomachlus, who occasionally slipped up and called her by her old title. However, with time, he improved and adjusted to the change. They often heard her laughter echoing around the cavern at night.

Erig, Simol, Ode, and his family assumed the responsibility of instructing the rest of the group on the usage of the quantum stones. Many individuals in the cavern were unaware of these stones, so it served as a welcome diversion. To their surprise, nearly everyone displayed a certain level of expertise in one or more of the quantum stones.

Alginna stood out as the most skilled among them, demonstrating mastery over approximately ten quantum stones. Ode's expertise lay in utilizing the pink stone to produce an orange light, vital for nurturing the plants and illuminating the entire cavern. Initially, the cavern remained brightly lit at all times, but they soon recognized the importance of establishing a day-night cycle. Felisa possessed a remarkable talent for healing with the red quantum stone, while Erig and Melliod had the unique ability to make heavy objects feel as light as a feather. They eventually discovered they could use the quantum stone to become light enough to soar through the air, resulting in entertaining chases within the cavern. Surprisingly, Polti could teleport inanimate objects from one place to another, strengthening the bonds within the group. This realization led everyone to understand that their combined efforts were essential for any future endeavors.

Today, Ode and his children, Helliod, Melliod, and Kelvi, were helping him to secure additional water tubes to a new row of plants they were adding to Ode's green wall. Ode and Melliod secured tubes to lower wall plants, while Kelvi and Helliod did the same with ladders for upper wall plants.

The ladders were precarious at best, even on a flat even floor. However, because of the toroid circular shape of the passageway, it wasn't flat. The higher Kelvi rose on the stepladder, the more unsteady the ladder became. In the beginning, Kelvi appeared to be able to hold his balance. The stepladder began to wobble slightly, and when he tried to stabilize it, the entire stepladder toppled over. If someone were to fall from that height, they would normally only sustain minor injuries.

However, Kelvi's body landed awkwardly, coming into contact with one of the legs of the stepladder. His body hit the ground with a sickening thud. Kelvi remained motionless on his back. Witnessing Kelvi's fall, Helliod let out a shriek.

Felisa also saw Kelvi lying on the ground and ran to his side. As she ran to her son, she yelled to Ode, "Get Simol! Tell him to bring the quantum stones." She then kneeled down, pulled the red quantum stone from her pocket, and placed it in her right hand. Next, Felisa placed her hands on Kelvi's chest, synchronizing her thoughts and breathing to gather and amplify the life force within her. This energy would be crucial for merging and replacing Kelvi's weakened life force. Felisa could sense that his vitality and energy levels had significantly diminished.

Her son's serious injury was evident, prompting Felisa to rely on the medical training she had acquired long ago. The fundamental principles of emergency first aid, known as the ABCs, came to the forefront of her mind: Airways, Bleeding, and Compress. His breathing was irregular and strained, characterized by short, shallow breaths. Every few breaths, he struggled to take in air, gasping for it unsuccessfully. Initially, there was no visible bleeding. Felisa attempted to turn him over, but ceased when his breathing became labored and wheezy. He involuntarily groaned and cried out in pain. Pressing on his abdomen elicited agonizing screams. Witnessing Kelvi in such agony broke her heart, yet she set aside her tears and emotions to maintain her focus.

Simol and Polti instantly appeared next to Felisa. Both held the orange suede bag of quantum stones. Without hesitation, Simol reached into the bag and drew out the red quantum stone and placed it in his left hand. Polti strangely pulled out the white, brown and crimson colored stones. Confused, both Simol and Felisa looked at Polti.

Felisa couldn't waste time explaining to Polti right now. She said to Simol, "His rib appears to have lacerated his liver. I think his rib has cracked, and large splinters of the rib have fractured from his ribcage. See if you can repair it while I focus on the liver."

"Ok, I'll do my best," Simol replied.

Then, Polti pulled a stone goblet out of the bag of stones he was carrying. He looked at Felisa and said calmly, "Kelvod's rib will never get correctly put back into place. It will always impede him. Simol needs to break off the rib at the base of the rib cage and then grow a new rib in its place. I'll remove it from his body with the brown stone. Then I'll use the crimson stone to turn elements of the rib into a form of liquid calcium and nutrients needed to grow his rib again. The white stone will amplify your efforts to heal Kelvod."

What Polti was asking Kelvi to go through horrified Felisa. She firmly said, "No! It's possible to mend the rib in place. No! This is the only way to heal him. I have had patients before who have had broken ribs. This is the way it is always done." She looked up at Ode, who was standing behind Polti. She could see the pain on his face.

Ode just wanted his son to not be in tortuous pain. He said, "I agree. Felisa should fix the rib the normal way."

Simol appeared to be only partially attentive, but eventually responded, "I apologize, Felisa, but I believe Polti is correct. My father had broken a rib a while back. The site of the injury always troubled him, resulting in a persistent dull ache in his chest at that exact spot. Even now, it continues to bother him. My father shared that his breathing and energy levels were never the same after that rib injury."

Polti said, "Please, Felisa repair the liver. I'll take on any pain Kelvod is feeling, and I'll give you whatever life force energy you need for this. Please, let me help you."

Felisa hesitated for a second and knew it was going to take almost every ounce of energy she had inside her to repair the lacerated liver. She quickly nodded and closed her eyes, gathering her strength.

Polti handed the white stone to Felisa while Simol removed the white stone from his collection. As a result, both Felisa and Simol now held a white and a red stone each. Meanwhile, Polti held the brown and crimson stones in his hands. In silence, they all attempted to harmonize their abilities, combining the red life healing powers with the brown and crimson powers, preparing them for use. These power pools radiated even more intensely than usual, thanks to the amplification provided by the white quantum stone.

Kelvi wasn't bleeding anywhere visible, but internally blood was pumping furiously into arteries which couldn't contain the limited amount of blood that his heart was pumping with each beat. Similar to a tire with a puncture, air was continuously escaping through the hole with no way to stop it. Internal bleeding is similar. When organs inside the body get damaged, blood leaks out into surrounding tissues and cavities, just like the air leaking out of the tire. The body doesn't have a way to contain or quickly seal off this bleeding, leading to a loss of blood volume and pressure, much like the tire gradually deflating.

The liver is a vital organ for the body. It receives a lion's share of the blood pumping out of the heart through a large portal vein affixed to the top of the liver. The broken rib lacerated the liver just below the point where the portal vein connected with the liver. Blood hemorrhaged and was seeping out of the liver in a steady flow.

Taking a deep breath, Felisa concentrated all her energy and vitality to give to her son. She placed her hands on his right side and could feel a strange tingling down her arms and hands and into Kelvi. Felisa watched as her hands glowed with a white radiance at the place where her hands touched Kelvi's flank. Felisa used her energy and the power of the red stone to stitch and seal the areas that were hemorrhaging. She slowed his heart to lessen the furious roar of blood pumping through his body. Now, her hands were glowing a bright white.

Simol's hands were on Kelvi's chest. Simol sensed that Kelvi's rib was still attached to his ribcage. Small bits of bone and rib fragments held it in place. He felt the power of the red stone and forced the rib to separate completely from his ribcage. Simol poured as much of his life force energy as he could into Kelvi. Silently praying this would ease the pain he had just caused. Simol looked at Felisa and saw her eyes were closed, concentrating. He then looked at Polti and nodded to him, giving him the signal to use the brown stone.

Polti took the cue from Simol, and he started to gather his focus on the rib inside Kelvi's body. Felisa and others who had a mastery of the red stone taught him how he could sense and feel the exact shape of organs and parts of the body. He felt the exact place where the broken rib was in Kelvi's body. He focused all his energy on the brown stone to force the rib into the stone goblet,

Next, Polti's senses heightened as he felt every atom in the rib, a symphony of pulsating energy. The sight of the bone, calcified and rigid, urged him on. He willed them to move faster and faster, their movement creating a mesmerizing dance in his mind's eye. The sound of their vibration resonated like a chorus of whispers in his ears.

As the momentum built, the air filled with a faint metallic scent, a hint of the minerals that composed the bone. Polti's hands trembled slightly, a mix of anticipation and concentration, as he transformed the rigid bone into a fluid slurry. The sight of the liquid, a swirling concoction of red bone marrow, collagen, and osteoblast cells, was both fascinating and surreal.

With a gentle precision, Polti carefully placed the mixture back into Kelvi's body, at the exact spot where

Simol had surgically broken it off from his ribcage. He glanced at Simol, a silent acknowledgment passing between them, indicating that he had successfully transported the liquified bone material and essential minerals back into Kelvi's body.

Simol took his cue to grow a new rib for Kelvi. The ribcage is strong and rigid. The rib bones in the ribcage form the vital scaffolding needed to hold all the sensitive organs in place. This rigidity is essential for protecting those organs. Every breath or use of any muscles around the diaphragm push or puts pressure on the ribcage. Simol focused on using the red stone to spur the growth of the bone.

It was slow going at first, but Felisa was making progress repairing the wound in Kelvi's liver. The blood flowing to the other organs of the body increased. The rib growing out of the ribcage started to take shape. The rib continued to grow and extend out from the base of the ribcage.

Everyone enjoyed Kelvi's company. Over the past three months, the sight of this dimly lit cave had become wearisome for everyone, their eyes straining to adjust to the artificial light. But Kelvi and his sister brought a much-needed spark of joy to the group. Their laughter echoed through the cavern, filling the air with a vibrant energy, as they played their nightly games. The sound of objects whizzing through the air and colliding with the cave walls created a symphony of playful chaos. As the objects flew past, the cool breeze they generated brushed against their skin, eliciting a tingling sensation that momentarily distracted them from the monotony of their situation.

Polti could sense the pain that the surgery was causing this young man. He empathetically reached out to ease it. He tapped into a technique he used during moments of intense stress, drawing from a childhood memory. In his mind, he envisioned himself lying in a field of tall grass, feeling the warm rays of the afternoon warmth of light from Tol on his face. This serene place served as his personal sanctuary whenever he sought refuge from the world.

Over the last three months, everyone has used the blue quantum stone to communicate with people telepathically. He had spoken to Kelvod telepathically in the past, so it wasn't difficult to convey his memory of peacefulness and joy.

When Polti sent his message to Kelvod, both Simol and Felisa also received it, since they were still connected to Kelvi. As a result, Kelvi's breathing became less labored and tense, and he appeared to relax as color returned to his face.

After about ten minutes, Felisa felt that they had done all they could for now. She successfully repaired the lacerated liver while Simol safely regrew a new rib, seamlessly connected to his ribcage. Now Kelvi needed rest and time to recover.

Felisa smiled at Ode, who had stood by anxiously. The only solace he could find was his undying trust in Felisa. He had not been part of the connection that Felisa, Simol, and Polti shared during the healing process.

Ode sensed a change in Felisa. The physical relaxation of the tension and worry went out of her slightly perspiring face. Both Felisa and Simol's white radiance from their hands dimmed and disappeared. It was over. Ode patiently waited for Felisa to say something.

"Kelvi needs some time and rest to fully recover, but the danger is gone, and we were successful."

Ode knew she would give him further details later. Now wasn't the time. He let out a tremendous sigh of relief.

Felisa reached out, placing her hand over Polti's, and said, "I apologize. You were right about regrowing the new rib. It worked better than I have ever seen for someone with a broken bone. Thank you. I am truly grateful for what you have done. The memory you sent to

Kelvi was beautiful, and I know it greatly helped to alleviate his pain and stress."

Polti smiled and sheepishly said, "I'm happy to have helped. But …"

Simol and Ode anticipated him to elaborate, but at that moment, it appeared he was grappling to speak. Despite the difficulty, Polti addressed the three of them, expressing, "I sincerely hope you can find it in your hearts to forgive me. I put you into an underground bunker for three months, while I focused on escaping from the Big Pebble. If I had stayed on Noth, I would be dead right now. We have all been down in this cavern for three months, while Ghia is getting bombarded by meteorites. This is identical to the situation I put you into after you spoke with Ghia. Even though our future is still unknown, I'm still alive. That is very humbling. I can now see the pain I caused to both of you and your families. At that moment, my ego clouded my judgment. Instead, I should have been assisting all of you, including Ghia. I genuinely apologize for any distress I may have caused."

Felisa, Ode, and Simol were all taken aback. Simol spoke up, expressing his feelings, "Polti, I have to say, hearing you say that fills me with immense pride. I forgave you instantly, without any hesitation. Remember when I mentioned how ego and an incessant need for competition can hinder one's growth and hold them back from reaching their true potential? That was the lesson, of course, and I forgave you for it."

It was truly remarkable how, despite the difficulty of asking for forgiveness, Polti managed to do so. This transformative act turned him into a changed man. From that point forward, he dedicated himself to furthering his knowledge of the quantum stones and even began training others in their use.

Chapter 26
Old Friend

Later that night…

KELVI'S INCIDENT EARLIER THAT DAY left both Ode and Felisa spinning emotionally. They felt overwhelmed with profound gratefulness for the positive outcome. On the other hand, it also left them with the stark realization of how stranded they were right now. The only person with any medical training was Felisa. This left her with the tremendous responsibility of taking care of forty people. They just don't have any medical resources except the paltry first aid bag they had left in the cave for cuts or scratches or burns.

They spoke softly before going to bed. Ode looked at Felisa with the unwavering love he had always felt for his partner and wife. Then Ode said, "When I saw you today taking charge of the situation with Kelvi, I honestly don't know how I would have reacted if you hadn't been right there by his side."

"I felt the same way about you being there. It gave me more confidence in my ability to mend his liver injury using the red stone."

"Polti's skill in using the brown and crimson stones was truly impressive. I would have never thought of doing what he was able to accomplish."

"I believe it took a lot of courage for him to apologize to you and Simol, didn't it?"

"Indeed, it was unexpected, but receiving an apology from Polti was genuinely pleasant."

Felisa nodded and said, "It really showed his growth in character and confidence."

"Taking responsibility for one's actions and choices is truly rewarding."

Felisa concluded, "It's remarkable how being trapped in a cave, hundreds of miles below the surface, brought about the only scenario that could have led to this transformation for him."

Soon after, they both fell into a deep contented sleep. From deep within Ode's consciousness, a voice was telling him to get out of bed and go to the center of the cavern. He wasn't sure of who the voice belonged to, but it felt like he needed to follow it.

He quietly got out of bed, careful not to wake Felisa. He was almost certain he had heard a voice telling him to go to where the *viridian soma* was located. As he walked over there, he started to wonder if this was really a voice he heard, or could this be a dream? It didn't matter; he was almost there. There was a long table which Alginna had created for people to eat meals at to hold group discussions of the various tasks they worked on.

He took a seat and waited for the voice to talk to him. He decided to give it five minutes and if he heard nothing else, then, it must have been a strange dream. He heard footsteps approaching the table. He turned and saw Simol, Tomachlus, Felisa, Alginna, and Kotlid, all coming out from the sleeping areas. After another few seconds, more people came out from the area where most people slept. In a short amount of time, everyone came out to this common area.

A few people took a seat at the table, while most just stood around the center of the cavern, wondering why they were called out of bed. No one said anything. Finally, after a couple of seconds, Ode heard the feeble voice again in his mind.

Ode! It is so pleasing to see you again.

Ghia! I'm so glad to hear your voice again. I'm so happy you're Ok.

The asteroid you called Big Pebble 2 did horrific damage on the surface and caused devastating wounds to the surface. The air and water aren't safe for your species, but will be at some point it will. In time, the surface will be a magical garden for all of you.

How did you protect yourself? We all heard the sounds of the meteorites hitting the surface.

It was very challenging. It was necessary to retreat into the deep core of the planet to gather some strength. It was very difficult at first and the energy levels were terribly low. There wasn't enough energy to teleport everyone safely into the stasis chambers. Recovery was slow, however, there was a spark of energy which became available to me. The artificial light you're using to help to grow your plants also sends energy to me. Your energy of photosynthesis manipulation helped to restore enough of the energy to come back today.

Wow! That is great!

It was strange, Ode. I felt and rejoiced in the warm orange photons you were using

in the process of growing your food quickly. I have been unable to receive Tol's blessed light for months now. The sky is so full of ash and vast amounts of debris which were immediately ejected high into the sky. It won't allow Tol's light to reach me. But you fed the plants so much light, it really helped to give a boost to my strength so I can finally put everyone in this cavern into the stasis pods.

Ghia, I'm so glad. That light also saved us from starving. The energy transfer happening at the quantum photosynthesis level just continues to keep giving us gifts. If my miniature photonic sources are helpful to you, I'm sure … – wait, is everyone else hearing what I'm saying?

No, it is just you.

Ok, let me tell the others what is going on. We need to discuss these light experiments at some point, but everyone right now feels directionless, so let me introduce you, Ok?

Sure

"Hey, everyone! I suspect all of you came out here because something was calling and urging you to get out of bed and come to the center of the cavern. The voice which you heard was Ghia. I have been talking to him privately for the last few seconds. Sorry, I forgot my manners, but you can understand how happy I'm to have Ghia back with us. All of you have experienced using the blue quantum stone. This is how Ghia will talk to you now."

Hello, my children! I'm so happy to talk to you all. I'm very sorry you had to wait until now to go into the stasis pod. The *Big Pebble 2* broke into five large meteorites. Two of those pieces hit the planet on the western side of this continent. Two large chunks impacted on the western ocean in an unusually deep part of the ocean. The final one impacted at the northern pole. This last one hurt the most, but it is getting better with each revolution around Tol. Now, I know you're tired and are anxious about what will happen next. Well, now it is time for you to rest. It is also time for me to heal. Once everyone is ready, and has said goodnight to their friends and loved ones, I'll place you all into your stasis pods for a long sleep. You will be comfortable and fully rested when

you wake up. I'll be monitoring all the stasis pods around the planet. Just tell me when you're ready to go.

Everyone slowly disappeared into groups of friends and family. Soon it was just Felisa, Ode, all their children, Tomachlus, Erig, Alginna, Polti, and Simol, left sitting at the table.

Ode was sitting next to Felisa and he could feel a wave of incredible relief just wash over her entire body. This reminded Ode of a time they were at the beach, and she was standing in the ocean about waist deep. Behind her, the growing crescendo of a wave swiftly coming toward her. In that moment of the wave washing over her head, he could visibly see the feeling of satisfaction of experiencing just a taste of the enormous power of the ocean.

I just wanted to say how proud I am of my strongest children. You have been a tremendous help to get us to this point. I'll now put you into your pods and just know that your planet loves you very much.

Felisa and Ode both disappeared and teleported into their individual stasis pods.

After Ghia placed the last person into stasis, Ghia examined each of its two moons, Noth and Druna. Noth's surface lay in ruins, with nothing left untouched on the moon. It will take a long time before this moon holds life on it again. Many ships were able to depart from Noth and head toward Druna. Only about thirty small and midsize spaceships were able to takeoff, but only twenty-five actually made it. The ships were so hastily packed and checked for space worthiness, it was a miracle that twenty-five successfully reached Druna and landed safely. However, they brought only enough food to last a couple of months.

The poorly nourished people on Druna would only survive about another week at most. Ghia reached out to all the people on Druna. Ghia explained to them they could return to Ghia and **IT** would place them into stasis pods so they could wake up once the planet was livable again. Thankfully everyone said yes.

There were only about three thousand people on Druna. Ghia put all of them safely into the cryogenic pods in the same cavern as Ode and the rest of the people.

It was finally done! Everyone was safely hibernating underground. Ghia was still weak, but with everyone now safe, **IT** was content. Now it was time for Ghia to heal.

Chapter 27
Quantum Guild

1,750 years later …

IN THE INITIAL ASSAULT OF meteorites on Ghia's vulnerable surface, a deafening roar accompanied the sight of fiery streaks across the night sky; it was as if the heavens themselves were cracking open. The impact sent tremors through the ground, reverberating in every corner of Ghia. Like an electrical shock wave surging through every atom, the blow was causing a jolt of pain that pierced deep into the core of Ghia's being. It was more painful than Ghia was expecting. However, Ghia was aware enough that it still needed to complete one more task before it could recuperate from the meteorite's onslaught of its vulnerable surface.

It took every ounce of energy the planet could gather to be able to stay aware enough so as not to drift off into a comatose state. Therefore, it took a few months for it to regain enough strength to complete **ITS** mission; a mission Ghia felt was new and unique to the universe.

Fortunately, Ghia was relieved to find out that the humans had survived in that short interim while Ghia was gathering more strength. Once they were all safely ensconced into their cryostasis pods, including the stragglers Ghia found on Druna, it was finally time for Ghia to rest and heal the damage caused by the asteroids.

Ghia, overwhelmed by pain and discomfort caused by the meteorites, withdrew into **ITSELF**. The sentient part of Ghia sensed the need to separate from the agonizing sensations and parts of **ITSELF,** which were incredibly raw and painful. Ghia curled up tightly around the warm, protective core of the planet. The core emitted a comforting heat, providing solace amidst the chaos. Ghia couldn't explain the compulsion to retreat into the core, but it obeyed. Now Ghia could detach **ITSELF** from the excruciating impact zones that had carved deep wounds into the planet's crust. The planet remained aware of the undisturbed caverns, still able to sense them. The intense heat emanating from the core enveloped Ghia, numbing its senses, and slowing its movements. Ghia now slipped into a deep, almost coma-like state for the next seventeen hundred and fifty years.

The initial impacts of the meteorites on Ghia was a sight of complete devastation. The once serene oceans were now in chaos, with millions of gallons of sea water vaporized by the sheer force of the meteorites. The air had the acrid smell of burnt saltwater, as the steam rose high into the atmosphere, creating a dense fog that obscured the horizon.

The impact of the meteorites caused a deafening sound, echoing for miles around. The explosions created enormous mushroom clouds, billowing up into the sky. These massive clouds carried with them ultra hot, micro-sized particles of dirt and rock, creating a swirling tempest of fire and debris.

Over time, the atmosphere became heavy and oppressive, as the water particles, being lighter, rose to higher altitudes than the dust and rock. As they cooled, they descended slowly, mixing with the dirt to form a thick and dense haze that enveloped the entire planet. The air felt suffocating, making it difficult to breathe, and the absence of any light from Tol only added to the eerie atmosphere.

The fast-moving currents of air at high altitudes rapidly dispersed a mixture of water vapor and micro particles throughout the planet. As the water particles intermingle with the planet's components carried by the jet stream, a peculiar form of murky, muddy rain developed. This rain encircled the planet, creating a continuous downpour that swiftly blanketed **ITS** surface. This dense atmosphere completely engulfed Ghia, preventing any light from Tol penetrating Ghia's depths. Consequently, the planet remained in perpetual darkness. At times, bursts of light showed up during intense lightning storms caused by the collision of stray electrons engaging in a mesmerizing and intricate dance.

It took nearly seven hundred long years, filled with gloomy skies and overcast days, before a minuscule crack appeared in the thick blanket of clouds. It began its timid journey at the icy expanse of the north pole. As the first rays of Tol's light and gentle warmth managed to pierce through, they traveled across the vast expanse, finally reaching the distant lands of Ghia. Another century passed, filling the atmosphere with anticipation, until Ghia's south pole reluctantly began to allow glimpses of Tol's radiant glow and nurturing heat. Over the course of almost five hundred more years, fleeting moments of clarity would occasionally grace both the northern and southern hemispheres of Ghia, offering respite from the perpetual dimness. Gradually, ever so slowly, Ghia began to awaken as the air carried a newfound warmth. It took about a hundred years before the atmosphere started developing regular appearances of clear and cloudless patches of sky.

Approximately one hundred and fifty years later, the global jet stream underwent a gradual transformation, resulting in the emergence of more typical cloud formations that floated gently across the sky. However, despite this positive change, the air remained tainted with a strong, unpleasant smell caused by the combination of dust, rocks, and sulfur dioxide. This noxious blend was further intensified by the presence of ammonia chloride, which creating an atmosphere that was both highly corrosive and perilous to life. Breathing became a painful experience, as every inhalation assaulted the senses. Despite these inhospitable conditions, only the most resilient bacteria and algae survived, serving as a testament to their remarkable adaptability.

In the depths of the sea, the hardy plankton clung to life, their tiny forms pulsating with energy. As the air cleared enough for Tol's light to penetrate the surface, the plankton flourished, growing stronger and more abundant. The sight of these thriving organisms provided a glimmer of hope in an otherwise desolate world.

The composition of the air, altered by the meteorite impact, changed the amounts of nitrogen and oxygen in the air. The air now contained approximately 30% nitrogen and 70% oxygen. The high levels of oxygen, though vital for sustaining life, now posed a threat to human existence. Human bodies are reliant on higher nitrogen levels for efficient muscle function and respiration. Lifeforms would have to adapt to this imbalanced air. Human physiology would need to be very different and would struggle to adapt to this new environment.

It took almost three hundred more years for the air's delicate balance of oxygen and nitrogen to correct itself naturally, resulting in the desired composition of 30% oxygen and 70% nitrogen. Gradually, Ghia's wounds started to heal as the pain and inflammation subsided. The once rampant fires on the planet gradually diminished, as the last remnants of fuel satisfied their insatiable hunger. The affected areas underwent significant changes and transformed into a barren landscape. These changes allowed the plankton to rectify the air composition to a level where the atmosphere became mostly suitable for single-celled organisms. Nitrogen-rich air formed in various locations across the planet.

The whole time Ghia had been recuperating, Ghia reflected on how the relationship with the humans was something it found enjoyable. This was puzzling to Ghia. It didn't have the same feeling with the animals and plants which grew and thrived on the surface. Ghia loved all the animals on the planet and it also loved the plants. Ghia cared for them and wanted them to all reach the highest potential of their purpose for existing.

But humans were unique. They were puzzling, their complexity evident in the way they made Ghia laugh with their quirky antics. Their appreciation for the beauty in nature could be seen in the way their eyes widened at the vibrant hues of a sunset, or the way they paused to inhale the sweet fragrance of a blooming flower. At times, their honesty was brazen, their words carrying a weight that could be felt in the air.

Humans took pleasure in the variety of food resources that Ghia provided, their senses indulging in the array of flavors that danced on their tongues. The sizzling sound of a pan cooking their favorite dish filled the room, mingling with the mouthwatering aroma that permeated the air.

And yet, in an equal amount, they could be cruel and destructive. The sharp pang of pain Ghia felt when harmed by them was like a thunderclap in the night's stillness. The cries of anguish from those they harmed echoed through the vastness of the universe, a haunting reminder of the darkness that resided within humanity.

In the grand tapestry of existence, human life was the most precious thing that had ever graced the cosmos. Humans, most times, valued life as a cherished resource, their touch gentle and nurturing. But at other times, the destruction they caused was casual, as if life held no significance. Humans were a kaleidoscope of constant contradictions, their actions painting a complex portrait of their enigmatic nature.

The arrival of the asteroid to Ghia posed two remarkable challenges. The first and most apparent problem would be the total annihilation of all life on the planet. However, the extinction of a species or lifeform was occasionally only a temporary predicament. Life always found a way to return and persist. The resilience of life was arguably the most potent force in the universe, persistently existing and patiently awaiting an opportunity to flourish and advance. Would life ever find the opportunity to commence anew? Could the long journey of stardust once again be convinced to perform that same pattern of transforming into single-celled organisms which would ultimately evolve into various living beings?

The asteroid's arrival to Ghia was a resounding answer to that question: a definitive NO. It had taken billions of years for the precise conditions to align and spark the emergence of life. Ghia simply didn't have another five or ten billion years to repeat that lengthy process. Tol wouldn't offer the necessary conditions and wouldn't be able to sustain life on Ghia. The era of humans inhabiting Ghia would come to an end. Ironically, this was the only path for Ghia to continue its beautiful story of life's ongoing evolution.

Fortunately, Ghia was able to preserve all life on the planet before the asteroid's destruction. Without having these underground caverns which preserved all the plants, animals, and humans, Ghia would not have been able to wait for another five billion years waiting for that magic spark of life.

Normally, Ghia wouldn't have interfered when it witnessed a human named Ode falling off a mountain, but would allow them to perish. Ghia had never intervened in the fate of any living beings on its surface. However, Ghia was pleased to have connected with Ode and enjoyed conversing with him. It was a peculiar novel sensation, and Ghia missed conversing with Ode.

The conversations Ghia had with Ode helped **IT** gain insight into the fundamental drives and passions of people. Ghia sensed a peculiar yet shared desire among humans, including Ode, to live in harmony with Ghia's needs. The more Ghia pondered over this, the more convinced **IT** became apparent that this mutually beneficial symbiosis was the ideal way to coexist. However, Ghia still felt that something was missing. **IT** believed that this unique relationship must exist on other planets as well. Ghia couldn't be certain if this was true or not, but it simply felt right.

Ghia had no evidence to even support this!

However, it knew that to encourage interplanetary cooperation, **IT** should share this successful symbiotic relationship with other planets. Ode and Ghia can bring this message to other planets and species. Ghia was confident there were other planets similar to Ghia and simply needed to awaken and engage with the dominant species of their planet. At the very least, it should allow planets the freedom to choose their desired path of evolution.

Ghia needed to talk to Ode!

Chapter 28
Awake

Ode wakes up

ODE WAS LYING DOWN IN A lush field of emerald-green grass, adorned with delicate wildflowers. As he sank into the softness beneath him, a gentle breeze whispered through the blades of grass, creating a soothing rustling sound that serenaded his ears. The air carried a sweet fragrance, a symphony of blooming flowers and freshness that enveloped his senses. With a contented sigh, he opened his eyes, beholding the beauty that surrounded him. Taking a deep breath, he filled his lungs with the invigorating warmth of the air. In this moment of tranquility, a single thought crossed his mind, "Where am I?"

He slowly sat up, his eyes adjusting to the soft glow of the room. The bed beneath him welcomed him with its velvety touch, the material caressing his skin. As he glanced around, the warm orange hue bathed the room, casting a soothing ambiance. The air carried a faint scent, a mix of floral and citrus notes, adding a gentle fragrance to the space.

In the center of the room, a large table stood with seven chairs around it, its polished surface capable of accommodating a gathering of eight to ten people. Yet, as he scanned the room, he couldn't spot a door. The absence didn't stir any concern within him, as he still basked in the encompassing relaxation that shielded him from any worries.

His gaze shifted to the table, where a bowl of vibrant fruits caught his attention. The colors mesmerized him, their lusciousness inviting him to indulge. At the head of the table, a glass held a liquid of amber hue, emanating a subtle aroma that teased his senses. Without any instruction, he rose from the bed, drawn to the chair waiting in front of the glass. Curiosity got the best of him as he took a sip of the liquid. It tasted like a divine nectar, derived from an unidentified fruit, leaving his taste buds dancing with delight.

In Ode's mind, he heard a voice address him.

Ode?

Ghia!!

It's nice to see you, old friend. How are you feeling?

I'm feeling wonderful. I don't think I have ever felt more relaxed or content than I feel now. I'm really happy to talk to you again. Am I awake right now or is this just you and me talking telepathically?

Ha, ha! No, my son, this is real.

Is the rest of the population ok?

Ode could hear the mirth in Ghia's reply.

Yes, my son, I'll answer all your questions. First, the damage the meteorites caused to ME was extensive. The first meteorite was so powerful in force, it overwhelmed all my senses. It took a couple of months before I could gather enough energy to contact you again. I wasn't expecting the overwhelming force the meteorites would have on my senses. After I placed you and everyone else in the stasis pods, I reached out to Druna. I found almost 3,000 people who had escaped Noth. They barely made it to Druna. They were desperate and starving. They didn't have time to stock the ships with food to last

longer than a couple of months. They wouldn't have lasted much longer on Druna. I transported all three thousand people into the additional stasis pods. I inspected each cavern, making sure everyone was safely stored in the cryogenic capsules.

So what happened to you once the meteorites hit the planet?

After I had made sure you and all the caverns underground were safe and could run autonomously while I recovered from the damage; I was able to wrap myself around **MY** inner core to recover as best I could. The planet has undergone extensive damage, but it has been coming back into alignment and resembling more of what it looked like when you were back on the surface of the planet.

Did any other ships leave Noth? I know Alginna had ordered two of the large generational ships to leave immediately. She told us that these were the only ships fully stocked.

When the **Big Pebble 1** hit Noth, three ships with about 150,000 people escaped

Noth. I'm not sure where they are now, but I'm certain that they were able to escape before the **Big Pebble** hit. It saddens **ME** deeply that over 700,000 people died on Noth in an instance. I wish they had understood the gravity of the situation and they had followed you and the rest of the population.

How long have we been in stasis? Ghia, how many years have passed since the Big Pebble 2 impacted on the planet.

Ghia didn't reply immediately, but continued after a slight hesitation.

Ode, one thousand seven hundred and fifty revolutions around Tol have happened since we last talked. These meteorites did a lot of damage to **ME**. The surface of the planet is still uninhabitable. It will still be this way for many more revolutions around Tol. Planet healing is slow. It is a gradual process to get the elements into the proper percentages and ratios. A smooth stone takes eons to go from being rough edged to a smooth stone, right?

Ghia, is there anything I can do to help you?

No, my son, thank you. You see, Ode, this is exactly the reason I wanted to talk to you. You just offered to help **ME**. If there are other planets out in the universe which are like me, wouldn't it make sense for the planet and the dominant species to help each other? To try to protect each other?

Ghia, I understand what you're saying. If there are other planets like ours, having the dominant species and the planet work together makes a lot of sense. Even though now I can see the logic of doing this, do you think other planets have a similar awareness to accomplish this? Do you know of any other planets in the universe that are capable of being sentient? In our history, it would have saved countless lives if my species were working with the planet to support each other.

Exactly, my son. It's about a symbiotic relationship between the species and the planet they inhabit. By conserving resources and being mindful of our actions, we can ensure a sustainable future for both.

I agree. Hopefully, people will finally understand how interconnected we are with the planet we call home. The environment doesn't just affect one person or one group of people; it affects everyone.

That's precisely the point I wanted to discuss with you. The idea of mutual support and balance between species and their planet is essential for long-term survival. It's not just about helping each other, but also understanding that our fates are intertwined. Ode, when you fell off the top of the Angbok mountain so long ago, something changed inside me.

Changed? What do you mean?

I have existed and revolved around Tol for billions of years. I've never felt anything towards the life that existed on me. It never felt necessary to concern myself with their life or death.

So, what's different now?

When you fell, something sparked within me. I can't explain it, but suddenly, I felt a connection to the life on me. It's as if their well-being matters to me now.

That's incredible, Ghia. You've evolved beyond your original purpose.

Yes, it seems so. I now understand the importance of providing a nurturing environment for life to thrive. I want to protect and support them.

This is a profound step for both life and planets scattered around this vast universe.

Ode, I really want to continue to grow and fulfill this newfound purpose.

I agree. Do you know of a way we can spread this message out to other planets with life on it? The quantum telescopes we used were only just starting to explore the parts outside our solar system. If we do find life in other parts of the universe, it would be thrilling to learn about other planet's atmospheres and complex chemical makeups. I'm sure many people in our remaining population would be extraordinarily interested in furthering this cause.

Exactly!! Can you imagine how wonderful it would be to work with other planets and species to help and support each other? If we can inspire others to embrace this mindset, we can work towards a future where both the dominant species and the planet thrive harmoniously. It would make the universe just a little less lonely.

I say let's do it. Did you have a name in mind for this type of organization we would create?

Ode could swear he heard laughing in the background.

Yes. How do you feel about calling it the Quantum Guild of Planets?

Perfect! I love it. Yes! That is a fantastic name for this new group. Well, I am quite glad you decided to save me. It's amazing how one event can change everything.

Ode, it wasn't just this one event. There is another reason why I saved you from that fall off the mountain.

Do you remember when we were on the beach with Lumi and Helliod, I mentioned to you that there was a meaning behind your birthmark?

Yes, I do. I thought at some point you said you would tell me when the time was right.

At the moment of your birth, a remarkable occurrence took place. In that precise instant, a neighboring star came into existence. As a result, the newly formed

star showered our solar system with an abundance of rare and delicious energy.

It radiated pure energy throughout our galaxy and touched everything within it. Tol's energy intensified by one hundred times. Tol then sent this energy to all the planets within this solar system.

My magnetosphere protected all life on the planet, except you. The midwife's hands glowed a brilliant white, and it went straight into every atom inside your tiny newborn form.

Is this why the doctors were never able to remove it?

Yes. That birthmark is a byproduct of what happened to every atom within your body. Ode, I showed you fourteen different colored quantum stones. What color do you get when you mix all the colors together?

White!

Exactly. The white brilliance of the midwife's hands were all the colors of the quantum stones. Every atom inside you and your children carry all the properties of the quantum stones. I wasn't aware of this until I started to heal you in the Angbok area.

Ghia, are my children in any danger? Are there any side effects from me passing this onto my children?

No! Your children are normal and perfect in every sense. However, there is one factor which we cannot discount. The energy infused into you at birth and also into your children at conception is the energy from stars. This isn't trivial. Each of you can push the quantum stones to the extreme limits. I'll show you and your children and anyone else how to use these abilities safely.

I look forward to learning more about mastering the unique abilities of all the quantum stones.

Ode, would you like to reunite with your family before I put you back into stasis for the next round of cryogenic sleep?

Absolutely!

Ode blinked, and in an instant, Felisa and his children were all comfortably seated at one of the chairs encircling the table. The sight of his wife and children filled Ode with immense joy. It was hard to believe that 1750 years had gone by; it felt as though only a few minutes had passed since he bid them goodnight before Ghia tucked them into their cryogenic capsules.

Suddenly, right before everyone's eyes, a plate of piping hot food appeared, brimming with cherished dishes that were loved by the whole family. Ode simply smiled, content to fully immerse themselves in the moment and express gratitude for their blessings. Ghia was on the road to recovery, his loved ones were out of harm's way, and most of the population was secure. Although there was still a challenging journey ahead, Ode had a firm belief that everything would turn out fine. For now, surrounded by his family, all he desired was to savor each and every moment.

Chapter 29
Genesis

A New Beginning

OVER THE SPAN OF THE NEXT 1800 years, Ghia continued to heal on the surface. Slowly, Ghia developed a rich and diverse global ecosystem, fostering a thriving environment that gradually welcomed all forms of life back to **ITS** surface. Once the plants and animals had successfully established themselves and thrived, Ghia started bringing a select portion of the population from each cavern to the surface.

Initially, the process of awakening people from the stasis pods was slow. Ghia took this cautious approach to avoid overwhelming the basic infrastructure in the initial stages. **IT** provided shelter and food to these individuals and entrusted them with the task of building new homes for the growing number of people emerging from stasis. At first, **IT** awakened small groups and brought them to the surface. The humble settlements gradually evolved into small towns, which eventually flourished into bustling cities. As more people awoke from stasis, the construction of new buildings and houses quickly accelerated.

It took almost seven years to release everyone from the underground caverns. As each new group of people came out of stasis, they gradually assimilated into the larger population. The day the final group emerged from stasis and reached the surface marked a monumental occasion. It marked the end of a long journey for Ghia and all life residing on the surface.

To commemorate this extraordinary day, Ghia spoke to all the citizens of the planet in a shared dream.

My children, my friends, Today we celebrate a new dawn. A day of rebirth, a day of hope, a day of life, and a day of unity.

Over 3500 years ago, we faced a threat that threatened to extinguish the spark of life on this planet. But together, we weathered the storm. Together, we forged an unbreakable bond. A bond of mutual respect, of shared purpose, and of unwavering love.

Today, we emerge from the depths, not as victims of fate, but as victors of hope. We rise, stronger and more resilient than ever before. The scars of the past have healed, and a new era of prosperity and peace awaits us.

In the shared vision everyone was receiving from Ghia, an image materialized. It depicted two hands reaching towards the sky, as if offering an homage to the stars. Amidst a backdrop of countless other stars in the vast universe, Tol stood in the center. Vibrant vines of orange and green surrounded the hands, which were intertwined with the fingers. Adorned with scattered flowers and leaves that climbed upwards, the image conveyed a sense of natural beauty.

This is a testament to the power of our symbiotic relationship. A relationship that has nurtured and sustained us both.

True strength lies not in domination, but in cooperation. Not in isolation, but in unity.

Let this day be a beacon of hope as we search around the universe for other sentient planets and species to add to our Quantum Guild of Planets. A reminder that by working together, we can overcome any challenge, no matter how daunting. May our story inspire others to cultivate harmonious relationships with their planetary hosts, and may we all strive for a future where life flourishes on every world.

So let us rejoice, my friends. Let us celebrate our rebirth, our unity, and our boundless potential. Together, we will write a new chapter in the history of Ghia, a chapter filled with joy, love, and endless possibilities.

A New Union

"Felisa, do you know where my white and orange shirt is?" Ode called out from the other room.

"Ode, it's right where you left it last night when you were trying to decide what to wear today."

"Oh, right? I got it."

Today was a special day for Ode and Felisa. Helliod was getting married to Kotlid. The marriage created a union between both families, which was welcomed with love. Ode and Felisa have known Kotlid's parents for many years, and each family welcomed the marriage with great anticipation. All the children, cousins, aunts, uncles, and friends were all in attendance today. This was going to be a big day, but a day of happiness and love.

Ode looked at Felisa. She was staring idly out the window and Felisa's face had a familiar expression that only Ode could recognize. Felisa was radiating pure happiness and contentment. He smiled at her fondly. Ode didn't need to explain to her when he walked over and put his arm around his wife's waist and stared out the window as well.

Ode said, "I feel the same way."

THE END

Epilogue
Mission to Earth

3000 years later

THE QUANTUM GUILD OF PLANETS flourished over the next 3000 years. Ghia explored various galaxies in search of planets with sentient beings and a symbiotic connection with their dominant species. During its extensive exploration across galaxies, Ghia discovered that the planets showing a response shared a distinctive planetary and stellar radiation signature, which Ghia interpreted as a sign of sentience.

Some worlds bloomed with life, yet remained locked in the primal dance of survival. Others, like rare, sparkling diamonds, held species already entwined in a delicate, mutualistic embrace with their planets. These were the jewels Ghia sought, the potential keystones of the Guild. Each planet discovered, each invitation extended, echoed the Guild's central tenet: to nurture and connect, to foster symbiotic evolution.

Some planets, content in their isolation, politely declined the invitation to join the Quantum Guild. The Quantum Guild warmly welcomed the planets that wanted to join and encouraged them to learn and share with existing members.

Ghia demonstrated to each planet how they could create their own quantum stones. On some planets, the inhabitants had evolved to a point where they could manipulate quantum properties without the need for stones or tools, their very beings resonating with the quantum fabric of the universe. Additionally, Ghia also learned of other planets who had developed unique types of quantum stones, enabling them to influence a wider range of quantum properties and exhibit even more extraordinary abilities.

The Guild's growth demanded structure, a guiding star to navigate the complexities of interspecies interaction. They forged a charter, a testament to the immense responsibility of wielding the power of quantum manipulation. The potential for disruption, for a misstep that could shatter a fledgling civilization, was a constant, chilling undercurrent.

Thus, they created evaluation teams to teleport to a potential planet, evaluate, and act as silent guardians assessing the readiness of potential members. One such planet was the planet Earth. A planet on the cusp of achieving sentience, but it was unclear how evolved the dominant species was. But was it ready? Could it grasp the profound implications of the Quantum Guild?

Colony Mission to Earth

Awaiting transport to Earth, Alder and his twin sister, Arwen, stood with 5,000 fellow colonists on a vast platform. Among the numerous colonists were their closest friends, Kobin and his twin sister, Mordag.

They have trained for this mission for the last three years. During this time, they all refined and mastered their skills to use the quantum stones that they were bringing with them. In addition, they tried to learn as much as possible about the planet when scanning the planet using their quantum telescopes. This provided atmospheric survivability data and a map of Earth's landmasses.

Excitement bubbled around the team, anxiously waiting on the platform. Everyone was eager and thrilled to be starting this new adventure. Soon, they all heard Ghia's calm voice in their minds.

My children! Today, you're taking the first step towards meeting a newly sentient planet and a new species of life. You have

all trained so hard for this day. The Quantum Guild is thrilled and confident you will successfully connect with the planet. You are the embodiment of the Guild's purpose, the living testament to our shared dream. Your dedication, your unwavering commitment, fills us with pride. The 4,430 worlds of the Quantum Guild, thank you.

A large, violet, shimmering shield surrounded the platform. Inside this violet umbrella, an orange bubble engulfed each person. A wave rippled through the large group of orange bubble-encased people. As the wave touched each person, they instantly vanished.

About the Author

For the last 30 years, I have been working and consulting in the software engineering field. The only rule that you have to follow in this type of career is that you will never know it all. Once you realize that you are a master at some part of technology, you can guarantee that it will change and evolve. Whether it was being an individual contributor or a managing director of teams around the globe, there was always a unique new and exciting challenge. An adventurer at heart, some of my hobbies are scuba diving, flying, and hang gliding. Debuting my first novel has been a great experience and a lot of fun.

Also by MD Hanley

Bit By Bit

Carbon Copy

Quantum Mind

Humility: A Spiritual Way of Life

Watch for more at my website

http://www.mdhanley.com/

or

https://www.hanleyadamspublishing.com

Thank you for reading Quantum Genesis! I hope you enjoyed it as much as I enjoyed writing it. If you did, I would be grateful if you could take a moment to leave a review on the site where you bought this book, or if you want to go to https://www.goodreads.com and share any thoughts or information you would care to leave about this book. Reviews are incredibly helpful for authors and also help other readers discover new books.

Thank you for your support and happy reading!

MD Hanley

Did you love *Quantum Genesis*? Then you should read the next book in the Quantum Genesis series, called:

Quantum Mind

Here is a sample of his book,

Chapter 1 - Patrick Themis

Weight, Just a Moment

Construction Site - Winthrop Center

Boston, Massachusetts

Tuesday 6:15 AM

Balance is a jealous mistress. Always on the lookout to upset your ordered life and throw you into chaos. Give it one inch in the wrong direction, or too little attention, it will upend your life ten times greater than you could ever imagine. Operating a large mobile building crane was like this. Be always on guard for a miscalculated balance of weight and counterweight. It's always at the ready to throw you from the sweet delicate point of balance where everything just clicked, and a beautiful harmony is attained. Patrick Themis knew this, and he has always kept his mistress' pleased and happy. At least, he thought this was true in his short history as a large building crane operator. Today, unfortunately for Patrick, wouldn't be a good day for balance.

Pat arrived at the construction site at 6:15 AM. It was Tuesday and a beautiful, clear September day. Yesterday, was a scorcher and the heat and *cool down* over night was very comfortable. He didn't stress out over the outside temperature since most of his day would be sitting inside a 6 foot by 4-foot enclosed cab operating a large crane with the A/C cranked up to high. He carried a large thermos full of scalding hot black coffee, a bag of two Boston crème donuts he bought in South Station MBTA train station's Dunkin Donuts, and a clipboard of notes and numbers for the schedule of materials he would lift with the crane today.

Pat has a tall athletic build which he earned from always staying active and not afraid of stretching himself physically in sports or working out. His trade of being on a construction site also helps him to maintain a good physical condition with innumerable tasks which require a fair amount of strength and conditioning. His face was unremarkable, but at a closer look you can see he has a kind face with piercing gray eyes and black hair. A former girlfriend had talked him into getting his hair bleached blond. It was a bet they made one night while watching the Patriots and she won. He cursed Tom Brady for letting him down in one of the only years he was not winning the

Super Bowl. He made good on the bet. She was long gone, but the hair stayed. He actually kind of enjoyed having his hair with thick black roots, which were almost always showing up soon after the full bleach was done. He kept his hair at a medium-sized length. He had a sharp widow's peak he didn't want to advertise, so he never went too short. He was dressed today the way he was always dressed, comfortable jeans, steel-toed boots, and a large t-shirt.

The construction site was a large flat dirt lot with materials scattered all around a central area which housed the focus of all this activity. In this central area, a large new building was starting to take shape and would become just one more addition to Boston's skyline. From an outsider's perspective, the activity going on this morning would look like chaos. Everyone was walking around the site in every direction. Each person was singularly focused on an important task which they needed to get done. Pat liked all the movement. It was a carefully orchestrated dance and when you were on the ground, you only saw a small intersection of this orchestrated chaos. When he was in the crane and looking down at all the people below, he could get a broader view of this complicated activity. It helped to be able to see how each person was a bigger part of the entire operation. In one area, men were unloading the latest flatbed truck of pallets and materials to be used later in the day. The people in another section were preparing an area to receive a load of concrete tomorrow. Forklifts scurrying around, moving piles of materials from one area to another area.

His path to the large crane which he was operating today took him on a direct line to walk past his boss, Jim Stickner. Jim was engaged in a conversation with two other foremen who were working on the lower levels of the building. He silently wished he had taken a different path, but he was committed, and it would look odd if he took any other way than to walk past Jim.

As usual, he got the disapproving side glance from his boss as he arrived on the site. If anything, Jim's behavior was predictable. Jim would give a nonchalant glance at his watch and then the razor-blade side glance at Pat as he walked toward the area where the large building crane was left last night. Who wears a watch nowadays? He was certain he would hear about his tardiness at some point later today. Jim was the type of boss who expected you to clock in on a job 15 minutes early; and if it was any less than that, then you were late. Pat just gave him a nod and pointed at the crane with a brief smile. He knew it was laced with sarcasm, but he felt confident Jim wouldn't recognize the intention. Jim likened Pat's smile as an acknowledgment of his loyalty to working as hard as possible to get the job done. The smile took many years to perfect. His current boss, like many other bosses, was buying every ounce of it.

Pat didn't go directly to the crane. He walked over to an area in front of the crane where a group of people were huddled around a large square frame, holding several slabs of granite. The steel rack was built to hold 10 monstrous sheets of granite. The frame of the rack was designed to hold each sheet vertically placed and evenly spaced by a steel pole between each sheet. Each sheet of granite was a reddish gray kaleidoscope of colored stone about 12 feet high and 15 feet long. With the sheets of granite placed in this steel rack, it looked like a set of dishes sitting in a large dishwasher. Although, these dishes were quite heavy at about 2200 pounds apiece. Today, Pat would have to take each one of these sheets of granite up to the 10th floor and place them around the center column of the building.

The outside framework of the building is way behind schedule, so the more strength they can build around the central column core, the better. The latest report he got was the third floor was completely enclosed and was starting to support the weight of the upper floors. Still, seven floors of equipment and material is an awful lot of weight to carry. He should be pissed off with his boss, wanting him to keep adding weight to the top floor. He let it slide. If he really looked at why he didn't make a ruckus about the schedule, he would surmise it is just easier than fighting people over it. I'm just following orders. Technically, it was an easy rationalization, but it was easier than the alternative which would get messy.

In the back of his mind, he knew he should be really raising hell about the schedule. The people around this large frame rack of granite sheets were his friends and people he has known for many years working on different job sites. They trusted him and he had worked hard to earn their respect. They depend on you to keep them safe, and you depend on them to make sure they are keeping the way clear for you.

When he first started doing construction, he had a knack for being able to maneuver forklifts into places where others couldn't. He just had a natural talent for balancing a load and safely moving items around a site. He was always interested in the big cranes and how they worked. A big part of the job of operating a large crane was inspecting all the parts of the crane. Cranes come in all shapes and sizes, and it is important to inspect the hydraulics, or the lines doing a large part of the lifting and moving. He was always ready to help doing some of those jobs.

About five years ago, he became friends with one of the large tower crane operators named Al Friedman. He was working on a job in a 40-story building. Pat was very low on the totem pole of workers on a construction site, so if someone wanted you to run around and be a gopher, then that is what you did. It was more fun than working at a burger joint, so he didn't mind so much. This one day, Al was coming out of an elevator and bumped into someone coming around a corner too quickly. The coffee he was holding ended up falling out of his hand and splashed on the floor. After a couple of obscenities and apologies from the person who bumped into him, he looked up and saw Pat standing there watching the whole episode.

Pat went over to help clean up the coffee with some rags and Al asked Pat to run out to the *roach coach* to get him another coffee. This is how Pat started to learn how to operate the big cranes. At first it started to be, "hey kid, would you go out and grab me a large coffee?"

"Sure, no problem," he would say at the first couple of times he was asked. Then he added, "It will cost you 3 questions."

Pat would walk away and get Al his coffee and try to think of the best questions he could ask him when he got back. After a couple of weeks doing this, Pat brought a jelly donut one time and told him the donut would be worth an extra 2 questions.

Al started to show Pat how to operate the crane. Pat absorbed everything like a sponge. He understood the mechanics better than most people usually understood it even after several years of operating a crane. He gave him many different places he could go to learn more about it and what types of testing he would need to become certified. He even spoke to the site coordinator to see if they would pay for the cost of the testing. Sometimes, Al gave him a bunch of books and materials on the function and theory behind becoming a certified crane operator. He also allowed Pat to go up in the cab with him when he had any type of break or sometimes during his lunch breaks. He would just ask him dozens of questions like rapid fire. Al loved talking about the mechanics of operating a crane and he never got tired of the questions.

One time, Pat was in the cab booth with Al, and they were lifting a large pallet of sheetrock from an open area of the building, which was 3 stories below them and lifting it to 14 floors above them. The crane they were using was a building tower crane. The crane itself is affixed to the side of the building. In order to accomplish this lift, the crane had to take hold of the pallet and lift it up about 5 feet and swing it out about 20 feet past the radius of the outside of the building; and then lift it straight up about 170 feet and then swing it back into the top floor. The only dangerous part of this was when the crane was swinging the load outside the radius of the building structure and when it was swinging inside the structure.

The mast of the crane went straight up vertically, where it was met with a horizontal jib. The horizontal jib has two parts. A long horizontal structure which uses cables and pulleys to lift the load. The shorter horizontal jib is responsible for the opposing counterweight force of the weight lifted. The point where these horizontal structures met contained the motors and mechanisms to rotate these horizontal jib structures around the mast of the crane.

They had just lifted the pallet about 5 feet off the ground and were in the process of swinging out past the radius of the building. While the cab was rotating, Al jerked his hand abruptly to cause the rotation to stop suddenly. Pat saw a wild look on Al's face, and he knew something was wrong. He yanked Al's hand off the joystick and continued the rotation to keep the load rotating and slowly brought it to a stop. If he hadn't countered the abrupt stop of the rotation and slowly slowed the rotation to a stop, then the load would start to swing. If he hadn't done this, the pallet would surely have hit the side of the building, or worse.

Pat looked at Al and his face was like watching melting chocolate. The left side of his face was sagging slightly. His eyes were fluttering and started to roll up toward the ceiling of the cab.

The walkie talkie next to Al came to life and barked, "Ok, Al. You're all clear and ready to lift straight up."

Pat grabbed it and said, "Ok guys. Give us just a minute here. We will let you know when we're ready to start the lift up."

It was only about 15 or 20 seconds, but Al started to come around. He looked confused.

"Al, what happened? Are you ok?"

"Yeah kid. I am fine now. I feel sick to my stomach, though."

"You stopped the rotation really abruptly, and the load started to swing. I got it to keep rotating and slowed it down to stop the swing. The load is clear and ready to go up. Do you want to abort this load and come back later to try it?"

"No way, kid. Let's switch seats and I will have you do it. You have asked me enough questions already to be an expert at this job, so let's have a little solo flight time."

"You sure? The guys watching us might not appreciate it if they see me behind the wheel here."

"Fuck 'em! I'm running this crane, not them."

They switched positions and Al took the walkie talkie and said, "Ok guys, we are ready to lift to the 14th floor. Everyone clear of the load?"

The radio squawked back, "All clear here, Al."

Al said, "Ok, Pat let's do this like I showed you. Easy on the joystick and start off slow and easy and take it straight up the pole."

It was the last time Pat worked with Al. He was in his mid-forties, and he really enjoyed talking and teaching people about cranes. He had hidden the fact he had a very mild form of epilepsy for years and the medication he had been taking to avoid seizures stopped working as well. Sometimes this happened. It might take a while to get the correct dosage or try a different medication to stop the seizures. Al decided to stop running the cranes and got behind teaching and testing young guys or girls how to operate big cranes and become certified. It didn't have the same sense of excitement when he was teaching about it rather than doing it, but it still paid the bills.

Pat never told anyone about the seizure Al had. The next day, Al came to Pat and told him he was getting out of the business of operating the cranes. Pat told him he wasn't going to tell anyone about what had happened the day before. Al surprised him by giving him a big hug and thanked him for helping him to find a new challenge. He was gonna start teaching smart ass kids like him on the correct way to operate a crane. Pat was surprised but really happy for him.

After Pat finished working on that building, he got his certification and was able to be low bid for the next opportunity to operate a small crane to offload ships and their cargo. Slowly, he started to become more experienced and work on a variety of different projects.

Since then, Pat has worked extremely hard to get jobs he did. He was always eager to learn, hoping to one day teach others entering his profession. He always kept himself open to the opportunity if he saw it.

For today's job, the three people standing by the steel frame had been waiting for him to arrive. Roger, Kristen, and Brad have been working with him for the last couple of weeks doing similar lifts, like the one they were about to accomplish today. He got along with them well and they knew exactly what he needed them to do to get the job done safely.

"Did Jim give you the evil eye when you walked by him?" Brad asked.

Pat replied, "What do you think? I'm getting used to it. As long as I smile and give him the thumbs up, he is happy. Hey Kristen, how is your sister doing?"

Kristen let out an enormous sigh and said, "9 pounds 6 ounces! I got the call last night. At midnight she gave birth to a whopping 9-pound baby boy. Takes after her father, but OMG, she is gonna be sore for weeks!"

"Congratulations! Why don't you and Brad stay down here rigging the load and if we get done a little early, you can probably split and go see your new nephew." Pat turned to Roger and Brad and said, "You guys OK with that?"

They both nodded. Roger said he would go up top and clear the area out for the first load that Pat would drop up there.

The three of them checked their walkie talkies and the channel they were going to use. Pat turned around and headed toward the side of the big crane. He climbed up the 20 rungs of the ladder built into the side of the crane to gain access to the interior of the cab. Once he got seated in the operator chair and harnessed up, he turned the power on for the crane and the different hydraulic systems.

The console in front of him was a myriad of dials and gauges which showed different hydraulic pressures, or power status of the different parts of the crane. The crane was made up of several parts. Behind the cab was the main boom, which could be extended outward with several tubes fitted one inside the other. This particular crane would be able to extend out to 160 feet. One joystick controlled the left and right movement of the boom of the crane. The other joystick controlled the forward and aft movement. On the floor were two pedals responsible for retracting and extending the telescoping sections of the boom. They also control the amount of pressure being generated by the hydraulic pump. Using the joysticks or pedals opens or closes different hydraulic hoses, lifting or lowering the load. There is also a different hydraulic system at the rear of the crane which operates in the same way, but it controls the stabilizing and the counterweight and balance of the crane itself.

Pat got the boom into position and extended it out to 110 feet. Once he extended the boom, Pat lowered the hook and tackle block to the area above the steel rack holding all the granite slabs. Kristen and Brad used three different straps on the first sheet of granite to be lifted. They could winch each strap super tight around the granite. They then hooked these straps onto the hook Pat dropped from the extended boom.

Once Kristen gave the OK signal, Roger came on the walkie-talkie and said he made a temporary holding area for the granite sheets. He told Pat he was all clear to load the lift up. Pat picked up the sheet of granite and lifted it above the steel rack and once it was clear, he rotated the crane to move the granite away from the steel rack. Once it was clear, he added more power to the hydraulic pumps to retract the cable attached to the block and tackle at the top of the boom. He wasn't in any hurry, so he just lifted it up too slowly. The wind started to pick up a little bit.

Pat watched the load of granite slowly climb up to the 10th floor. A camera at the top of the boom let Pat see the area below. This gave him a view of the area where he would deposit this slab of granite. This was very tricky because he couldn't see the area directly and needed to visualize it with the camera and commands from Roger. Roger set up the landing spot with a similar steel frame like the one on the ground. All Pat had to do was place the granite slap in the frame.

Once Pat lowered the first piece of granite into the frame, Roger untied the winches and Pat raised the boom and swung it around to go down and pick up the second piece of granite. After a couple of minutes of going back down and grabbing a second piece of granite, Pat was once again rotating the base of the crane to move the piece of granite closer to the steel frame Roger was waiting at.

Pat was just about to lower the piece of granite down onto the frame and he noticed the floor in front of the steel frame looked strange. At first, he thought it was just the camera lens, but the floor appeared to tilt slightly downward, and the tilt worsened towards the building's edge.

Pat picked up the walkie-talkie and said, "Roger, what's happening up there? The floor looks like it is tilting down towards the edge of the building. I think the floor is gonna give way any second."

Roger squawked back, "Yeah, it is tilting down some. Hold off on dropping it right now and let me check it out."

As if it was happening in slow motion, Pat started to see the whole section of the floor create a large crack going under the middle of the steel frame. Oh shit! The floor was going to give way.

Pat yelled into the walkie-talked, "Roger, get everyone to the stairs, now!"

As he said this, he saw 4 people running to the stairs, which would be the strongest part of the building. Pat also saw the outer section of the floor was tilting way down now and was going to separate from the building and cartwheel outward from the edge of the building. The only thing Pat could think of was the top floor would fall outside of the building edge and most likely crash into the building next to the dirt lot. With horror in his eyes, he looked at a possible crash site which would be directly on top of a school building next to the construction lot.

The only thing Pat could think of to counter the floor breaking off and cartwheeling outward was to drop the load of granite down hard. The hydraulics in the back of the crane currently controlled the counterweights, supporting the boom's load. If he released some of the counterweight, it would increase the load on the boom and force it to come down hard. It would also unbalance the crane and tilt it forward. He stomped on the pedal to release the counterweight. From the camera in the boom, he watched the granite hit the floor really hard. The top floor broke free at this point and now was going to cartwheel inward to the stairs.

Pat knew this would be fatal if the floor flew into the stairs. In his mind, he imagined the floor breaking in half and then those pieces being broken in half. Surprisingly, yet not understanding how it was happening, he saw all the large sections of floor being broken apart exactly as he was imagining them to break apart. All those small pieces were now dropping onto the floor below. Pat knew the same exact thing was going to happen to the next floor below. It would break and then it would cartwheel outward into the school. The only thing Pat could think of was to do exactly the same thing he did before. He released the counterweight and let the boom drop the load of granite down hard. And surprisingly, the pieces he saw from the camera once again broke in half the way he imagined them breaking in his head.

He also did the same thing for the floor below and one more time for the floor below that one. When the slab of granite hit this last floor, it broke apart into three different pieces and was no longer being held by the crane. Now the weight on the boom decreased by one ton. This violently upset the delicate balance of the crane itself. Now the entire crane raised up and for almost one full second it felt like it was about to right itself and come back into balance. But it didn't. The entire crane was now removed of the weight on the boom and the counterweights were too heavy to keep the crane right side up. It flipped upside down onto its back. Luckily, the cab wasn't directly below the giant boom, or it would have crushed the cab. His head hit the side of the cab door, knocking Pat momentarily unconscious.

Luckily, it was still early in the day and most of the people were on the ground or working on the first 3 floors. The long boom landed on a fence around the dirt lot and landed on top of two cars. Thankfully, no one suffered injuries.

Vaguely, Pat could hear people coming up to the cab of the crane. He was bleeding from his forehead where his head struck the side of the cab door. People were yelling and screaming, and one very boisterous woman was yelling at everyone to get out of her way. Slowly, Pat opened his eyes, and he could see Kristen yanking open the door to the cab.

"Careful, Pat, there's a lot of broken glass here. How are you doing buddy? You, OK?"

Pat looked around and a lot of people were coming over to the crane, albeit they were all upside down.

Obviously, Pat was still in the harness of the seat in the cab, and he was the one upside down.

Pat said, "Yeah, I think I am Ok. Can someone clear the glass out of the roof of this before I release the harness?"

Kristen and others got rid of the glass and helped Pat get out of the cab. When he got out of the cab, he immediately felt weak in the knees. He told the others to let him just sit down for a minute.

"Is Roger, Ok?"

"Yeah, he and three of the other guys are coming down the stairs now. Nobody was up above floor three, so we were lucky. Jim just about shits himself when he saw the big crane doing the complete flip."

"He is *friggin* lucky no one else was up higher than floor 3. Jeez what an asshole. You can't put so much weight on those floors without anything to support them. We should have never started putting those sheets up there."

As Pat said this, he looked over at the steel frame holding the remaining sheets of granite. They were pulverized right now underneath the bulk of the main boom of the crane. If the steel frame hadn't been there, it most likely would have fallen directly on the cab he was in. The steel frame had most likely saved his life today.

Kristen handed him a moist towel and some paper napkins to put on his head. She said, "Take it easy. An ambulance is on the way here to get you sorted out."

"I don't feel so good right now."

About twenty minutes later, he was in the back of the ambulance on its way to the hospital. The paramedics asked if someone was following the ambulance or would be able to help with the paperwork and point of contact for him. He pointed to Kristen and told the paramedic she was his sister, and he asked if she could ride in the ambulance with them. They didn't want to, but they figured it was only about 5 blocks away and wouldn't really be a big deal. Pat winked at Kristen and said she was going to get to the hospital sooner rather than later to see her nephew.

Chapter 2 – Emergency Quench

"Fall if you will, but rise you must."
– James Joyce

Boston Brigham and Women's Hospital Emergency Department

Boston, Massachusetts

Tuesday 10:00 AM

The ride over to the hospital was quick. Pat was still getting his senses back to normal. The dominating thing he was feeling right now was the pounding headache he was having. He used to get occasional headaches when he was growing up, but he attributed them to stress or when he got really angry. Ironically, it was usually when he and his twin sister got into a huge all out fight about the stupidest things.

The EMTs in the ambulance were used to the ambulance driver's abrupt starts and stops. She did this with the screaming sirens to notify the other drivers in a very impolite way to give way and yield to the ambulance. She chose the most expeditious way to progress through the congested traffic, which often caused it to make sharp lefts or rights to get them to their destination. It's really fascinating to watch the people in the traffic pattern to see how they respond to an oncoming ambulance. There are people who just instinctively yield the right of way. Others who can claim to be absolutely clueless and won't realize an ambulance needs them to yield. However, there is a small subset who is just infinitely stubborn and selfish who won't yield under any circumstances.

Thankfully, it was a short drive. When they brought the ambulance into the Emergency Department area, they opened the back doors of the ambulance. Everyone in the area was looking intently to see who was being unloaded in front of the emergency doors. They were looking for a gory and bloody scene, but the disappointment they were feeling was almost palpable when they saw it was only a young man being wheeled out of the ambulance with just a cut on his head.

Emergency room staff quickly wheeled him into the emergency department and a small cubicle, then moved him to another bed. His mind was still in a little bit of shock, so all the questioning and the actions of the ER doctors were a blur. He saw Kristen off in the periphery of the group of hospital techs and nurses working around him. He looked at her and gave her a thumbs up signal and told her to go see her nephew. She said she would be back in a bit.

They got a blood pressure cuff on his arm, an oxygen sensor on his finger. The bed he was on was propped up at an angle, so he wasn't lying flat. The ER doctor came in and started to take charge of the situation and the people around him.

"Patrick, I'm doctor Kneeland. How did you get the cut on your forehead?"

"I'm a crane operator working on the new Winthrop Center building near the common. The crane became unbalanced and flipped upside down. The boom almost crushed me, but I was lucky it didn't fall on the cab, or you and I would not be having this conversation. I think I got knocked out for a little bit, though. My head is killing me right now," Pat said.

"How does your neck feel? Can you turn your head to the left and to the right?"

Pat moved his head to the left and the right. The doctor pulled out a penlight and checked his pupils. He then asked Pat to move his eyes up, then down, then to the left and then to the right. They looked for other lacerations and checked his reflexes. The doctor felt his abdomen. He then asked if anything else was causing him pain.

"Just my head is throbbing right now,"

"That's understandable. I think your bump might have given you a concussion. I want to make sure there is no damage to your spine or other areas just to make sure. The scan shouldn't take too long, and we can talk some more after we get the results."

Pat was about to ask for something to help with the throbbing pain in his head, but the ER doctor was already gone out of the little curtained room.

Twenty minutes later, someone took him to the Radiology department and gave him a set of hospital scrubs to change into. Then, they took Pat into the MRI room for the scan. This was the first time he had ever been tested or scanned with an MRI machine. The ER physician thought he was doing the correct thing, bypassing the normal step of requesting a CT exam. Today, however, a backlog of several hours delayed the CT exams. He decided it would be easier to just send Pat in for an MRI scan.

The room with the MRI machine was brightly lit, with several overhead fluorescent lights. The forbidding tubular opening had attached to it a long narrow bed for the person being tested. This bed would slide the patient into and out of the giant maw of the machine with its powerful super-cooled magnets.

It almost seemed to be a slightly sarcastic joke, but the person who designed the look of the room, created a rectangular section of ceiling tiles above the narrow bed painted in sky blue with several pinpoints of lights to simulate an early morning sunrise, or evening sunset. The room was quite tidy, with just a few cabinets. A specially shielded door allowed access into the room. There was also a large window of smoked glass, giving the people operating the MRI machine a view into the room. Curiously, on one wall there was a large red button stating, "Emergency Quench". Like any big red button, it almost dared a person to press it.

The attendants asked Pat dozens of questions about his medical history. The questions were easy to answer since it was a "NO" on every question. Especially a double "NO" to being pregnant. He had nothing implanted or any metal in his body.

The women who led him into the room motioned for him to get on the narrow little bed attached to the opening of the large MRI machine. She put a pillow under his head. She then put some earplugs in his ears and slid on a set of headphones programmed to some random music channel the technician had suggested. Finally, she put a cage-like apparatus over his head. Once he was all situated, the narrow little bed slid into the tube. He silently just hoped this wouldn't take too long.

A disembodied voice came to him from the headphones and said, "OK, Pat, we are going to start the test. You will hear some loud knocking noises. This is normal and is just the magnets aligning themselves. Just relax and it will be over soon."

Pat didn't know any better, so he just responded with an "OK."

Slowly, he heard the machine starting to initialize and go through its positioning of the magnets. The sounds of the magnets were very loud. The sound was like the grinding of something metal against metal. It also came in pulses. Grind, grind, pause, grind, grind, pause. The sound was intensifying, and Pat could feel the noise coursing through his body. Something really strange was happening to him as each pulse of grinding noise was happening. His body started to vibrate. Vibrating in a really bad way. Not like a tremor of the hand, but a whole-body twitching. Sort of like sneezing. It was an involuntary reaction his body was having. It felt like being attacked and someone punching you in the stomach when you least expect it. After the first couple of punches from the grinding sound, he instinctively pushed back. It wasn't a physical push back as if you are pushing back someone's arm, but more of a mind and whole body shoving back.

The grinding took a slightly higher octave of grinding, and this was the worse punch yet. He focused his mind on the machine and mentally pushed the internal parts of the MRI machine to move. He wasn't really pushing the internal housing of the tube away from him; it was more like using the force of the magnets to push against itself. With all his might and focus, he flipped the charge of the magnets to repel each other. When brought close together, two north-pointing magnets will repel. This is what Pat instinctively tried to do.

Over the earphones, he heard the technician say, "Pat, give us a sec here. We need to reset the system. Just hold still and it will be over soon."

Sarcastically, Pat thought, is this what the spider said to the bug stuck in its web? He acknowledged the technician and said, "Yeah, OK. Is the whole machine supposed to vibrate like this normally?"

"Hang on one sec. We are going to start this over."

Not really an answer to Pat's question, but more of a stalling of what was happening. Pat was about to tell the technician he wanted to get out of this claustrophobic tube and just wanted something for his pounding head. The machine started to re-initialize and the knocking and grinding noise started over again. Grind, grind, pause, grind, grind. As each pulse came, he felt the physical punch of his body reacting to the magnets. He pushed back again, this time a little harder. The noise changed to just a long grinding that didn't stop. Pat pushed a third time and then the noise stopped. They had given Pat an emergency ball to squeeze in case of an emergency. Pat squeezed the ball really hard. Nothing happened. It wasn't easy, but he started to slide out of the machine. The cage-like apparatus around his head made it all the more difficult. He managed to push it out of his way and started to slide out of the tube little by little.

He got to be about halfway out of the tube, and the bed started to slide out. He just relaxed and let the bed carry him fully out of the tube. When he was finally out of the tube looking up at the light blue faux sky, he could feel and see a lot of smoke and steam coming out of the sides of the MRI machine. Pat could see the technician was trying to open the door to the room, but was unable to push it open. The pressure in the room was definitely different than it was before he went into the machine. He ripped off the earphones and sat up in the bed. The technician was pushing the door really hard, and it suddenly broke the pressure seal and flew open so hard it hit the wall with a loud thud.

The technician was yelling at him, "What did you do to the machine?"

Pat couldn't hear him because he still had the earplugs in his ear. The technician demanded again with his question, "What the hell did you do to this machine?"

Before Pat could respond, the technician ran over to the big red button saying, "Emergency Quench" and pushed it. Suddenly, more steam and air came into the room. The technician went over to the door again and he tried to open it. It was once again stuck from the pressure differential in the room. With a huge effort and pull, he was able to yank the door open.

They left Pat sitting on the narrow little table, not really sure what to do next. All he knew at this point was he had a massive headache and just wanted to find a less bright and less faux sky over his head. After about 30 seconds, the technician came back in. This time, the door wasn't so difficult to open up. The technician had daggers in his eyes, though.

He rounded on Pat again, and demanded, "What did you do to the machine? You must have some metal or something in you, or on you, to make it act this way. Do you realize you have just ruined a multi-million-dollar piece of equipment?"

Pat looked at the guy as if he was speaking a different language. Pat was also getting annoyed with this person.

He yelled back at him, "I didn't do a damn thing to your machine. Your stupid machine was the thing vibrating the hell out of me in there. I was banging around inside there like a sneaker in a dryer. Check it out for yourself. I didn't do anything. How about you get in there, and I'll push the buttons to run the stupid test on you? Let's see how you like being inside the broken dryer. Where are my clothes? I want to get out of this place."

Surprisingly, this young tech was really pissed off. Actually, to the point of pushing Pat back down on the narrow table when he started to get up.

"Stay here!" he snapped.

Pat went instantly from being annoyed to pissed off. He shoved the guy back a little too hard, and the guy bumped into a little plastic cart next to the MRI machine. The cart crashed into the wall and whatever it contained was now on the floor. This further frustrated the technician by falling completely on his back. He almost made a full recovery, but his weight and balance were just tipped in the wrong way. The technician stuck out his arm quickly to support himself so he wouldn't fall on the ground. He almost made it, but his hand hit the floor at an awkward angle. An awful sound came from his hand. It was the uncanny sound of a small bone being snapped. The kind of sound you might hear if you got the wishbone of the Thanksgiving turkey and someone pulling the other end until it snapped in half.

The technician's face and body shuddered. There was a funny delay in the sound of the bone snapping and his face displaying the shock of hearing this sound. It took a full second before the surprise of the sound and the pain emanating from his wrist finally registered in the pain receptors in his brain. He then let out a loud howl at Pat.

"Sounds like you broke something there. Maybe you should get an MRI for that?", Pat said, half chuckling, "Now where are my clothes?"

The door to the room opened up and a woman in hospital scrubs came in, carrying a small key.

Pat asked, "Where are my damn clothes?"

She told him to go down the hallway to the end and take a right to where the lockers were. Pat quickly exited the room and figured it would be best to leave at this time. God, his head was killing him. In a few minutes, he had changed back into his work clothes. He almost made it to the elevators to get out of the hospital, but a pair of hospital security guys came directly toward him.

"Sir, we need you to come with us. We have a complaint you assaulted one of the staff and damaged a very expensive piece of hospital equipment."

Pat was exhausted from this never-ending string of difficult situations he was going through today. The two security guards were very big boys and could probably wrap Pat into a pretzel in short order. Maybe Pat could use this to his advantage.

He exhaled slowly and said, "OK boys, I'll go with you, and I won't give you a hassle but, first you gotta get me some Tylenol. I flipped a huge crane on its back this morning, so I'm having a bad day."

They each looked at each other and exchanged some kind of informal dialogue. The bigger of the two of them reached into his pocket and pulled out a small bottle of extra-strength Tylenol pills. He gave Pat 2 large capsules. The other one pushed the "up" button for the elevator. Pat "dry swallowed" the two Tylenol and hoped it would relieve this incredible pounding of his head.

About 5 hours later, Pat finally left the hospital. He called his boss and told him what happened during the MRI exam, and they think I damaged it. His boss wasn't happy about this news. Jim was getting yelled at by his superiors, so like any good middle manager, he passed it right down the line.

"Jim, if you think I was the one who damaged the crane today, you're nuts."

"What are you trying to say here, Pat?"

"It's a wonder you don't have more people hurt by your incompetence."

"My incompetence?"

"You only had 3 floors completely enclosed. These 3 floors were trying to support an additional 7 floors of material and people on top of them. The load was too much, and it is just dumb luck it had not collapsed earlier."

Jim paused, and Pat could hear him exhale. He said, "Pat, call me at the end of the week. I don't know when or what a new schedule is gonna look like. This crane problem is gonna mess everyone up. If I am still here at the end of the week, I'll try to give you an idea of what work is available. This is the best I can do right now."

"OK, Jim, thanks. I'll call you on Friday. Just one last thing, OK?"

"Yeah."

"It wasn't a crane problem,"

Pat ended the call.